KISS ME DEAD

DALE IBITZ

SOUL MATE PUBLISHING

New York

KISS ME DEAD

Copyright©2014

DALE IBITZ

Cover Design by Rae Monet, Inc.

This book is a work of fiction. The names, characters, places, and incidents are the products of the author's imagination or are used fictitiously. Any resemblance to actual events, business establishments, locales, or persons, living or dead, is entirely coincidental.

Published in the United States of America by
Soul Mate Publishing
P.O. Box 24
Macedon, New York, 14502

ISBN: 978-1-68291-789-3

ebook ISBN: 978-1-61935-463-0

www.SoulMatePublishing.com

The publisher does not have any control over and does not assume any responsibility for author or third-party websites or their content.

To my family,

who is always there without fail:

Wayne, Wayne Jr,. and Cassie.

Acknowledgements

Some people make all things possible.

Linda C., Chrissie, Mary Beth, Linda S. and Jen, my fab critique group for their unfailing support, and who put up with cluttered email boxes and an endless supply of questions.

Debby at Soul Mate Publishing, the first one to see something beyond a rough story of Kiss Me Dead and took a chance, and then Kim, editor extraordinaire, who was beyond generous with her time and insight, pushing me to make my best efforts and turning my rough story into a polished novel. And, of course, Rae, for the awesome cover design.

Chapter 1

1938

Christian watched the dying girl and did nothing.

He longed to do something—anything—to save her, but it wasn't his place, his calling, or his duty. His duty was to wait for her death, then act.

Giltine, Goddess of Death, had branded the girl for death, the mark on her cheek glowing like slick silver while wet moonlight clung to her breasts. Her flailing arms and flooded gasps forced Christian's eyes to close and his hands to clamp over his ears.

Nothing could stop the sound of death.

He could taste the girl's fear; blood-metallic, like pennies. Even though he yearned to run, he wouldn't. He would stay. He'd wait for her death then reap as he was bound to do.

Inhaling, he closed his eyes, scenting Giltine's addictive poison, sweet nectar reapers craved. He was a slave to her and to his addiction, just as the girl was a slave to death. Neither could escape their fate.

But no matter how many times he tried to abstain and break his addiction, no matter how fervently he wished for death to claim him, to awake and find Giltine's mark glowing silver on his cheek, he would continue to exist, if only to hunt for death.

The girl's hands slapped the water. She slid deeper into the shadowy lake. Pulse in his neck throbbing, he swallowed, trying to remain detached and unemotional as a proper reaper should. Unfortunately, he was also human. His humanity made him suffer.

As he edged closer to the water, sweat formed along his hairline. The mark on the girl's cheek shone brighter, sweeter. He licked his lips. It was almost time.

Trembling with need, he rubbed his thumbs along his pants' seams. He'd gone too long without a soul-hit, and cold rotted him from the inside. The longing for poison that tightened his stomach also made his lips twist in disgust. Not wanting to watch this beautiful girl die with hungry anticipation, he turned his head away.

Water covered the girl's mouth, sucking out one last, drowning breath before consuming her nose and fear-glassed eyes. She sank below the surface.

Christian sighed. It was done. The silence, however comforting, didn't dispel the echoes of the girl's dying breath lingering inside his head. He shuddered.

The girl's stillness revived the nocturnal silence: the grinding cheeps of tree frogs, an owl's chirruping hoot. Wooden docks stretched into the water like skeletal fingers. A red fox's tail flashed. Not willing to enter the water, he waited on the shore for the girl's soul to emerge. The spring lake water was snowmelt frigid, and he detested both the water and the cold, as all his kind did.

Moments later, like dust motes in a sunbeam, the girl's soul appeared. Her skin shone with an ethereal glow, a result of Giltine's poison, and her hair hung in damp ringlets. He could almost taste the sweet poison, so saccharine as to make his teeth ache.

He studied the drop of water that tickled down the girl's neck and trailed between her breasts. To him, her soul appeared as alive as her living form had been. Once she crossed to the other side, the embodiment of her physical being would dissipate, and he'd no longer be able to see her, feel her, smell her. Until then, however, she was real to him.

Realizing he was staring, he bit his lip and focused on the ground. The girl might be dead, might no longer care about decency or modesty, but he believed in dying with dignity. He scooped up her dress.

"Put it on." His voice squeaked like an adolescent boy's.

The girl hesitated then took the dress. He averted his gaze until she slipped it over her head. The dress was old, with a frayed hem and torn collar. Most of the buttons were missing, and it barely covered her nakedness. The loose flapper-style made her seem like a young girl, but he'd seen her nude, and her figure suggested she was one or two years older than him; maybe twenty-one.

Unable to stop himself, he slid a fingertip along her cheek, the silver mark sweet and sticky like icing on a hot bun. When he licked his finger, Giltine's poison shot like bathtub gin down his throat and seared his lungs. His sigh bordered on a groan.

"Who are you?" She was pretty, with cat-green eyes and hair he was sure would lighten like honey when it dried.

"Christian."

He held still, watching her while sweat collected along his back. Despite the aching need, and despite the small taste he'd just sampled, he couldn't take her soul completely. He had to wait until he took her to the Void, and for her to make the decision to cross to the Other World. If he didn't follow the rules, there would be punishment.

Lines wrinkled her forehead. Her pain leaked fragile ribbons that looped around his chest. His Other World senses allowed him just enough information to lure her there, and he could taste the earthy flavor of her confusion. Some might consider such knowledge cheating; Christian considered it a means to an end.

She turned to the lake. "I'm in there." She smoothed her dress. "But I'm here."

He concentrated, looking inside her. Mary. Her name was Mary. She was twenty-one, her mother had died, and she left behind a baby sister and a father.

Christian swallowed, focused on keeping his voice level. "Only your body's in the water, Mary. You don't need it now."

She peered past his shoulder at the dark house tucked into the woods. Her fear increased, the taste pinching his tongue.

"I'm dead?"

"Yes."

"Oh, bugger." Now she frowned at the lake.

"You don't need to be afraid. I'm here to guide you."

A girl appeared on the porch of the dark house. He froze, trying to melt into the shadows. Mary, however, was invisible to the living.

She stared at the girl and murmured, "I know her."

Setting empty milk bottles by the front door, the girl tossed her light hair over her shoulder and slipped back into the house. He studied the spot where she'd stood, a tiny ray of sunshine in his darkness. Shaking his head, he released the breath from his lungs. It was time to dust this place.

Mary's poison-drenched soul made him dizzy with need, and he licked his lips. "Take my hands," he said. "It's your time."

A pause, then warm fingers slipped into his. He closed his eyes, focusing on that reaper essence residing in his core. A tingling fizz burst upward from his toes, enveloping him in an evanescent fog, sending them adrift into the darkness where glacial air shivered through him. He clung to Mary, his teeth chattering until the warmth of her soul batted the cold aside. Poison filled a need that had been rotting him from the inside. A shudder swelled along his spine.

His cells and muscles solidified. Time stopped flowing, and the air stilled. White walls loomed on either side, and behind them the dark gray entrance to the Void shimmered like a silken sheet. Christian swallowed, trying to ignore the cries of souls.

She clutched his sleeve. Her hair had dried, turning the color of sunlight, long locks tangling around her face. Her soul cracked open, sending her broken thoughts tumbling through his head.

It's dark, and bitter. I want to go home.

Not that Renkin slob.

Poor Izzy. Who'll protect her?

She squinted down the tunnel. For the dead, the tunnel held only darkness; the darkness of the unknown, the darkness of eternity.

He brushed her fingers. "Take my hand. I'll guide you."

Hand-in-hand, they crept forward. Giltine's poison oozing from Mary dried his mouth with longing. Reapers craved not only the sweetness of Giltine's poison, but heat. When her poison combined with a soul's warmth it became an all-consuming need, and one that couldn't be ignored. He wanted to take her soul, right there, but the girl needed to climb the mountain before she could cross over. A soul couldn't be forced; that would be stealing, which was against Giltine's law.

He was panting when a mountain stretched upward and out of sight, licking the whiteness like a long, black tongue. Its rock exterior was cracked and gouged from centuries of reapers and mourning and death.

Souls who hadn't yet climbed the mountain to cross over moved within the whiteness. Some clawed their way up, only to tumble back down. Others crouched into recesses as though in hiding, yanking their hair. And still others rocked back and forth with their heads tucked under their arms. Christian's head throbbed with their moans.

Like an ethereal ballet, reapers drifted among the pale shadows. Silver eyes glinted below dark hair, their black coats swirling a ghostly fog. Without expression, they watched and waited for their next soul-hit. Waiting for a soul to cross over was torture. Occasionally, one would shudder when a reaper touched it, taking a taste of the poison-drenched soul without fully enveloping it. While not strictly adhering to the law, it was a transgression Giltine typically overlooked.

Mary whispered, "Who are they?"

"The dark ones are reapers. The others are souls who are undecided or lost."

"Undecided about what?"

"Some don't want to climb the mountain to meet their fate. They stop, or try to turn and go back."

"Can they?"

He glanced at the mark on her cheek. "Not if they've been marked for death by Giltine."

"And the lost ones?"

He considered his answer before speaking. "Those are people who haven't been marked by Giltine, yet are on the edge of death. While their physical bodies are in a comatose state, their souls are caught here in the Void, neither alive nor dead."

He didn't explain that those unfortunate souls could be lost in the Void for a very long time. Squeezing her hand, he refused to dwell on that.

"Who's Giltine?"

"Goddess of Death. Once she marks you, you're slated for death."

"The dark ones frighten me."

"Don't be afraid. They're merely guides."

Her tongue traced her bottom lip as she studied the mountain.

He tugged her hand. "Come on. I'll be with you."

She hesitated, and then let him lead her around gouges that tripped the unwary. He had to let go of her hand as they climbed higher, and the mountain became steep, using pits and ledges for hand and footholds. His muscles burned.

It was an eternity before they reached the top and were met by an iridescent white wall that glimmered with rainbow streaks. Mary didn't breathe hard, but his lungs ached with his labored breathing. He needed a soul-hit very badly.

On the other side of the flimsy wall, fields of green riddled with vibrant flowers lay to the right. Tall grass waved in a gentle breeze beneath an azure sky. To the left was a barren wasteland, dry and flat, with vultures circling in a blood-red sky.

She bit her lip, hesitating.

"Once you pass through, you'll be judged by the Goddess of Life," he explained. He waved to the right. "If you pass her judgment, you'll stay in her world and enjoy peace and tranquility for all eternity."

"If I don't?"

He pointed to the left, where Giltine reigned. Mary's fear scalded his tongue. She took a step back.

"Wait," he said. "I've sensed your goodness. I'm sure you'll be sentenced to an afterlife of tranquility and not torture."

It was a lie. Christian had no way of knowing how she would be judged, had no way of knowing what happened on the Other Side, as he'd never witnessed a soul's judgment. He only knew what he could see through the curtain, only knew the lives of those who crossed over would be judged and sentenced to one side or the other. But the trembling need for a soul-hit nearly buckled his knees. He'd say anything to get her to cross over.

Reapers, attracted by her soul, skimmed behind them. He took her by the chin. Heat and poison throbbed toward him like warm, seductive arms, holding him captive.

"It's time." He ran his tongue over his cracked lips. "Your mother's waiting for you on the other side. You miss her, don't you?"

"No."

His head snapped back. Gods below, she couldn't back out now; he *needed* her warmth and her poison.

"I can't go. Who'll protect my baby sister?"

He answered in a hoarse whisper, "Your father."

"No, he doesn't know. That pill, Renkin, will come after her next." Her lips twisted over the name. She glanced down the mountain. "Who'll protect Izzy?"

Christian reached for her, but she drifted away, her warmth receding.

"Will you?" Her eyes, so deeply green that if he stared too long in them he would become lost, widened.

He turned away. He couldn't promise her anything. His tongue stuck to the roof of his mouth when he tried to wet his lips.

"Yes." The word barely slid through his cracked lips.

"Promise?"

Of course he couldn't promise such a thing. "Yes."

Mary's mouth relaxed. The trust and gratitude that shone from her eyes wrapped him in warmth so foreign he had to blink. He almost corrected the lie, but he couldn't.

"Thank you, thank you." She took his hand in both of hers and kissed his knuckles. "I'm ready."

She stepped into his embrace. He absorbed Giltine's poison and the delicious, dizzying warmth of Mary's soul. A small flash of light signaled her entrance to the other side. An explosion burst inside his chest; heat and poison flowed throughout his body.

Christian tilted his head back and drifted in ecstasy.

Chapter 2

Present Time

When Brooke woke up that morning, dread had risen like flood waters over a dam. Her premonition of doomsday was very vivid; vivid because reapers converged on Connecticut in apocalyptic proportions.

Brooke knew. She could see them.

She had no intention of leaving her room, her house, or even her bed. She'd been resigned to spending her life in her phobic cocoon, alone and afraid, hiding from reapers and memories of her brother's death.

But here she was in Simsbury, contemplating Talcott Mountain, a rocky ridge that wound northward through Connecticut like a colossal snake. At its one-thousand-foot crest sat Heublein Tower, a castle-like summerhouse built in the early 1900s by the wealthy magnate, Gilbert Heublein. The phallic tower was a local landmark.

She traced her temples with her fingertips and tried to keep her breathing even. Thick trees surrounded her like a cage, patches of blue sky peeking through their twisted branches. The shadows were dark and smothering. Not even the riotous chorus of birds could lift the anxiety constricting her chest.

Rolling her head to ease the tension in her neck, she checked the road, but her only company was a handful of cars parked on the grass. A crow screeched overhead, and she flinched, bringing one shoulder up to her ear for a moment before forcing herself to relax.

Sucking her lips between her teeth, she glared across the street at the gate barring her access to the trail. As far as she was concerned, it was the gate to Hell. Even though spring treated these northwestern hills with cool indifference, moisture slid down her face, her palms and thighs damp with sweat.

Her gaze jumped the gate to the path that snaked into the woods. Branches tickled with the fuzz of spring growth strained toward the trail, dragging her focus downward as though pointing the way for her to follow. She didn't want to follow that path . . . she wanted to bolt home, back to her safe bed, in her safe house, in her safe town of Bakerville.

Clearing her throat, Brooke shifted to her other butt cheek and pushed those thoughts aside. No. She refused to bolt. Today, after all, was the day she'd finally decided to face the Outside.

Okay, now she was being overly dramatic. She'd been going to school—it was safe there since students didn't usually drop dead or attract those damn shadows from Hell—but she'd quit working at Panera Bread and going to the movies and to school basketball games and on dates. Abby, her pierced-to-the-nines best friend, was all kinds of slanted over it, telling Brooke she was committing social suicide and that Paul would move on to a more-willing-to-leave-the-house kind of girl.

She bit her thumbnail. While she didn't really care if Paul moved on—in fact, she was pretty sure he already had—she had to admit her nosedive into agoraphobia was starting to piss off her own damn self.

Outside, after all, had been one of her favorite places in the whole, wide world; especially Heublein Tower. Heublein was where she spent hours writing poetry, and the long days of spring break spent cooped up in her house had morphed into long days of monotony. Today was the day that crap ended. Today she was hiking.

Despite her mental pep talk, however, she stayed velcroed to her car.

"Brooke," she said. "You are one big-ass chicken."

She glanced up and down the road, then toward the trail. There was no one around, human or Hell shadow. She took three deep breaths. It was time to get level. Grabbing her notebook from her car, she darted across the road before she could change her mind.

Following the path snaking around the gate, she attacked the trail to Heublein Tower with the fervor of a fitness instructor.

It wasn't long before she was engulfed by the shadows and that muffled kind of silence only experienced in a deep forest. Fallen trees lined the trail like corpses, the path littered with holes, rocks, and tree roots. As though trying to exorcise her demonic thoughts, she kept a solid pace. The steep incline made her leg muscles burn.

Her steps snapped to a halt when a dark-haired guy in jeans and windbreaker stumbled toward her.

"Morning," he huffed and strode by.

Brooke's breath shot out of her lungs. She slapped a hand to her chest and hauled in steadying breaths. Her paranoia had finally developed into full-blown hallucinations. He'd just been some random guy with dark hair and clothes, and brown eyes—not silver—so he couldn't be one of those F-bomb demons.

Demons, yes. She'd been watching reapers going about their business since she turned fourteen, reaping the souls of people who had strange, silver marks on their cheeks. While she really didn't understand what any of it meant, or why she could see this other world when no one else could, she'd learned to keep her reaper radar secret and her mouth shut. Keeping a healthy distance from them and having a healthy awareness of them had been enough . . . until she'd seen a reaper kill someone. Now she outright feared them.

She shook her head. No, she wouldn't think about that. She pressed on.

She squeaked when a squirrel leaped through the branches over her head, and then flinched at a crow's mocking laughter. Her steps slowed. Above the trees, a hawk screamed. The trees crowded her, the breeze made her shiver, and the path seemed to forbid her from going any further as she tripped over another damn tree root.

Stopping, Brooke clenched her fingers, wiggling her sore toes inside her sneakers. The urge to hide in her room flooded her mouth with the sour taste of failure. As much as she'd wanted to break from her bout of agoraphobia, she couldn't. She was out of there and going home.

Grinding her teeth, she gave the trail the finger then spun to race back to her car. She halted when she saw a guy standing ten feet away and watching her.

Her chest went tight, and her bladder ached with an urge to pee. She checked herself. She'd already been a hyper-doofus over one guy she'd wrongly assumed was a reaper. Deciding not to be a coward and so quick to judge every guy she met on the basis of looks, she held her ground and faced him.

He wore a black hoodie hanging open to reveal a black shirt, jeans, and boots. Her gaze drifted back to his chiseled face complete with dimpled chin. His eyes came up at the same time as though he'd been checking her out too.

She bit her lip. Her reaper radar buzzed faintly, unsure, zaps inside her head like mosquitoes hitting a bug zapper. No, not a reaper . . . but what?

"You okay?" he asked.

She nodded.

He sauntered by her to sit on a log-hewn bench, and she caught an overly sweet scent, like wild grapes in the heat of summer. It was a trademark of the reapers who took unmarked souls. Her hand went to her throat, her pulse quickening. He didn't *seem* dangerous, lounging on the bench with a small smile as he watched her.

"What's the matter? Do I smell or something?"

"Yes."

One side of his mouth curled, as if he knew her answer before she'd spoken. She scratched her neck while studying his strange, silver eyes that were somehow mixed with blue. Maybe her reaper radar was broken, and this was just some random, normal guy with weird eyes who liked to drink a lot of grape juice.

Biting her lip, she tried to puzzle him out. He was solid, human, real; as real as the pimple she discovered on her forehead that morning. He had the reaper-dark hair and pale skin, but there were blue shards in his reaper-silver eyes. He had the body of a guy who liked to work it, standing even with her 5'11" height. Abby would totally be in to him, but Brooke wasn't into the Jersey Shore steroid type. She sidestepped away.

Glancing at windbreaker-guy just disappearing at the bottom of the hill, he asked, "Was that guy bothering you?"

She shook her head, her mouth too dry to unstick her tongue enough to speak. Maybe the guy wasn't a reaper, but he was some kind of hybrid. Part reaper and part . . . what? Human? What the hell was going on? Brooke swallowed, the sound audible in the silence.

"Then what are you afraid of?"

"I'm not . . ." Before it had a chance to form in her head, the lie evaporated.

Unfortunately, she was genetically coded to always answer a question with the truth. How or why, she didn't know. She only knew that after she'd turned fourteen, she couldn't spit out a lie no matter how small or white.

She could, however, ignore him. A lie-loophole she'd discovered halfway through her freshman year.

"I asked if you were scared." His gaze was intent, focused, and he held very still as if the fate of the future rested on her answer.

Her heart squeezed out several, annoyed thumps. She crossed her arms over her chest. "A little."

One corner of his mouth lifted in a satisfied smile, like a cat that had just gobbled up a bowl of cream in front of a panting dog. "I see," he said and stretched his legs.

She decided she didn't like that smile, because it made her think he knew things about her, things he couldn't possibly know. Holding completely still, like prey hiding from a predator, she debated whether to ignore him or shove him off the bench or just bolt for her car. "Whatever."

"Are you alone?"

She squeezed her eyes shut, intending to not answer, but then whispered, "Yes."

Damn, damn, damn!

She glared at him. A trio of panting girls dressed in tank tops and barely-there shorts—apparently they thought it was July, not April—hiked past them, twisting their heads to ogle the guy. He smiled as he eyed their asses, then ran his tongue over his upper lip. Her throat constricted. Were the girls safe around him?

Running was no longer an option. Even though her heart slammed and her palms itched and her teeth ground with the urge to hide behind the nearest tree, she had to stay and figure out what the hell he was because she was the only one able to detect demons.

Fear won out. Someone else would have to save the day. She spun to head back down the trail.

"Wait," he said.

She turned but, unable to quite face him, her gaze slipped to the woods. "What the hell do you want?"

"Why do you want to leave?"

Because you might be a freak. Because you might be a demon. Because you scare the hell out of me.

She finally settled on the most innocent truth. "Because I don't know you."

"We can fix that. I'd like to get to know you."

"Too bad, because I don't want to know you."

He waved a finger between them. "You don't think this is nice? Talking?"

"Hell no."

"Come on, doll, don't be like that," he said in what he probably thought was a charming, can't-say-no tone, and rose from the bench.

"Back off."

"Wow. Bitch much?"

Could he feel the angry heat blasting from her gaze? "Only with tools. Look, I don't know what you are, but . . . "

The gray in his eyes brightened. "Don't you mean who?"

"No. I said back off. I mean it." Her stomach sizzled as though a cigarette had been jammed into her belly button.

His tone lowered to basement-level proportions. "And what exactly do you think I am?"

Brooke was too fevered and dizzy to even try to evade the question. She whispered, "A reaper . . . sort of." She couldn't seem to stop her mouth. "You don't look exactly like them, but you're some kind of reaper hybrid, aren't you? A demon wanna-be. A freak . . . "

He stepped toward her, fury unfurling in the force of his glare, and the silver in his eyes flashed. Literally flashed, like sparks.

She backpedaled, her eyes bugging and mouth gaping as her mind gelled in a silent scream.

Chapter 3

1938

Christian lay atop the Void mountain, his legs and arms stretched out. Giltine's poison, which he'd soaked from Mary, filled him with sweetness. And though the girl's soul softened the sharp edges of ice from his joints, small aches still plagued his body. He'd abstained too long from a soul-hit. He'd have to cruise for another number.

He staggered down the mountain, brushing past reapers and souls until he reached the gray, wispy entrance to the Void. His stomach wrenched. He doubled over and sailed into the frigid darkness, his body fragmenting and molding again before landing topside.

Shivering, he let his sight adjust to the waning gloom and his hearing to the quiet cacophony of night sounds, and then moved like a sleepwalker to the lake. He searched for Mary's body, but all he saw were ripples highlighted by pre-dawn shadows. He squatted, picking up a stone and turning it in his fingers.

Christian wanted to drift, but his promise to Mary held him there. He studied the house that had so interested her. It was an ordinary cottage; dark brown with white-paned windows and a stone chimney. A porch broke through the mountain laurel and into the small yard. Rocking chairs and milk bottles completed the picture.

Like Mary at the bottom the lake, unfeeling and lifeless, unease settled in his gut.

He stroked the back of his neck. A soul had never requested a favor, and never had he made a promise to one. It was an odd feeling, this promise, lying so heavily upon him. He rolled his shoulders and stretched his arms. The feeling didn't lift.

He snorted. He was being utterly ridiculous.

Christian should walk away, right now. He didn't like this place anyway. Unlike territorial reapers who rarely strayed from their regions, he wandered south every fall when the Berkshire Hills' icy nights slid into icy days. Yet every spring he drifted back to these remote, northwestern hills of Connecticut. New Hartford was close enough to remind him of home, but not close enough for him to be home.

He could never go home.

He tossed the stone into the lake, where it awakened a round of ripples. Would Mary know if he kept his promise? Was she watching him now, like some religions believed? He didn't think so, but he didn't know for sure. Because of his humanity, the afterlife was as big a mystery to him as it was for other people.

He stepped toward the woods, and then paused, the lie pressing on his shoulders made his body too heavy to move.

Glaring at the house, he swore softly at the dawn.

The memory of Mary's eyes floated before him like mist from the lake; the *trust* that had shone from them haunted him. What fear had motivated Mary to make her linger in the Void to ensure her baby sister's safety, to be so bold as to ask a reaper to watch out for her?

It wasn't as if he could help. As much as he wanted to, he didn't belong in this world, with humans and relationships and houses with white-picket fences. Giltine didn't tolerate such nonsense.

An image of Giltine's punishing ring flashed through his head. Her ring was the epitome of cruel and vindictive punishment; a punishment he couldn't escape.

Christian clenched his teeth. No, these human problems weren't his concern. He had his own problems. He was leaving. Right. Now.

He'd taken two steps into the woods when a voice behind him chimed like church bells. "Mary? Mary!"

He darted behind a geriatric oak tree. The girl from the night before stood on the porch, the wind tossing her pale hair and curving her blue cotton blouse against her breasts. She appeared to be his age, around nineteeen; too old to be Mary's baby sister. He scowled. Why couldn't this dame protect the fool baby?

She stepped from the shadows. The sun tarnished her honey hair with strands of red dawn. Her blouse was tucked into a pair of denim trousers, the bottoms rolled up to show a great set of gams. Standing with her hands on her hips, she surveyed the woods and the lake.

"Mary?" She stomped her bare foot and swore, the harsh word an intriguing contradiction to the soft lips that uttered it. She clumped down the stairs.

"Izzy?" a man called from the front door.

The girl spun toward the house. Christian's eyes widened. This was Mary's "baby" sister? Gods below! Had Mary been blind?

"Daddy, have you seen Mary this morning?" A trace of Izzy's petulance lingered in the air.

Her father stepped from the porch, skin flashing through the holes in his denim overalls. "She at work?"

"It's her day off, and she's supposed to pick strawberries with me."

"She swimming?" Her father scratched his armpit and yawned.

"I don't see her." Her gaze swung past Christian's hiding spot, and then swung back. "Mary? Is that you hiding back there?"

He ducked behind the tree, tensing his leg muscles.

"Mary!" Izzy giggled, and he imagined rainbow-laden bubbles escaping from those velvet lips. "I know you're back there."

Her soft footfalls padded through the grass. He swallowed hard. Reapers were invisible to humans, but being half-human, he was plainly visible, and now it was too late to drift.

Her father screamed Mary's name. With a gasp, her footfalls retreated. Christian peered around the tree to find her father clutching Mary's dress.

She fled to her father's side, searched the water, and shrieked, "Mary!"

"Dear Lord in heaven." The dress slipped from the man's fingers.

Her father dove into the lake. Again and again he resurfaced, yelled, "Mary!" and plunged back into the dark depths. The girl crumpled to her knees, crying like a forlorn kitten.

Christian didn't want to see this grief. Curse Mary, curse Izzy, and curse that ridiculous promise. He was dusting this place and would never return.

He ran as though Lucifer's hellhounds were on his heels.

Chapter 4

Present Time

The birdcalls and squirrel chatter were lost in the thunder of blood echoing between Brooke's ears. The gloom from the trees couldn't hide the almost-reaper coming at her, the silver in his eyes flashing like demonic fireworks. She backpedaled three steps before tripping on the uneven trail. Her scream snapped short when she slammed backward, her head smashing into the ground.

She gasped when he knelt next to her and cradled her head. She tried to twist from his grip, but every movement was like pressing her scalp into glass. The gleam in his eyes and the overwhelmingly sweet scent sent a shudder raging through her body.

Warmth trickled from her. She couldn't focus. She couldn't scream. She couldn't remember what she needed to do. She wanted to shout, "Go away," but the thought whisked from her mind before she could say the words.

Her mind went numb, and her head dizzy. She floated toward something; something dark and quiet. The floating was nice, euphoric almost, except for the wintry air. Then the darkness deepened, consuming, suffocating. She struggled to breathe, then decided breathing wasn't as important as the dreaminess enveloping her. Her muscles slackened, and an empty feeling burrowed through her center. One epic shiver rippled through her body, seeming to take years to subside.

He let her go and leaped up. Her head plopped into the dirt, making her wince. The chilly ground seeped through her clothes. She grabbed chunks of cool air into her lungs then pushed herself onto her knees and finally her feet. Swaying against a tree, she pressed a shaking palm to her temple and tried to still her trembling.

Watching the almost-reaper, she blinked in order to better focus. The scattered remnants of the last few minutes—or had it been hours?—slowly emerged, making her lips go numb. It might have been an epic mistake to call the demon wannabe a freak, because he'd been seriously pissed, and he'd . . . what?

Touched my soul.

She knew it with certainty. After several minutes of hard breathing, Brooke said, "You *ass*hole."

He shoved his hands into his pockets. "You fell. It's not like I pushed you."

Propping herself with one hand against the tree's wrinkled trunk, she used her free hand to brush her hair as though he'd given her cooties. Assorted twigs and dead leaves shook free and floated to the ground. "Get away from me."

"Can we start over?" He stretched his hand toward her, eyebrows raised, the lightning in his eyes settling to a simmering glow.

"No." The last bit of coldness was consumed by the fire forming in her stomach. His sweet smell made her nostrils flare. "Get away from me. Get . . . away . . . from me!" she repeated when he stepped closer.

He paused, gave her a lazy grin, and then said, "I'll be seeing you around." He pivoted and sauntered up the path.

She pressed a hand against her chest. Clenching her muscles, she willed the shakes away until her panting slowed.

When he touched her, frosty fingers had reached inside and tugged her soul. She touched her cheek. There'd been no silver mark there this morning. Had she been on the edge of a soul-stealing death? She knew stuff like that happened . . . she'd seen it.

Brooke absorbed another epic shudder. Her breathing calmed. The canopy of trees swallowed the noise of a plane, the scent of forest decay once again evident. Up the trail, the almost-reaper disappeared around a bend.

It was time to jet. She picked her way through the loose rocks back toward her car. Behind her, a girl's scream burst out then pinched into silence.

She took two more steps before the sound registered in her brain. She halted, cocked her head, listening to rocks rolling down a hill. Pain seared her gut, and she had a sudden . . . feeling . . . as though a black fog filled her brain with one word: death.

She gripped her hands behind her. What did she think she was, psychic? Not only was that ridiculous, it was bat-shit crazy.

She studied the path. That wanna-be reaper was up there. Had another girl fallen when trying to escape that lethal stare? Was he touching her soul?

"Oh, crap."

She tossed a look down the trail, and then sped upward. She slid to a stop as she rounded the bend, panting. A girl sprawled on the ground, one leg twisted at an odd angle, her hair sprayed out like a chocolate wave around her unblemished face. Her head tilted awkwardly against a bloodstained rock. The girl, Bekka, had been captain of the cheer squad in Brooke's senior year at high school. Almost-reaper knelt beside her.

Brooke's head raged like an inferno. Her fingers itched as though covered in bug bites, and she had a sudden desire to leap onto the guy's back, grab him by the throat, and shake him.

She'd felt like this before, when Ryan died. Only then she said nothing, did nothing, and now her brother was dead.

There was something infinitely wrong when Bekka's body trembled and then jerked as though possessed.

"What did you do to her?" Brooke snapped.

"Nothing. She fell."

Just like she had. "Get away from her."

Almost-reaper flicked a glance at her. "Why?"

"She's not marked."

His head snapped back, then toward Brooke. "You know about that?"

"Well, yeah."

She wiped her palms on her jeans, and twisted her head to glance behind her, twice. She couldn't stand there and say nothing and do nothing and let someone die again. There were no do-overs and her brother was dead and gone, but she believed in second chances.

"I said get away from her."

He scraped his teeth together. "And if I don't?"

She opened her mouth then shut it.

"I could kill her, and I could kill you," the guy said softly. "You think you can stop me?"

She swallowed, irritated at the amplified sound that echoed between them. "I don't know." She could barely hear her own words.

He hesitated for eons before snorting and turning his attention to Bekka. "Do you have a cell phone?"

"A . . . what?"

He gave her a look that could make a cactus sweat, then repeated his words slower and louder, as if there was an invisible dunce cap on her head only he could see. "Cell phone?"

"No."

"Then do something other than annoy me, and go find help."

Brooke hesitated, sucking in her bottom lip. If she left, he might kill Bekka. If Brooke stayed he'd maybe kill them both. The itchy burn returned to her fingers, and she clenched and unclenched her fists. He locked gazes with her, and she hoped he couldn't see the sweat shivering over her forehead.

"I don't need to be watched," he said.

A tiny voice, *her* voice, whispered inside her head. *Watch.*

She inhaled. Exhaled. "You're seriously whacked if you think I'm leaving you alone with her."

"Don't trust me?"

"Damn straight."

His lips quirked in a smile, then he laughed. Brooke narrowed her eyes. A couple sauntered around the corner, holding hands, giggling. Their conversation died when they saw Bekka lying like a corpse, and Brooke and almost-reaper eyeing each other like two cocks about to battle.

"What's going on here?" the guy asked.

His girlfriend clutched his arm and slid back a step.

"She fell," Brooke said, never glancing away from almost-reaper. "Either of you have a cell phone? We need 9-1-1."

"Yeah." The guy fished his phone out of his pocket, his Adam's apple jumping in his throat.

An older couple with a small boy made their way down the trail toward them, and their boisterous arrival shushed the birds overhead. In unison, they came to a halt. The father dropped to his knees by almost-reaper's side and pressed two fingers against Bekka's neck.

"Did anyone call 9-1-1?"

"My boyfriend did," the girl offered.

The added safety in numbers lifted some of Brooke's anxiety, freeing the tightness in her lungs so she could breathe again.

She froze mid-swallow. The almost-reaper's eyes were closed; his lips parted, and sweat glistened on his upper lip. Slowly, he licked his lips, and a wave of cloying grape tsunamied toward her.

"Is she dead?" the boy asked.

"No," Brooke almost shouted.

Almost-reaper blinked, then focused on her. She wanted to spit that sweet taste from her mouth. He struggled to his feet and swayed, reaching toward her.

Bekka's soul was safe now. The pee-urge overwhelmed Brooke's bladder, so she did what any self-respecting agoraphobic would do when facing a demon after venturing outside the safety of her house in a dumbass attempt to be brave in the shadow of death.

She bolted.

Chapter 5

1938

Christian trekked into the Bakerville section of New Hartford. His deathbed promise to watch over Izzy clung to him like skunk vapor, and he couldn't seem to wash his thoughts of it. Every time he attempted to drift, his drifting brought him back to that grief-stricken lake house. He felt as though he'd turned into a homing pigeon.

He neglected the dirt main street and its solitary gas station, old mill, and the lone, lurking reaper. A two-story schoolhouse nearly linked arms with a small white church with a squat steeple. He haunted the mourners when they exited the church, shuffling behind them as they moved down the road that led to the cemetery behind the church.

He loitered outside the cemetery, a patch of space chopped out of the woods. Some headstones were tilted by the annual cycle of frost heaves brought on by arctic winters and warm springs. Clouds darkened faces gray with grief, while birds warbled threats at the intrusion.

Standing next to a tiny headstone that overlooked the open-mouthed grave, the preacher clutched his Bible in one hand and gestured with the other, occasionally pounding his chest in lieu of his pulpit. Christian ignored the man's words.

Izzy leaned on her father. The pink rose she clutched to her chest shone against her dark-gray blouse with capped sleeves. Her gray skirt flared below her knees, blonde hair snaking in a long braid from beneath a laced hat.

Face muscles slack, Izzy stared at the headstone emblazoned with the words, *Mary Vincent, Beloved Daughter and Sister, 1917-1938*. Next to it a similar headstone read, *Sara Vincent, Beloved Wife and Mother, 1899-1934*.

Why was he here? Even if Christian was inclined to keep his promise, he'd begun to think the menace against Izzy was a result of Mary's imagination. For three days, he watched Izzy endure the days like a brain-dead soul, watched her not brush her hair, watched her not eat the food brought by neighbors, and for three days nothing had threatened her.

He sighed. Gods below, but she was a beauty.

Shaking his head, he crossed his arms and squeezed his biceps, hard. He had to make a clean sneak, and fast. This sulky girl wasn't worth risking Giltine's ring. Though he clenched his jaw, he couldn't seem to take the steps to leave. Though he cursed Mary, it seemed he was the one cursed.

"Did you know Mary?"

He snapped out of his internal battle with the suddenness of lightning lashing a weathered barn. People strolled from the cemetery. Hugging his Bible to his chest, the preacher bowed his head while denim-clad workers holding shovels lingered near Mary's grave. And Izzy stood five paces from him, giving Christian the once over. His thoughts twisted and he couldn't make words form.

Damnation!

"Sir?" Izzy prompted.

"I . . . I . . ." He swallowed. "I met her once."

"Oh. Not well then."

He dipped his head.

"Have we met?"

"Why?"

She twirled the rose. "You were staring at me."

Christian looked sideways from her and cleared his throat.

"In fact, you were looking quite fierce."

He shifted from one foot to the other, tension coiling in his gut like a cornered snake.

She went on, "Anyway, I guess to notice you watching me I'd have to admit I was watching you."

He studied her. Her eyes weren't as green as Mary's; instead the green was permeated with flecks of gold and brown. Even though red and puffy from tears, they were still beautiful. And she smelled good, like lilacs.

She touched her earlobe, drawing his attention to her long, smooth neck. "Are you from these parts?"

He tore his gaze from her neck to study his boots. "In summer."

She considered him as though he was an errant puzzle piece. He glanced behind him, intending to escape, but her next words yanked his attention back to her.

"I'm Elizabeth."

Without thinking, he blurted, "I thought you were Izzy."

"Izzy's childish, don't you think?"

He nodded, unable to resist sizing her up. She certainly was no child.

"How'd you know my name?" she asked.

"Mary."

"And you are?"

"Christian."

"A pleasure meeting you, Christian."

He scratched his neck, and checked the path once more. An elderly woman touched Elizabeth's shoulder. He shifted so she couldn't see his face.

"We're ready to go to the house, Izzy."

"Thank you, Mrs. Marsh."

"Your father's having a hard time with it."

"I know. I'm at a loss."

"Don't worry, dear; we women will help you at the house. We'll get through."

"Thank you." She sniffed.

Mrs. Marsh patted her back and shuffled toward the girl's father, whose face was colorless below his soft cap, his hands shoved into the pockets of his dark work pants. An unshaven man sporting a charcoal, pinstripe suit and a wide, red-striped tie stood next to him, tapping a walking stick on the toe of his wingtips.

Her father choked out, "Thank you, Ray. We all miss her."

Ray's gaze drilled into Elizabeth like a nail in wood, sharp and penetrating. His cinnamon lust stung Christian's tongue.

"Who's that man?" he asked, jutting his chin toward Ray.

"Mr. Renkin." She tried to smile, failed, and then bit her thumbnail.

Renkin, the man Mary mentioned. The coiled snake tightened, ready to strike, but Christian swallowed his whisper that he'd protect her. The girl wasn't his concern.

She peeked at him through her lashes. "Would you like to come to the house? We have sandwiches."

"Of course," he lied, if only to placate her. He would simply vanish, and she'd be left to wonder who that dark stranger had been. He'd soon forget her and Renkin and that irritating promise.

"We're just down the road, on Lake Wonksunkmunk."

Christian glanced in the direction she pointed.

"See you there."

He turned west, toward Torrington, intending to cruise for a number, get a hit of poison, and forget about Elizabeth. Moments later, however, he found himself tracking to her house. He settled in the woods to watch, unable to ignore the bitterness gnawing his gut. Or maybe that was hunger; he was starving.

The autos rattling into the yard popped and belched smoke, many seemingly held together by rust instead of paint. He hadn't paid much attention to the social decline brought on by the depression, but he knew enough to know not many could afford Renkin's cream-colored convertible that tore into the yard. Boys and men alike descended like dust, caressing its rounded fenders, chrome bumpers, and white-walled tires. Renkin strutted with his bowler perched at a sly angle on his head.

The boys moved on to chase chickens through the yard. Men set wooden planks on sawhorses. Girls helped the women cover the makeshift table with white cloths, and then laid out dishes of food and pitchers of lemonade, their chatter mingling with the chirps of an egret swooping over the water. Christian's stomach rioted with hunger.

Elizabeth joined her wilted father by the lake, linking an arm through his and resting against his shoulder. They studied the water that claimed Mary. Christian remained at the edge of the woods, unable to socialize with her, or anyone. Yet the longer he watched, the more his muscles trembled with a sudden longing to touch her mouth with his own. He scoffed. A pair of kissable lips wasn't reason enough to get ringed by Giltine.

Finally, Elizabeth towed her father to the table. Renkin's gaze trailed after her like a lusty bull's. Christian choked, then muffled a cough behind his hand.

Renkin's voice boomed over the subdued crowd. "You there, hiding behind that tree, you've no business here. Scat, you punk!"

Christian froze, caught by the man's glare and the mourners' questioning glances. Elizabeth whispered to her lethargic father, thrust the plate of food at him, and glided in his direction.

"Oh, Mr. Renkin," she called over her shoulder. "He's been invited."

Shock and surprise propelled Christian into the yard. Sound, movement, and time seemed to stop, as though he was death itself absorbing life from the crowd. Renkin's lips peeled back over the cigar clenched between his tobacco-brown teeth.

Halting in front of Christian, she said, "You found us."

"Yes." He barely heard his voice over the low humming in his ears, which he realized wasn't from the dread pounding in his eardrums but the crowd returning to their conversations.

She studied him with that look someone uses when they're sure they've met you but can't quite remember where or when. He rocked on his toes.

"Are you hungry?" she asked

"Yes."

"Come on then."

He did need to eat, and he was already there, so he followed her. The choices seemed endless: meatloaf sandwiches, potato salad, chicken, baked beans, pineapple cake, and oatmeal cookies. He took some of everything.

Elizabeth, whose plate seemed empty with a dab of potato salad and one cookie, nudged her chin in the direction of the dock. "Let's sit over there."

The sway of her hips and her tanned gams forced heat into his cheeks and his knees to go weak, and he found himself wondering where her shoes had gone. Swallowing, he turned his attention to the dock. The air was thick with the smell of wet dirt and algae, and water licked the pilings.

Settling at her elbow, he beat back the urge to gulp the food. He bit the sandwich and counted to five before taking another bite. She nibbled her cookie and stared at the water. He'd eaten his sandwich, chicken, and one cookie before she spoke.

"I don't understand how Mary could drown. She was a good swimmer."

Watching her, he crunched into another cookie.

Her cookie dangled from her fingers. "Her dress was torn."

He pointed to a post rising from the water at the end of the dock, its top frayed from decay. "Perhaps she caught it."

"Maybe." She swung her feet over the water. "I know we haven't met before, but you seem vaguely familiar."

He froze. Had she fingered him from the day Mary died? Sweat popped up along his forehead, a warning that this conversation had escalated from relaxed to risky.

"How'd you and Mary meet?"

He studied his answer from every angle, but couldn't see any way around, or harm in, speaking the truth. "Swimming."

"Where?"

"Here."

She stiffened. "When was that?"

Suddenly his drink tasted as bitter as her uncertainty.

"You see, it's been a while since Mary swam. She worked at a dairy farm, and she was too exhausted at night to do anything but eat and fall into bed."

"Izzy?" Renkin's voice slithered through the narrow space between them.

"Oh, hello Mr. Renkin." Her nose twitched before she sprang to her feet.

"Want to introduce me to your pally?"

Christian stood. Gray-tinted, black whiskers poked through Renkin's skin, and the sun highlighted the wrinkles around his eyes.

"Christian, this is Raymond Renkin. Mr. Renkin, this is Christian . . . ?" She raised her eyebrows.

"Graves."

Renkin pointed his cigar at him. "What kind of name is that? You one of those foreigners sneaking into this country?"

A flash of color rolled up her neck. "Graves doesn't sound foreign, and even so, it's a free country."

The man shrugged. "Eh."

She said to Christian. "Maybe we should . . . "

Renkin interrupted, "What are you doing here? This here's friends and family only."

"Mr. Renkin!"

Christian sized up the older man, whose blazer extended over his farmer's muscles. If it came to a fight, he thought he could take him.

"He's . . . was a friend of Mary's."

Renkin's teeth tightened on his cigar. "You knew Mary, eh?"

When Christian remained silent, she added, "They swam in the lake together."

Renkin rolled back his shoulders and threw his chest out. "I don't think I like you sniffing around here, Christian Graves."

Her face flushed. "I don't think that's your concern."

"Your father would consider it a favor if I kept an eye on you, seeing that he's, ah, preoccupied."

She tugged her braid and pushed a stone with her toe. Her father slumped in a chair, the forgotten plate in his lap. Several women fussed over him, pressing a glass of lemonade into his hand, chattering in his ear. He seemed oblivious.

"I came to pay my respects to Mary, and Elizabeth invited me here."

"Elizabeth?" Renkin snorted. "You putting on airs, Izzy? You're nothing but a beat country dame whose beat father lost his farm."

Christian tightened his lips at the insult to the girl and her father; from what he'd seen, he wouldn't consider them losers.

Her head jerked back. "How dare you speak about my father that way!"

"Someone ought to teach you to have some respect for your elders, Dizzy Miss Izzy." His smile held the dark promise of a secret untold. "You want to end up on ice like your sister?"

She gasped, the color melting from her face. Her lower lip quivered, and even Christian raised his eyebrows at the heartless remark. In his mind, Mary's eyes accused him, beseeched him, demanded he protect her dear, baby sister.

"Gods below," he blurted. "Leave the girl be."

Chapter 6

Present Time

The next day, Brooke hovered by her car on the east side of the nearly vacant strip mall in Canton, Simsbury's neighboring town. She'd been channeling an ice sculpture for twenty minutes, shivering while rain jiggled puddles awake and pattered the rooftops like squishy marbles. Panera Bread occupied a desolate corner, its soft lights glowing dimly through the murk. The weather had intimidated all but the hardiest of shoppers, most of who were running toward the grocery store the next block over. Reapers cruised the wet sidewalks, and she clenched her teeth against the buzzing in her brain.

She would not bolt.

She stumbled when a woman brushed by her, her umbrella nearly taking out Brooke's eye.

"Excuse you," Brooke said.

The lady gave her a snarky look. A silver streak grazed her cheek from her prissy-tight lips and ended at her clenched forehead. A moment later, a reaper's damp breath brushed the back of Brooke's neck, the chill luring a tremble down her spine.

Their gazes locked; the reaper's eyes were a dead sea of gray that burned with excitement. Her breathing escalated.

The reaper said, "She's marked."

Brooke staggered into the car behind her. The reaper drifted away, following the woman like a black shadow. Another reaper strolled along the far end of the sidewalk, and a third one crossed the parking lot, flashing his teeth at her when a car buzzed through him.

The reapers' silver-eyed stares caused an uprising of goose bumps over her body. Fleeing across the parking lot, she plunged through the door of Panera Bread, pausing to tug off her hood. The gray skies outside muted the orange interior. Tables were scattered by the door, and the far end of the shop hosted intimate booths. Most of the tables sat empty.

She raised her eyebrows, surprised she didn't recognize the two women preparing food behind the counter. How long had she been gone from work anyway?

To her right was the glass display-case showcasing the day's goodies. Abby fogged the glass with her breath, then made dots on it with her index finger. Her usual Goth clothes were replaced by a pastel-green, collared shirt—Abby detested pastel—and tan khakis, over which she'd tied an olive-green Panera Bread apron. A thin chain snaked from a silver ring on her middle finger to the wide cuff on her wrist.

She didn't quite get Abby's passion for piercings: her ears were lined with studs, her eyebrow and lip had tiny hoops, and one side of her nose flashed a small diamond, though at least she'd removed the chain hooking her right ear to her upper lip before showing up for work.

Her best friend wore her individuality like a badge of honor, and Brooke loved that about her, though she was somewhat jealous over Abby's ability to embrace her inner weirdness. Brooke didn't have the courage to stick out in a crowd; she was noticeable enough with her head rising above it. And while Abby believed in ghosts and psychics, when Brooke mentioned reapers once, Abby was adamant they didn't exist; that was the stuff made of fairy tales.

Brooke approached the counter. "Hey, Abby, what's up?"

She looked up at Brooke from her lowly 5' 3" height and raised one black-lined eyebrow. "Stilts? What are you doing here?"

"I'm out," was all she said, hoping Abby wouldn't make an epic issue out of her being Outside.

"I see that. So did you take my advice and channel Ryan through the Ouija Board? Did he tell he was going to haunt your ass for playing mouse stuck in the house?"

"No, and before you ask, Ryan's not haunting me."

"It's because you're not opening yourself up to the possibility. You're very closed-minded."

Brooke shrugged.

"So what in God's name happened to your hair? It looks like a cat puked a hairball on your head."

She eyed Abby's dyed-black hair with the neon-blue skunk stripe. Brooke knew full well her shoulder-length, bobbed, blonde hair frizzed in the rain, but she simply said, "In case you haven't noticed, it's raining like three cows pissing on a peach pit."

The other girl giggled, a light sound that cheered the otherwise-desolate coffee shop. "You're slightly confused; sewer mouth doesn't mash with pre-teen fashion."

She glanced at her jeans with their holey knees, lime-green Converse sneakers, and loose Nirvana t-shirt. "I don't dress like a kid."

"Ditch the shirt. You've got rockin' boobs, and you're hiding them under that tent. Ryan's t-shirts are too big for you."

She smoothed an imaginary wrinkle from the shirt.

Abby snapped her fingers. "I know! We'll dress you like a Catholic schoolgirl. Guys are into that kind of thing."

"How would you know?"

Her BF winked and slid a cup across the counter. "Anyway, despite your obvious lack of wardrobe sophistication, you have impeccable timing. I'm on break in a few."

"Coolness."

Brooke made a cup of very blonde coffee from the self-serve station, and then dropped into a chair at a table near the window. Her shoulders tensed when a reaper licked the glass from the other side. She switched chairs so her back was to the window, and then wrapped her fingers around the cup, trying to warm her shaking hands.

She would not bolt.

Not for the first time that day, she regretted her venture into the Outside.

Abby fixed her own cup of coffee then settled in the chair opposite her. "I have it from a very reliable source that Bekka I'm-the-Cheer-Captain-Don't-Fuck-With-Me Thomas is getting a muffin top." She wiggled her eyebrows.

"No way."

"Way. And I heard you were there when she bit it at Heublein yesterday. So is the rumor true? Did you knock her on her ass for calling you a giraffe in heels at the spring dance last year?"

"Of course not. She just fell."

"Too bad. I'd like to see someone pop that witch in the mouth." Abby clucked and pretended to punch Brooke in the jaw.

"You should be nicer. She could have died."

Abby rolled her eyes. "It's just a concussion. She'll be back to kicking by the time spring break's over. Besides, you'd think with her talent for being flexible she could've landed on her feet."

"Still, she's nice enough."

"She's a Barbie, all plastic and fake." She tapped her chin. "Though I'm pretty sure her boobs are real. They're not perky enough to be plastic."

"Maybe, but deep down I think she's just insecure."

"So she's insecure every time she calls me Elvira?"

Brooke bit her lip.

"Don't you get tired of giving everyone the benefit of the doubt?"

"Not really." She sipped her coffee. "Everyone has good and bad sides."

"God, Brooke, you get more angelic by the day."

"Okay, maybe she can be mean, but she probably has issues we don't even know about. Even Barbies have problems."

Abby sucked in her lips and let her silence speak her disagreement. Brooke squirmed in the chair, trying to mind-block the other girl's gaze drilling the space between them.

"So, you're Outside," Abby finally said, making air quotes with her fingers.

"Yup, my New Year's resolution."

"It's April."

"I'm a late bloomer."

"Coming back to work?"

Brooke shook her head.

"How about a date, then? If you're Outside, you should give Paul another chance. It's been, like, forever since you went out."

"He's not really my type."

"Seriously? He's totally boss, and he's got fabulous lips."

"Seriously. Move on."

"Have you even looked at those lips?" Abby puckered hers for extra effect.

"Of course I've looked at those lips," she admitted. "I'm just not feeling it with him. He's too, I don't know, jockish."

"He *is* seriously jacked."

Brooke dealt with the uncomfortable subject matter in the most mature way she knew how; she changed the subject. "How about you? Didn't you have some epic hook-up the other night with Willy?"

"It's Will, and you know it." Abby sighed dramatically, but then gushed, "He's majoring in psychology. Says he wants to be a sex therapist, so we have to practice like, a lot."

What a dork. Brooke counted to three before saying anything. "But he's, like, twenty-three years old." And a drug dealer, she silently added.

"So?"

"You're only twenty." Even to her ears, the argument was lame.

"And?"

Brooke drummed her fingers on the table. Abby, a year older, was a sophomore living on-campus at Central Connecticut State University. Brooke, a freshman at the same college, was too afraid to live on-campus and instead commuted back and forth. She hated how isolated that thought made her feel. Even now when everyone was home from college on spring break, no one bothered to call her anymore—except Abby.

"You're being totally lame. If you don't like the guy, just say so."

Brooke knew when she'd lost a battle with her friend. "Honestly, I don't know him well enough to like or hate him. What did you guys do?"

"Hung in my dorm room, watched a movie, sort of. We made out like the world was ending, and I had to sexile my roomie."

"Nice." Being sexiled meant being kicked out your room so your roomie could have sex.

Abby sighed. "Talk about fabulous lips. I think he's the one."

Brooke groaned. She'd heard that proclamation on a weekly basis since the seventh grade. Abby fell in and out of love each month with the consistency of the moon waxing and waning.

"You're not in love." Brooke's voice had the weary edge of a tired argument.

"Bite your tongue. He's total coolness."

"Since when does having a record for selling drugs cool?"

"It was just pot. Like you said, you don't even know him. Don't judge."

She kept her mouth shut on her argument.

Abby snapped her fingers. "I know! Maybe he's got a friend, or a brother, or knows some other boss hotcake who could de-virginize you."

"I don't think so."

"It's time to retire the wimple, Sister Brooke. If you're not feeling the Paul thing—which quite frankly stuns me—I'm finding you a guy." She lowered her voice. "Maybe that guy who just walked in. Holy shit, but he sure knows how to rock that shirt."

Brooke's muscles clenched when a grape scent rode the draft that drifted down the back of her neck. Her mouth opened. Her eyes widened. She looked away, then back, but he was still there. Still smiling and bringing the draft of death with him.

The almost-reaper from Heublein strolled to the counter.

"Got to go." Abby tripped over her own feet to get there to serve him.

"Coffee, black, and as hot as you," he winked, "got."

Her cheeks flushed, never looking away from the almost-reaper's face as she found a cup and slid it over the counter. "Anything else?" Her voice squeaked, sounding as though she was having trouble breathing.

"I'm good." He laid money on the counter. "Keep the change."

"Yeah, right. Thanks."

She started around the counter as though wanting to follow him, but was held back by another customer. Almost-reaper dumped about a pound of sugar into his coffee before settling at a table, where he watched Brooke with a smirk.

She leaped from her chair and slammed to a stop three feet from his table. "Are you freaking stalking me?"

He smiled. "Small world."

"What are you doing here?"

"Having coffee."

"You can't."

"This is a public place, isn't it?"

"Yes, but . . . "

"Are you refusing me service?"

"No, but . . . "

"Okay then. I want coffee; they serve coffee. What's the problem?"

Her lips tightened. "You are. Go to the Panera Bread in Torrington."

The silver in his eyes flickered, and her heart stuttered.

He said, "I like this coffee."

"It's the same coffee."

"The service here is better." He ogled Abby as she leaned her elbows on the counter to watch them.

Brooke slammed her palms onto the table. "Stay away from her."

His gaze tracked down her neck to her chest, and then trailed back up to her face. Her temperature rose with his gaze.

"Jealous?" he asked.

She snapped straight up. "No."

"Hey, you guys know each other?" Abby called from the counter.

"No!" Brooke shouted at the same time he said, "Yes."

"Oka-ay," Abby said, and then turned away to ring up her customer.

"What do you think you're doing?" Brooke demanded.

He leaned back, stretched his legs, and lifted his cup. "I thought we already settled that question."

She rolled her eyes and snorted. "Not that. Why are you stalking me?"

"Not stalking. Hunting."

His widening smile kept pace with her widening eyes.

"Stay away from her."

"I'm not interested in her."

Her lips went numb.

He laughed softly. "It's you I want."

Chapter 7

1938

Elizabeth and Renkin's mouths dropped open in unison. Christian realized too late that he shouldn't have used a curse so common in the Other World; now they both looked at him as though demonic horns had sprouted through his hair. His words seemed to sap the song from the birds and the shine from the sun. All that existed was the buzz of dread in his head.

"What did you say?" Renkin asked. "You a devil worshiper?"

He shook his head.

"'Gods below' sounds like you're talking about the devil. You lying?"

He shoved his hands into his pockets.

"Speak up, boy!"

"No."

"Dark clothes . . . "

Tension tightened Christian's jaw.

"Dark hair . . . "

His gaze swiveled left and right, unable to land. Renkin was getting much, much too close to the truth.

"And you got hinky eyes."

Christian shifted from one foot to the other. His eyes were a mix of silver and blue . . . human blue from his mother, and reaper silver from his father. He glared at Elizabeth . . . it was her fault Mary conned him into making that promise.

Renkin thunked his walking stick on the dock. "Explain

yourself before I haul you off to the coppers and let them put the screws to you."

The girl tilted her head, her eyes boring into Christian's as though she could see inside him. The older man chewed his cigar. Christian had no idea how to extricate himself from this situation. He swallowed twice to hamper his developing fury.

"It's just a saying where I'm from," he finally said.

"And where's that?"

"Down south."

Renkin spat. "Hinky southerners. Wouldn't surprise me one bit to hear they got devil worshipers."

Elizabeth flicked her braid over her shoulder. "It's just slang."

"You know nothing about this grifter." Renkin waved his cigar in Christian's direction. "You can't keep picking up every stray you find."

"He's not a stray."

The man's gaze raked Christian's threadbare clothes. He glowered at the potato salad crusting over on his plate, but his appetite had vanished.

"Why don't you just take a powder, will you?" In a swift movement, Renkin jammed his walking stick into Christian's chest.

He stumbled back, his heels catching the edge of the dock, his weight carrying him backwards. Lake water smacked into his backside. His boots dragged him downward. Icy water closed over his head, freezing what little breath he had in his lungs. His coat cocooned his arms. Panic froze him for long, motionless moments before he finally kicked his feet and stretched a hand toward a pinpoint of sunlight wavering above him. His toes touched bottom. He thrust upward, stretching his fingers toward the sun, but it was out of reach.

His lungs burned. Spots sparkled in front of his eyes. The sunlight dimmed. He longed to release his hoarded breath and gasp in another.

A tug on his arm. A water sprite's golden braid wafted like a silky snake, her green eyes determined beneath her furrowed brow. All things considered, it wasn't a bad way to die. At least he wouldn't be alone as Mary had been. He smiled.

She grabbed him by the armpits and pulled him through the water until they broke the surface. Christian sucked in large quantities of air, choking, gasping, his lungs aching and his eyes burning. As the water tried to claim his body once again, he slapped the surface.

"Don't fight me," Elizabeth said.

He obeyed, relaxing in her arms as she towed him to the dock. He scrambled atop its dry safety and sprawled onto his back, coughing up a surprising amount of water.

She hovered over him, her braid dripping onto his face. "Can't you swim?"

He shook his head. Biting her lip, she sat on her heels.

"Izzy?" a woman called from shore. "Is the boy all right?"

A young lad knelt next to him. Soundly vaguely disappointed, he said, "He ain't dead." He scampered back down the dock.

"Are you all right?"

Christian spit out another mouthful of water and nodded.

"He's fine," she said, and the gawking onlookers dispersed.

Christian stood, his wet clothes sticking to his skin. His feet squished inside his boots, and he shivered. Breathing aggravated his sore lungs, and another spate of coughing wracked his body. Drops of water traced her face while she studied him, a different Elizabeth from the petulant child who had annoyed him. Her wet clothes molded against her curves, and heat flicked along his skin.

"Thank you," he said, surprise whispering through his tone.

Renkin's cigar wobbled between his grinding teeth. He stepped close to him, his tobacco breath hissing through his lips. "This family don't need any more trouble. Take a powder and leave them be. And you . . . " He gave Elizabeth the up-and-down. "Change your clothes." He stomped down the dock and across the yard.

Two shots of pink sharpened her cheeks. "Mr. Renkin's not usually so rude, just odd. Mary hated him, said he was a trouble-boy."

Christian squeezed water from his coat.

"I think he's too old to be a gangster, though."

Was her smile always lopsided, or was she simply too tired to move her lips?

"Izzy!"

Her father stood, his shoulders hunched, gesturing to her. Next to him, Renkin tapped his stick.

She brushed Christian's arm with her fingertips. "I need to change."

He nodded.

"I'll be right back."

She strolled away from him, turned and parted her lips as though to speak, then moved toward the house. Hurrying down the dock, he dusted the place without looking back; if he saw Elizabeth again he would stay . . . and he'd already lingered too long.

He sloshed into the woods, groaning when he saw William leaning against a tree, tossing an apple with one hand.

William stared, his lips flat. His eyes, a marbled mix of silver and blue, roved Christian from head to toe to head. "You look like a drowned rat."

He slowed. It had been a long time since he'd spoken to his one-time protector and great uncle, and he didn't want to talk to him now. Straightening his shoulders, he marched past him.

William grabbed Christian's arm. "What do you think you're doing?"

"Walking."

"I heard you tried abstaining again, you sap."

He didn't answer. When reapers abstained from Giltine's poison, longing ate their bones like a disease; a torturous existence at best. William and Christian weren't full-blood reapers; they were secucron, half-reaper and half-human. Because of their humanity, he thought they could live without Giltine's poison, so he'd tried abstaining a number of times. So far, he'd been wrong. The pain always proved too much to bear, and Giltine always punished him for refusing to reap.

"How long did you last this time?" William asked.

"Four weeks."

He whistled. "That's a personal record. Better look out, or Giltine will send her watchers after you."

"They don't exist."

His great uncle laughed. "Poor Giltine. She has no watchers to keep her reapers in line."

"Lucky for you."

He waved his apple. "Remember how the reapers tailed you like hellhounds when Giltine first dragged you to the Other World? You were lucky to have kin to protect you."

Christian started walking. It was true. He didn't know what secret William held, but reapers let him be. And when Christian was with him, they let Christian be.

"Was all that effort just a trip for biscuits?"

Christian said, "Sorry if I wasted your time. Maybe you should have let the reapers kill me when I was fourteen."

"I'd never let you die, Thomas, you know that, right?"

Christian's feet dragged to a halt. Thomas, William's twin brother and his grandfather, died decades ago.

"What?"

William took a large bite of apple, and then went on as though Christian hadn't spoken. "Why have you been hanging around here?"

"I made a promise that I'd, ah, look out for someone."

"So? Break it. Giltine doesn't care about human bargains. It's not worth getting ringed for it."

Christian shrugged.

"I saw that dame pull you out of the water."

"Spying for her?"

"No, but if you're looking to pitch some woo, I know a few secucron babes who'd be glad to relieve your tension." William bit the apple and wiggled his eyebrows.

"She saved my life."

"So did I." His silent gaze accused. "Giltine has only three rules." He ticked them off on his fingers. "No interacting with humans. No suicide. No taking souls that haven't been marked by her." He winked at this last point. "They're not that hard to follow, especially that last one."

"You don't follow that last one."

"We're not talking about me. We're talking about you. Besides, you know she only punishes us secucron if we break her rules; it's the reapers who have to worry, because she'll sentence them to death. But right now you, my friend, need more than a hit of poison."

"No."

"I've always liked you, you know that." William tossed the apple. "Gods, but you remind me of Thomas. He was a stubborn jackass too. And so *nice*."

He tightened his lips. "I'm not so nice."

"Because you stole a few souls once upon a time? Gods, you get sappier by the day."

Christian winced inwardly. For years he'd followed William like a lost soul. Young and scared, he'd mimicked him, even going rogue and stealing unmarked souls—an intense experience that was highly addictive, not to mention illegal—but a stolen soul couldn't cross to the other side. Stolen souls became lost in a remote abyss for eternity. Stolen souls were murdered souls.

He swallowed. He despised himself for the souls he condemned to the abyss. In the end, he couldn't live a rogue reaper's life, or with himself. He left William to find his own path, and his great uncle had never forgiven him. Still, the guilt weighed on Christian's soul, making it impossible for him to stand fully erect.

William said, "If you're worried about Giltine finding out, don't be. I can protect you. There's not a reaper out there who'll rat me out."

He didn't want to be like William, family or not, protection or not. The man was nothing but an Other World thug. Christian couldn't undo his past; all he could do was vow to keep his distance from his great uncle and follow the rules . . . until he found a way to free himself from Giltine, the Other World, and William. Then Christian would dust this place, never look back, and find some way to redeem himself.

"I can't."

"But we're kin!" William slapped the tree by Christian's head, and he flinched. William breathed slowly through his nose before saying, "You can't change who you are. Once a rogue, always a rogue."

"I've changed."

"Suit yourself. But you can't have the dame, so forget her. I mean it. Do you know why we're not allowed to get cozy with humans?"

"So we don't get found out. Someone like that Renkin could have me jailed, or have me dancing on the end of a rope."

"No, genius, it's because emotions get in the way of duty. Emotional secucron die trying to bargain with Giltine for their freedom."

He crossed his arms. Even if he liked Elizabeth enough to risk a bargain with Giltine—which he didn't, even if she did save his life—he wouldn't admit that to his uncle.

"Fine." William walked a few steps, then stopped and snapped his fingers. "Oh, right, one more thing." He twitched a grin. "Giltine wants to see you."

Christian kicked the dirt, shooting a spray of dead leaves into the air. Several crusty ones stuck to his wet boot. "I thought you said you weren't spying."

"I wasn't spying. I'm fetching. Let's go."

Shit! Once again, the image of Giltine's ring spun through his head. He wanted to scream or break something or sock William on the chin. Instead, Christian turned his back on his smirking great uncle and fell into the Void with a violent shudder.

Chapter 8

Present Time

Hunting.

The gloom of the coffee shop competed with the doom of the almost-reaper's words. Brooke stared at his smirky smile, the word *hunting* pummeling her brain Ali-style and muffling the chatter of two older women debating whether the chocolate or the raspberry pastry was worse for their hips.

The almost-reaper was hunting her. She was as good as road kill.

All the feeling slid from her body. She stumbled back on numb feet into the table behind her, and a chair clattered to the floor. The sound barely squeaked through the deafening sound of blood pounding between her ears.

"Are you scared?" he asked.

"Yes," she whispered.

She snuck a peek over her shoulder, thankful for the handful of witnesses in case this guy pounced on her like a feral fox. With trembling fingers, she picked up the chair and set it back on its feet.

The almost-reaper gave her a half-smile. "Sorry. I was just messing with you, having fun with your, ah, curse."

"My what?"

"Not a curse really. More like a limitation."

Brooke crossed her arms, hugging herself tightly in order to support her upright position. "Cut the riddle crap. What are you talking about?"

He leaned his elbows on the table. "You can't lie, can you?"

"I *can* lie, unless I've been asked a direct question. How'd you know?"

"Just a guess."

"You're really slanted, you know that?"

"I said I was sorry."

"Too little, too late."

He crossed an X on his chest with his index finger. "I swear, I was only messing around, and I'm not some loser who's out looking to hurt girls. I just think you're interesting and want to be your friend. That's all. Is that okay?"

She brushed the tip of her nose. Abby drooled from across the room, the glint in her eye unmistakable. The girl would soon be on a mission to play the new game in town. He'd invaded Brooke's space, a puzzle that needed to be put together before Abby started toying with the pieces. Would the finished picture be a friend, or an enemy?

Before Brooke could answer, a wet draft blew through the door with a couple of guys from her old high school. Her spine stiffened when she spied the two stoners heading for Abby. Oh, great. Why now? How could she watch over her friend while this almost-reaper was distracting her? Why did she ever leave her F-bomb house?

One of the guys, Matt, brushed back his long, dirty-blond hair, plastering it against his head. His friend, Jake, leaned against the counter and gave Brooke a small wave. She sucked in her cheeks, but waved back.

"Trouble?" almost-reaper asked.

"Maybe," she murmured.

Abby set down two coffee cups, and Matt, after slinking a glance around the coffee shop, slid a small baggy with his money across the counter.

"Is that what I think it is?" almost-reaper asked.

"Yup."

"Judging by the tone of your voice, you don't approve."

"Nope."

"Amazing how easily one can get addicted to poison."

Though she didn't approve, she hardly thought pot was poison. This almost-reaper was getting on her last nerve, so she ignored him. Abby poked the ring in her lip with her tongue, hesitated for a second, then scooped up the package and the money. The baggy went into her pocket, the money into the register. She giggled at something Matt said, and the guys wandered to the self-service station.

Brooke strode across the shop. "Are you completely off your nut?"

"I wasn't the last time I checked, Nurse Ratchet."

"If you keep walking in a pasture you're bound to step in shit."

"Is that your way of telling me I'm hanging with the wrong crowd?"

"You're going to get fired . . . or arrested."

Abby grinned. "Chill, I'm not going to get caught."

"I bet that's what Willy said before he got arrested."

"It's Will."

"I thought you said you were going to lay off that stuff?"

"It's just weed."

"It's a gateway drug."

"That's bull." Abby whipped out a rag and attacked a spot on the counter. "Look, I don't tell you to get out of the house or to get a life or to get laid. Okay, I do tell you to get laid, but you could at least return the favor by butting out."

Brooke tapped her fingernail on the counter. "I'm sorry. But you know . . . "

"You're just worried about me, yada, yada, yada," Abby finished for her. "I've heard it a hundred times. But chill, I'm good, I don't need saving. I'm a college girl just having fun, and I'll lie low . . . soon."

"Promise?"

"Promise. So, how's tricks?" She raised her eyebrows in almost-reaper's direction.

"Too tricky for me."

"You really need to loosen up."

"And you need to tighten up."

Abby laughed before disappearing into the back room. Brooke slumped against the counter.

"Trouble in paradise?" the almost-reaper asked.

She sighed. "Are you still here?"

"Well, duh."

Wetting her lips, she asked, "Why are you here? Somehow that getting-to-know-me excuse sounds like some lame pick-up line from the 1900s."

"Ow. That one stung."

She shrugged.

He tilted his head. "You see them, right? The reapers?"

"Yes."

She studied the silver glistening in his eyes. Her dry throat locked when she tried to swallow, and she mentally smacked her palm against her forehead. Talking to a reaper, even if he wasn't quite all reaper, was stupid. It was time to get level.

She made to push past him, but he moved in front of her. She bounced off his chest.

"I'm not just a reaper, Brooke. I'm half human."

"How is that possible?" she whispered.

"Long story." He inhaled deeply, closing his eyes. "Gods below, but you smell good." It seemed to take an eternity for him to open his eyes again. As though hypnotized, he twirled a strand of her hair. "Did you know your hair is the color of honey?"

She slapped his hand away.

"You know, I came to warn you, but you've been so incredibly bitchy maybe I won't."

"Warn me about what?"

"You can't hide behind walls. Reapers can sense you—your body is like a marquee of heat—and someone's noticed. Someone like me."

"An almost-reaper?"

He laughed. "Almost-reaper, I like that. Technically, though, I'm a secucro."

"Why does this secu-whatever care about me?"

"You're kind of a descendant of a watcher, and he wants you."

"I'm a what?"

"Isn't that what you do? Watch us?"

"Not unless I can help it," she muttered, wishing she'd stayed locked in her room. "So, who is this guy?"

"Just do me a favor and don't talk to any almost-reapers but me. Promise?"

Brooke was about to agree, but something inside her stalled her words. She was very careful about making promises, because she had a tendency to knock herself out trying to keep them. Why should she promise this almost-demon anything, anyway?

"No," she said. "I'm not even planning on talking to *you*."

Almost-reaper chuckled and headed for the door.

"Wait," she called. "What's with the warning? What's in it for you?"

He smiled slowly. "Maybe I have my own plans."

A creepy-crawling feeling inched down her arms. "Who are you?"

"William, but my friends call me Billy."

She poked her tongue in her cheek. "So tell me, *William*, what this guy wants with me."

"Well, Brooke, it's simple. He wants to kill you."

Chapter 9

1938

Christian's feet slammed into the ground, his teeth chattering from taking the Other World journey in sodden clothes. He bent his knees to absorb the impact then, without missing a beat, hurried down the tunnel and climbed the mountain. His trousers, still wet from his fall into the lake, chafed his legs, and his boots felt like cement, while his heart lay heavy in his chest. Being summoned by Giltine was one of the most petrifying events in his sorry life, and could only mean one thing. The good news was that her punishments weren't lethal.

Usually.

"Come on. Don't be mad."

He ignored William.

At the top of the stairs, he swept his hand toward the wall. "After you."

"Piss off," Christian muttered, and stepped through.

A field of dead grass stretched toward a red horizon. Endless, red sky, bloated with shrieking buzzards, sizzled with heat. The air was excruciatingly dry, sucking the moisture from Christian's body. His tongue swelled in his mouth, and he couldn't swallow. William whistled, seemingly unaffected—one of the benefits of the souls he'd stolen. Would his great uncle ever get caught breaking that cardinal rule? Christian snorted. Somehow the man always managed to skate by.

Rows of shacks, built of gray, aged wood, crawled across the sand like crippled snakes. Chimneys burped columns of smoke upon which rode the smell of roasting rat-like creatures and other vermin that slunk through the Other World. Occasionally a buzzard was captured and put on the spit.

Christian preferred human food that could only be found topside, which was difficult to obtain unless a secucro was adept at lying, cheating, and stealing.

Over the years, he'd become very adept at lying, cheating, and stealing.

Secucron lounged in doorways, watching him. Most preferred to live in the Other World, bartering for human food and other topside goods on the secucron black market.

Christian glanced back at William, but he'd wandered toward the shacks, chatting up a female secucro.

Skeletal souls worked at dead soil with rusty tools, clouds of dust pillowing around them. Flies buzzed into the souls' infected sores. He tasted brine and sulfur and bit his thumbnail to keep from screaming, just like the first time he'd come here with Giltine five years ago, the day of his fourteenth birthday.

Christian had to trot to keep up with Giltine as she marched across the dead grass.

She instructed him with a brittle tone. "This is the first level of the Other World. Since you are too weak to survive the other levels, this is where you'll reside. You are to usher souls to the Other Side. You will identify these souls by the silver mark I leave on their faces."

"Why me?" he asked.

"Because your father has given your life to me in exchange for his freedom. You're my *child now."*

Christian swallowed and tried to ignore his trembling lips. They reached a stone wall. Men and women climbed ladders and fitted stones into vacant spaces with bloodied hands. *Their faces were drawn, eyes dark hollows, worms crawling over their skin and clothes.*

"Who are these people?" He winced. It hurt his throat to speak.

She watched them with the calculated interest of a scientist studying microorganisms under glass—interested but detached. "These are the souls who have not passed judgment. These are the souls who do not deserve to live after life."

I'm in Hell, he thought.

"You are only to take those souls who are marked."

"Why?"

Her gaze was sharp as an ice pick. "Only I have power over death. If you take that power away from me, if you disobey me and steal an unmarked soul, you will be punished. Do you understand?"

He nodded and flinched, realizing he'd bitten his nail so far down it bled. Giltine snapped her fingers. A man, crippled by dehydration, offered her a leather pouch. She sucked greedily, and her gulps echoed in his ears.

He reached for the pouch, begged, "Please."

"I'm afraid not, my dear Christian. When you usher souls you will be rewarded with poison, which provides you with the sustenance you require to survive the Other World. The more souls you usher, the more comfortable you will be within my domain. But don't worry. I love my children, and as long as you obey me, we'll get along just fine." She touched his cheek, an icy finger that made him shiver. "But as all good mothers do, I will punish those who misbehave."

He dropped to his knees, covered his face with his hands, and wept. Instead of tears, dust streaked his face.

"Hello, my dear Christian."

The throaty voice snapped him back to the present. The woman's filmy, white dress brushed the ground when she sauntered toward him. A crown of tightly woven feathers perched on her wild, dark hair, with a white streak that sprouted from one temple to sweep behind her head. Her eyes were dark as deep caves, and her red lips pouted, crinkling the leathered skin around her mouth.

"Giltine," he whispered.

"Welcome back." She brushed back her hair, her sleeve puddling around her elbow and exposing a leathery, pale arm. One gnarled finger was entwined by a gold ring of a snake eating its tail.

He ignored his thirst, his burning feet, and the staring secucron. The arid air made his clothes steam.

She peered at him over her steepled fingers. "My spies have been watching you."

Air suddenly seemed in short supply; there wasn't enough to reach his lungs as he panted.

"You see, my dear Christian, after three attempts at abstinence, I decided it would behoove me to pay closer attention to you." She turned the ring on her finger. "Four weeks is a long time to go without my poison. I was prepared to send for you, until you acquiesced and ushered that girl's soul."

Wiping his fingertips across his sweat-greased forehead, his gaze slipped to the ground.

"Look at me when I speak to you!"

He jerked his head up, staring at her flaring nostrils and tight lips.

"You broke two rules. One, you abstained, and by abstaining you think to leave me, which will not do. You're mine, and you're here to reap. " Giltine's low tone was as menacing as a rattlesnake's rattle.

"Why should I be sacrificed for my father's freedom?"

Her smile softened her lips but her eyes remained hard. "Because your father didn't give me what I wanted. So I took what I wanted from him."

A child. He plucked the seams of his pants, unable to swallow, unable to blink, unable to look away from the ring on her finger, spinning, spinning.

"Then there's the girl," she said.

He didn't think his mouth could get any drier, but now terror scorched his tongue. She knew about Elizabeth. Did she know about his promise to Mary?

"I needed food."

"For three days?"

"But . . . "

"Do you think I don't *know*?" Giltine's tone was glacial.

"Know what?" Not only did his voice crack, it rose in pitch.

She grabbed his chin and forced him to look at her. Her ring froze the hairs on his face. "Do not test me, my dear Christian."

A commotion drew her attention—and her ring—from him. Two reapers dragged another through the wall.

"We've discovered a rogue," one reaper said.

Giltine advanced upon them like an enraged lioness. "How dare you?"

Her voice was almost as sharp as her hand slapping the rogue reaper's face. The rogue jerked back, but the other two reapers held her in place.

"Do not for one moment believe I do not know reapers flaunt my laws and steal souls. Do not for one moment believe an absence of watchers means you will not be discovered. Do not for one moment believe you will not be punished!"

The rogue's fear was rank on Christian's tongue. He couldn't keep his gaze from flashing to William. Grinning, his great uncle shrugged and leaned against the shack with his arms folded across his chest. At the sound of Giltine's raised voice, the other secucron had fled inside their shacks.

"Take her to the third level," she barked.

The reapers relinquished the rogue to two black-hooded disciples, who'd materialized as though they were heat-induced mirages. Christian dipped his head in order to see their faces, but all he saw were endless shadows accompanied by the stench of death, like rotting eggs. The disciples hauled the resistant rogue across the dead field.

"No!" the rogue screamed. "That'll kill me. No!"

Giltine's frustration vibrated along her spine before she took a deep breath and regained her rigidity. She spun toward him. "And you, my dear Christian, are as untrustworthy as your maggot father."

He blinked. "My . . . my father?"

Her nose flared. "Take my hand. Now."

The ring gleamed. He swallowed, rubbed his palms on his trousers, felt and smelled the sweat springing from beneath his arms and along his back. *No*, he longed to beg. *Please don't make me do this.*

He would not beg.

Pulling in as much air as he could, he held it and looked her in the eye. Fear gripped his heart as viciously as she gripped his fingers.

Ice flashed over his hand, scratched and bit its way up his arm, across his shoulder, crawled into his mouth and nose, scraped against his lungs. He clenched his teeth, air hissing between his lips, but every breath brought arctic air into his chest and his veins, encasing his body in agony.

The ground wavered in front of him. He crashed to his knees. He tried to drag his hand from Giltine's icy grip, but it was as though their hands had been frozen together.

His body convulsed, clenched in a rigor mortis of pain. A shriek punctured his eardrums. The shrieking went on and on and on. He longed for Giltine to put the tortured soul out of its misery so he could die in peace.

She released him. He arched his back, his lips peeled away from his teeth, eyes bulging as though his lids had frozen open, fingers bent like fish hooks. The painful spasm unclenched its grip and, gasping, he curled into a ball and opened his eyes, cracked slits in his icy face. Surprise and shock pierced his frozen senses.

The screaming came from him.

Chapter 10

Present Time

After dropping the he-wants-to-kill-you bombshell, William gave Brooke a wink and strode out of the coffee shop. More than one girl's head—and even some guys'—turned to watch him go. Her legs collapsed. Thankfully, a chair caught her before she crashed into the floor. *Kill* her? Why would some almost-reaper want to kill *her*?

Abby grabbed her arm. "You okay?"

"No."

"What did that horn dog do to you? Shit, you're too nice for the bad boys. Just say the word, and I'll kick his righteously fine ass."

"It's okay, just lightheaded."

"Maybe you should switch to decaf."

"Maybe you're right."

"You sure you're okay? Maybe I can channel some of your angel complex and save *you*. Are you sure you don't want me to chase him down and kiss his ass?"

"Don't you mean kick?"

Abby winked. "Well, obviously."

Brooke chuckled weakly. "I'm good."

Abby wiped down tables, humming to herself and tossing protective looks at Brooke. After ten minutes of splitting napkins into a pile of spaghetti with fingers that trembled like an addict's, and enduring a firestorm in her gut she feared would morph into a puking episode, she decided to jet. She said goodbye to Abby—who promised to call later—and paused outside on the sidewalk to grab some much-needed fresh air. The earlier rain had ushered in a warm front, and now a humid mist roiled across the parking lot. A low growl of thunder warned that the storm hadn't left.

Partly secreted by the fog, a shadow leaned against a motorcycle parked three spots from her car. Legs stretched in front of him, arms crossed over his chest, watching.

She sniffed. There was a sweet, soul-stealing residue in the air, though not nearly as strong as with William.

Her heart bungee-jumped to her knees, and her reaper radar almost buzzed . . . what she was guessing was her almost-reaper radar. This guy had to be the other almost-reaper William warned her about.

The one who wanted to kill her.

Her chest muscles constricted and stopped the flow of blood to her head. She tried to wet her lips, but her tongue was like sandpaper. She wanted to run back inside, but she didn't want to drag Abby into this nightmare. For a brief moment she almost wished William was there.

She scanned the empty sidewalk, and though cars powered their way down Route 44, she was alone. She needed a weapon. Leaning against the brick building, she fumbled inside her purse. Her fingers played over useless objects: hairbrush, make-up, iPhone, keys.

She white-knuckled her car key like a tiny sword. She didn't know anything about these almost-reapers . . . were they fast? Strong? She didn't even know if they could be killed, though being half-human, she thought the least she could do was jab out his eyes.

He still hadn't moved.

Oh, why hadn't she parked closer to the door?

She crept across the parking lot. Her bladder muscles loosened as she inched forward, sweat clinging to her armpits. He was still channeling a statue by the time she reached her car, though his head turned slowly to track her movement. Silver eyes gleamed in the dark. She hesitated, lowered her pathetic weapon, and dove into the driver's seat. She flipped the locks, jammed the key into the ignition and, with a shot of squealing tires, peeled out of the parking lot.

Brooke checked out the almost-reaper in her rearview mirror. His head turned as he watched her drive off.

By the time she got home, rain pelted her as she raced to the front door. She paused on the porch to shake water out of her hair. Flashes of lightning lit the white rocking chairs, creaking in the ghostly wind, and a peal of thunder rolled through the darkness.

She took her shoes off in the foyer, and then paused by the living room. She was surprised to see her dad watching TV. As a contract lawyer, he had a tendency to work long hours, though he tried to make it home by seven each night. Her mom, a medical assistant for a local doctor, was more punctual about her hours, and was settled in her usual spot in the leather recliner, cuddled with a book and a blanket. The iridescent-green curtains and the soft glow of a lamp accented the room's oak-wood floors and chocolate-colored furniture. The air was rich with the scent of Murphy's Oil Soap.

The warm light didn't hide how much older her parents looked, and Brooke couldn't help but wonder if her dad had been that bald and her mom's face that lined before Ryan died.

"Where've you been?" her mom asked, sticking a finger between the pages of her book.

Shivering, Brooke said, "Panera Bread. I left you a note."

She couldn't ignore the look that passed between her parents.

"I know, I just didn't expect you to be gone so long," her mom said, and a small smile tickled her lips. "It's good seeing you get out again."

No one mentioned the reason why Brooke shut herself away. No one mentioned Ryan's death. No one mentioned how his room sat closed off from the family, lifeless and empty. She shifted from one foot to the other.

"Everything okay?" her dad asked.

"Everything's cool. I'm just wet, so I want to go change."

"Okay, dinner's in half an hour," her mom said.

She ran up the stairs to her room, shutting the door and then leaning against it. Lola, her overweight calico cat, stretched on her bed, digging her claws into the moss-green comforter. Her gaze traveled the room.

After months holing up in that small twelve-by-twelve space, she had every speck of dust memorized on the green-flowered curtains, her white-pine dresser cluttered with make-up and hair bands and knick-knacks, the full-length mirror that she used to hang scarves and belts and bras, the chocolate-milk stain on the cream-colored rug next to her nightstand, and the cobweb that had taken residence in one corner of her ceiling.

As much as this room comforted her, she was kind of glad she'd gone Outside. Kind of, because even though she faced the Outside and kicked her phobia's ass, she seemed to have stumbled into an almost-reaper nightmare.

"What an epic mess," she muttered.

After changing into flannel polar-bear lounge pants and one of Ryan's high school wrestling shirts, she nudged Lola off her side of the bed. Flipping open her laptop, she went straight for Google. She drummed her fingers on her thigh. What had William called her? She thought a moment and then typed "watcher".

She toggled through a gajillion sites: weight watchers, bird watchers, whale watchers, suicide watchers. She hovered over a religious site about fallen angels, called watchers.

"Oh, please." She clicked anyway.

Watchers were angels sent by God to watch over Earth, but not to interfere. Some watchers became corrupt, lusting after women, marrying, and living among men. These sons of God taught men things they shouldn't know, and went to the daughters of men and had children with them, called Nephilim. These sins could not be tolerated. The angels fell from God's grace, were banished from heaven, and imprisoned.

Brooke wasn't religious, and had never believed in angels. There was life, and there was death. Her gaze settled on the corner of the ceiling where the cobweb undulated in a current of air. She snapped her laptop closed. This was lame. Watchers didn't exist. She knew at the heart of her bottom she was no angel, fallen or not.

But reapers existed. Could things get any more slanted than that?

Why would a reaper want to kill her anyway? It wasn't like she'd done anything to piss one off, had she?

Brooke pressed her palms to her head. The only thing she'd ever done was witness a reaper taking an unmarked soul . . . her brother's. Her insides twisted like a French braid. Maybe that was a crime where reapers came from. Maybe this almost-reaper who wanted to kill her was the one who stole her brother's soul. Maybe he was after her to shut her up . . . permanently.

A motorcycle put-putted down her street, and she peered through the window. The rain had retracted its icy nails like cat claws, leaving a steady drizzle behind. Streetlights didn't exist on the road she lived on, though the lights in her driveway bounced off the flat-black motorcycle tooling slowly past her house. The rider was dressed in black, and she couldn't see clearly enough to see his features, but she could see him turn his head to study the house.

Gasping, she jerked away from the window and leaned against the wall, her heart spitting nails in her chest. Was it her imagination, or had she seen the glint of silver eyes in the darkness?

Chapter 11

1938

Christian tried to convince himself Giltine's reference to him being as untrustworthy as his father was meant to provoke him. He hated his father; hated what he'd been and what he'd done. Unlike his father, he would never sacrifice another's life in order to be free from Giltine's servitude.

Still, her words haunted him.

Despite her crippling punishment, he left New Hartford and traveled east, traversing the towns of Canton and Avon until he reached Simsbury, hugging the shadows like a defeated dog.

The windows of his former house stared like lifeless eyes. The curtains were drawn, the windows sealed. A white-oak tree stood as a solitary sentry over the single lawn chair in the yard. Despite the deceased feel, the lawn was manicured, the window boxes nested flocks of purple petunias, and pruned rhododendron and azalea bushes circled a stone terrace.

"Christian?"

Forrest, an old friend of Christian's parents and caretaker of this property, had come around the corner of the house and froze by the front door. Dirt scuffed his chin and clung to the knees of his denim overalls. He held a clay flowerpot in one hand and a trowel in the other. His gaping mouth was almost as round as his green-silver eyes.

"Gods of the Other World." The trowel slipped from Forrest's fingers and bounced off the concrete stoop. The pot shattered.

"Hello, Forrest."

He held out his hand. Forrest ignored it and hugged him instead. Slowly, his warmth released the tight ache in Christian's chest. It had been a very long time since someone had touched him without inflicting pain.

Forrest patted his back. "You're a block of ice." Grabbing his hand, he studied the fresh, red mark flaring across the pale scars of past punishments. "Giltine's been giving you a taste of her ring."

"Yes."

He guided him to the lawn chair. "It's good to see you, boy."

Christian lowered himself stiffly into the chair. "You too."

"Wait there. I'll get another chair."

The older man trotted to a gray shed tucked into the corner of the yard. Christian leaned back in the chair, letting the sun warm his face. Next to the shed, a caretaker's cottage gleamed with fresh paint. Across the street a cut in the trees revealed how the terrain rose sharply, giving birth to Talcott Mountain. The Heublein's summerhouse dominated the horizon.

Mr. Heublein, master of his personal piece of Talcott Mountain, his freedom, and his destiny . . . until he'd died the year before. Even free men couldn't escape Giltine's poisonous tongue.

Unfolding another chair, Forrest asked, "So, what brings you to Simsbury?"

Christian shrugged.

"I haven't seen you since you turned fourteen. You've aged."

"So have you."

Forrest ran a hand over his weakening hairline. "I stay topside mostly."

"Me too." Christian hesitated, and then asked, "How's Grandmother?"

He harbored many a vile thought about his grandmother, a puritanical, religious woman who never cared for his reaper-turned-grave-digger father and never spared a kind word for Christian, although she'd been quite fond of the rod she used for punishments. Despite her religious rigidity, she was the only family he had left, and he felt obliged to inquire of her.

"Dead," Forrest said.

"When?"

"Just a few months after your parents passed. Riding accident. You're the sole heir of her estate."

Christian snorted, wiggling his frozen toes inside his boots. "I find that hard to believe. She hated me."

The other man scratched his ear. "She hated everyone."

Christian dug deep, but felt nothing at her passing. Still, his sigh dragged his shoulders downward. He was truly alone now. He only had Forrest, his father's best friend and his pretend uncle whom he'd avoided for the past five years. And William, of course, but he didn't count anymore.

"Gods below, I feel so alone."

"Do you hate me?" Forrest's voice was heavy.

"You're not the one who traded my life to Giltine."

"You hadn't been born when your father bargained. He did it for your mother."

Irritation snapped inside Christian's gut. "Don't defend him. He was a liar."

Forrest folded his hands across his stomach, which had grown wider over the years. "He saved my life."

Christian raised his eyebrows. Because Giltine favored her secucron children, reapers hated them. It was true, for while she punished secucron for breaking her rules, he never heard of her sentencing one to death . . . unless they tried to bargain for their freedom. "Why would he save you?"

"He had a soul by then; and because I saved your mother's life."

"Mom?" A forgotten kind of warmth flickered in his chest, and Christian sat straighter. "Tell me."

"You know how Giltine bargains with reapers, offering them souls in exchange for becoming her mate. But like the reapers she propositioned before him, your father fell in love with a human. Not one reaper has ever fallen for Giltine." Forrest jutted his chin toward Talcott Mountain. "Your mother was out walking when she took a fall, knocking herself unconscious."

Christian nodded for him to continue.

"I'd been cruising for a number when I saw her. I didn't understand what the reaper was doing with her. It wasn't until I was overpowered by this sweet aroma, like wild grapes, and her body started to convulse I realized he was a rogue and he was snatching her soul."

Did Forrest know about Christian's rogue years with William? Had Christian stolen the soul of some child's mother? He shifted in his chair. "What happened?"

"I stopped him."

"But you're just a secucro. You fought a reaper? And won?"

Forrest cleared his throat. "No, he whooped me but good, and then started grabbing my soul. The feeling was surreal. I was chilled and disoriented and . . . euphoric. But then darkness closed in, and I started falling, lost in a dark abyss. I tried to hold onto something . . . color, feelings, thoughts . . . but it was like grabbing dank air. Nothing existed . . . nothing . . . and you can't see . . . you can't hear . . . not even your own voice . . . you can't scream . . . "

The man's words died out.

"And?" Christian prompted.

He shook his head. "Your father came along. I don't know where he got the strength, but he was like a beast, and he hauled that rogue to the Other World for Giltine's punishment. Then we carried your mother down the mountain." His voice softened. "The end."

Christian dropped his chin into his palm and the corners

of his mouth drooped. "Then he traded me to Giltine for his freedom. And yours."

"Not exactly. He had to trade your sibling as well. Two lives for two lives."

Christian's heart gave a massive pump, and blood rushed to his head. He clenched the sides of the chair. "Henry?"

"Right; but then he died when he was just a lad."

Polio had stricken his twin brother at the age of four. Christian always felt guilty—and lucky—that he lived. Now he knew Henry had been the lucky one.

His parents never had another child.

Through numb lips Christian said, "So, my father didn't fulfill his bargain with Giltine?"

"No."

"Shit." Christian leaned his elbows on his knees and ran a hand through his hair. He was the product of an unfulfilled bargain. That must be why Giltine picked on him.

They sat in silence. Two robins flitted through the branches above them. A beetle crawled across the toe of his boot. The sun finally did its job and warmed his bones.

"If you're free, why do you still usher souls?"

"It's who I am. I choose to reap. There are a lot of souls who need guidance. Is it right to turn your back on them, to leave them lost in the Void?" Forrest patted his stomach and grinned. "Besides, Giltine's poison helps me keep my youthful figure."

Christian didn't smile, deciding to ignore Forrest's question, since it wasn't one he wanted to consider. He wanted to be free; completely. He flexed his fingers. "Would you bargain your child's life for a woman?"

Forrest licked his lips before deflecting his question. "Would you?"

"Never."

"Maybe you haven't felt passion for a woman, but that

passion inflates your head and body and soul until you would do anything—anything!—for the woman you love."

"How can you say that? You were betrayed so your father could be free. You've lived the nightmare of being ripped from your family to be enslaved to Giltine. You've seen the horrors of the Other World." He slapped the armrest. "We both have!"

They stared at each other for a long moment, Christian panting.

Forrest leaned back, the chair creaking against his weight. "You can't break free from her by abstaining. The only way to leave Giltine's enslavement is to bargain with her."

"So you'd trade your child's life for a chance at a woman?"

"I'm not immune to love." Forrest turned his head to study Talcott Mountain.

Christian's thoughts tumbled like a combination lock. The pins all hit and the truth opened, as did his eyes. "You were in love with my mom, weren't you?"

Forrest grunted and crossed his arms over his chest. "Why'd you come here? Why all these questions about bargains and dames?"

He wasn't as blameless as Christian thought. If he married his mother instead of his father, if Christian had been Forrest's son instead of his father's, his life would still be the same. Forfeit. The truth pushed him deeper into the chair, making him feel small and insignificant.

"Well?" Forrest asked.

"I'm just trying to figure it out." Christian studied the Heublein summerhouse. "Because of my father, Giltine will make it impossible for me to be free of her, won't she?"

"That's not why she punishes you."

"Why then?"

"It's because you're trying to leave her. You're her child, and leaving her is a betrayal."

"I can't stay there."

"She got a name?"

"Yes," Christian murmured. He cleared his throat. "I mean, no. I mean, I don't know."

"You sound dizzy over this dame."

"I'm not. She's pretty; spoiled but nice." Christian ran his thumbs along the seams of his pants. "I was drowning, and she saved me."

"Ah, then."

"It's not like I'd bargain with Giltine and condemn a child to this life, not for any dame." Even if she was someone he promised to protect. Even if she had saved his life. Even if she was the most beautiful girl he'd ever seen.

Forrest traced a scar on Christian's hand. "I wouldn't let Giltine know about her. Stay away from the girl, for the girl's sake."

Christian's heart pounded *shut up, shut up, shut up,* but his brain forced his mouth open. "Why?"

"Because your father didn't fulfill his bargain, and she just might think to collect through you by taking someone you love."

"I don't love her."

And he didn't love her; he didn't even like her. His heated blood and fluttering heart whenever he saw her meant nothing. Christian studied Heublein's house, rising from the mountain like a slim, white finger, as though Giltine herself was sending him a message. A message as threatening as the history of warfare, when enemies cut off the middle fingers of captured archers so that they could no longer shoot arrows. A message meant to destroy any hope of life.

Chapter 12

Present Time

The morning rays of sunshine trying to drill holes through Brooke's closed eyelids beckoned her to wake. A heavy weight constricted her chest. Yawning, she stretched, laughing when Lola licked her nose. She scratched the cat's chin and then, gasping with memory, shifted the cat's weight off her chest and leaped out of bed.

She bee-lined for the window and checked the street for suspicious motorcycles and almost-reapers. Chewing her thumbnail, she scrutinized every shadow slinking around the trees. There were at least two almost-reapers stalking her—maybe more—and for all she knew, they were sneaky bastards out to steal her soul.

Brooke relented on the thumbnail gnawing only after she decided the street was reaper-free. She flicked her hand across her sweaty forehead. That sizzling belly-button-brain-sludge feeling was back, and it was like an itch deep inside her she couldn't scratch. An army of pins and needles marched up her spine.

Watch.

She blinked at hearing her own voice in her head. As if seeing reapers wasn't bad enough, now she heard voices. Okay, technically her voice, but still, it seemed bat-shit.

Glancing at the clock, she groaned. She'd slept late . . . it was almost eleven. Pulling on yesterday's jeans and a clean t-shirt, she stumbled down the stairs. She grabbed a chocolate-covered granola bar before bolting from the house.

Unlike the day before, shoppers, cars, and reapers saturated the strip mall. She worked her way through the parking lot, staring at the door to Panera Bread, trying to dodge what seemed like an anthill of reapers. They brushed against her, leaving her shivery and out of breath. Her radar buzzed so loudly her brain vibrated.

She huffed into Panera Bread, trying to ignore the reaper that trailed in behind her, panting on the back of her neck. She stood immobile by the door, wishing he would back off. From behind the counter, Abby flicked a tired glance at her and tossed a smile.

Brooke shuffled to the counter. "Hey."

"Hey." Abby set a cup in front of her. Circles edged the bottom of her eyes, the corners of her mouth drooped, and even her blue skunk stripe seemed to wilt against the black backdrop of her hair.

"You okay?" Brooke asked.

"Yeah. Why wouldn't I be?"

"Just checking." She spun the cup between her hands. Had the weed Matt given Abby been laced with something stronger? Was she breaking her promise and letting things get out of control?

A man came from the back with a tray of M&M cookies. "Can you re-stock these in the case?"

"Sure thing." Abby yawned as he vanished into the back room. "Brooke, when are you going to dress more, I don't know, like a babe?"

She one-shoulder shrugged.

Abby snapped open the goodie-case door and stacked cookies in a sloppy row. "How many times do we have to talk about this? You're never going to hook up dressed like that."

"Maybe I don't want to hook up."

"*Every*one wants to hook up." A cookie crumbled under Abby's fingers. "Damn." She scooped up the cookie pieces, then slammed the door and drummed her fingers on the counter. "You know, if you got laid once in a while, you wouldn't be so starchy."

"I'm not starchy."

"Uh huh. Okay, prove it. A too-tall-for-me guy just walked in . . . wait! Don't look," she said when Brooke started to turn around. "Trust me, he's just your type." She wiggled her eyebrows. "He's got that adorable, puppy-dog look, and holy shit, is he ever tall. Dark hair, a little scar thingy on his cheek, and he's wearing black jeans and a black, leather jacket over a hoodie. If you promise to ask him his name, I'll lay off the subject of your virginity."

"That's slanted."

"Promise, or I'll be relentless."

Brooke pinched her lip. For her, breaking a promise was harder than levitating. Besides, she wasn't in the mood to start talking to random dudes; she'd done that yesterday, and that turned out to be a reaper-mare.

"So, how long are you planning on being a virgin anyway?" Abby asked so loudly a woman standing near the counter with her boy clucked her tongue and tossed Brooke a sharp glance. The boy poked a finger in his nose.

Her eyes widened and she blurted, "Fine. I promise to ask that random dude his name. Happy?"

"Totally." Abby winked as she turned to the woman, who eyed her BFF as though she'd just spoken with a forked tongue. "Go get your freak on, girl. And then get a table, and I'll take my lunch break. There's something I have to tell you."

Brooke whirled from the counter, bumping into someone behind her. Her cup smashed into a firm chest before tumbling out of her hand and landing at the toe of a scuffed, black boot.

Bending to pick it up, she froze when her hand met with another, an electric jolt zipping through her as they touched the cup at the same time. His hand was solid looking with long, scarred fingers. Her gaze crawled up a black-leathered arm to a boyish face with a round, purple scar marring one cheek and another slashing through an eyebrow. Other small scars were scattered across his skin like thin, pale freckles. They made him look sexily dangerous.

He had longish black hair tousled in a just-got-out-of-bed kind of way. Slowly, they both stood. Rock-star thin, he towered over her. Glints of gray stabbed his blue eyes like steel shards, and the gaze he narrowed at Brooke was arctic.

She veered away from his intimidating eyes, and her gaze wandered over his leather jacket with silver-studded cuffs. Heat swirled in the pit of her stomach. She whiffed a faint grape smell, and her almost-reaper radar gave a weak buzz then died, as though it too was mesmerized by him. He held out the cup.

"Would you like this back?" His voice was like a magnet, drawing her attention back to his face.

She blinked. It was time to get level. "No."

Despite her slight—albeit misguided—attraction to him, she didn't want to touch him, didn't want to feel that reaper chill, didn't want to feel the warm glow spreading through her.

He stared at her, still and silent, as though he stood in Hell and it had just frozen over. "Someone has some issues."

She shifted from one foot to another as she tilted her head back to look at him. Her toes itched to run, but her promise to Abby held her there, because he was most definitely the random guy she'd promised to ask for a name. Which was a big-time suck.

"Did I do something wrong?"

"No," Brooke murmured. "But that cup's dirty now."

"Why, because I touched it?" His voice was like an ice cube sliding down her back.

"No, because it hit the floor." She wiped her sweaty palms on her jeans.

"You're all twitchy."

"I'm not."

"You look like you've seen a ghost."

She snorted.

"Do you see ghosts?"

She narrowed her eyes, tension writhing between her shoulders. Refusing to play this game with an almost-reaper, she turned to leave, but her feet defied her. Her mouth opened with the ready-fire message to piss off, but instead she shot blanks.

The question built in her chest, growing like a hot-air balloon. She ran her tongue over her teeth, poked her tongue in her cheek, and then bit her tongue, trying to stop the words from exploding through her lips.

"What's your name?" she snapped.

Defeated, she crossed her arms over her chest and glared at him. Maybe her pissy attitude would get him to leave without answering her question.

He raised his eyebrows, but said, "Christian."

She couldn't stop the snort. A demon named Christian, as though he was religious? Get level. "Seriously? Is that some kind of joke?"

His lips tightened. She couldn't help sliding her gaze down his body and then back up. This couldn't possibly be the almost-reaper William had warned her about. He didn't look deadly. He was so thin she thought she could knock him off his feet by poking his chest with a Q-tip.

Yet who else could he be?

She said, "Yeah, um, I'm not supposed to talk to you."

"No?"

"No."

One side of his mouth lifted mockingly. "And do you always do what you're told? Are you a good girl?"

"It depends on how you define good."

He chuckled, a low sound that thrilled her ears. Alarmed at her body's reaction to him, she blurted, "Do you always do what you're told?"

"Depends on who's doing the telling."

"What if I told you to leave and never come back?"

He stepped closer, forcing her back as he leaned toward her.

His gaze grazed her throat before moving to her face. "Now *that* I can't do."

The spit in her mouth evaporated.

"Brooke?" Abby said, her glance bouncing like an echo between them. "Who's this?"

"Christian."

He gazed at Brooke for a long moment, not giving an inch on the invasion of her personal space, and a shiver shimmied up her spine.

"See you around . . . Brooke."

The way his voice caressed her name, like melted, dark chocolate, sent heat at warp speed through her body. He turned and strode through the coffee shop.

"Well, damn. He is so your type," Abby said, her gaze crazy-glued to his ass.

Brooke was still staring at the door after it closed behind him. She snapped her mouth closed before she started drooling. What was she thinking? Doing? *Feeling*?

"I hope you got his phone number, too."

"No."

"A name? That's it? Nothing else?" Abby fired at her.

"Yes. Yes. And yes."

"You are seriously whacked. That guy was practically licking you."

She turned her head to hide her blush.

Abby sighed. "You can be so lame sometimes."

She shrugged, not trusting herself to speak, because she wasn't lame. She was insane.

"Anyway, let's sit. I have to ask you something."

When they settled at a corner table with their coffees, Abby poked her lip ring with her tongue, studied Brooke, then her coffee, then Brooke again.

"You remember that guy you were talking to in here last night? The one who was seriously, *oh-my-God*?" Abby emphasized "oh-my-God," as though those words were the absolute-highest form of compliment.

William. Brooke's fingers tightened around her cup. "Yes."

"Are you, like, into him or anything?"

"No."

"So, what do you think of Billy?"

She spit her coffee across the table, spattering Abby's shirt.

"Brooke! What the hell?" She rubbed her sleeve over her chest. "Shit, this'll never come out."

"Sorry." Brooke grabbed napkins and wiped the table. "How do you know his name?"

"He came back last night after you left."

The air got caught somewhere between Brooke's lungs and her nose. "What?"

"Are you sure you're not into him?"

"Definitely. Are you?"

"Yeah."

"What about Will?" Anyone, even an over-sexed drug dealer, was better than an almost-reaper.

Abby lifted one shoulder. "Meh."

Brooke's mind wasn't whirling crazy thoughts or racing to conclusions or functioning at all. It was numb, as were her lips. "You guys hung out?"

"Oh, yeah. He's seriously jacked, and he's got stupid-hot lips that, I might add, are stupidly delicious."

"You kissed him?" One side of Brooke's mouth curled as though her friend had just admitted to kissing a warthog with cold sores.

"You bet I did."

"Did you, um, do anything else?"

Abby winked. "Not yet."

"Tell me you aren't seeing him again."

"Yeah, can't do that. Why do you care, if you're not into him?"

What could Brooke tell her? That he was a monster? A soul-stealer? A demon? Abby would have her committed to the nearest straightjacket. "There's something off about him."

A small smile curved Abby's lips. "You're right. He's got a dark side, mysterious. Bad boys are so boss."

She groaned. "Please think about this."

"Why?"

"Because he's dangerous."

"And you know this . . . how?"

Brooke, of course, couldn't answer the question without telling Abby about seeing reapers, so she said nothing.

"You know, I don't get you. It doesn't matter who I go out with, but you always tell me to back off. Why don't you want me to have fun?"

"I'm all for the having fun part, I just don't want you to get hurt."

"When do I get hurt?"

"All the time."

"Why are you always on my ass?"

Brooke yanked in a breath and counted to three. She had to keep this conversation level because Abby wouldn't listen if she was pissed. "It's just you fall for these guys and then they act like dicks and dump all over you. I worry about you."

"Well, quit it, I'm a big girl." Winking, Abby stood. "I'm getting some food. Want anything?"

She shook her head. "I'm in the mood for pizza."

Abby snapped her fingers. "See? Now you're stressed because you didn't get that dude's phone number. And why can't you crave chocolate like a normal girl?"

"I like pizza."

"Lame, like I said." Abby darted to the food counter, a pouty twist to her lips.

"This is fan-freaking-tastic," Brooke complained to her coffee cup.

She had a sour taste in her mouth and a sour feeling in the pit of her stomach. She didn't know what William's game with Abby was, or Christian's game with her, but the pulse throbbing in her neck warned her none of it could end well.

Chapter 13

1938

Christian left Forrest at the house and marched through a patchwork of fields until he reached the wooded base of Talcott Mountain. The mountain rose steeply, with scraggly trees clinging to the rock face. Two hawks thrust off from the cliff and soared beneath puffy clouds, their cries sharp in the air.

He strode through the trees, thrashing at ferns and wild phlox with a stick. Crickets lazed in the afternoon heat, pulsing messages. Queen Anne's Lace spread its feathery fingers along an unpainted, wooden fence. Pretending the half-cylindrical white flowers were Giltine's wrinkled face, he whacked off their heads with his stick.

He took the road leading to the Heublein summerhouse at a jog. The first mile was steep, gutted by rain and littered with sharp rocks. A constant breeze hummed through the trees and made the leaves shiver. His leg muscles strained through the climb, and by the time he reached the precipice, his breathing had elevated. Small-scale pine trees wedded to the edge interrupted the view of the distant Berkshires.

He made his way to the mountain's rim. The hills of the Berkshires rolled over one another in the distance, and at one point a white church steeple broke through the trees. Below, a farm's round barn and silo sprung from the field amidst Jersey-cow polka dots.

His thoughts tumbled. Despite the years of taunting by Giltine, this was the first she ever mentioned his father. In fact, he'd never seen any of his family in the Other World. It could be that they weren't there, or they were confined to a lower level. His father deserved to rot in the third level of the Other World, but what about his mother, who'd taken her own life? Had innocent Henry been condemned for eternity because of what he was? Would Christian?

Groaning, he locked his arms behind his head. He had a soul, but what good was it? It was just another form of torture, witnessing the guilt and pain and despair of the souls he ushered. Why couldn't he be more like William, drop those emotions into the abyss and do his duty with indifference? Or embrace his lot in life with compassion, as did Forrest?

Christian growled at the scenery spread before him, and then loped up the road as it wound south along the mountain. Minutes later, he followed the stone path to Heublein's summerhouse.

The one-hundred-sixty-five-foot, white, square tower jutted from the front of the stone house, which had afforded the one-time inhabitants a spectacular view of the Berkshires. Scraggly bushes disguised the drop that plunged to the valley below.

Settling on a stone wall that circled a stone terrace and outdoor fireplace, Christian caught a deep breath filled with pine. The quickening breeze nudged him in the chest, and a chill tremored through him, but not from the wind or the vertiginous drop. Climbing a thousand feet hadn't freed his thoughts.

Elizabeth had saved his life, and now he was forced to abandon her. He slapped the fireplace, and his red scar flared with pain. Swearing, he studied his hand. All he wanted was a normal life. All he wanted was to watch Elizabeth. And all he received was punishment.

He grabbed a branch from the ground and hurled it over the cliff. Branches snapped, and crows shot into the air, squawking insults.

"It's not fair!"

His words echoed over the valley. He dropped to his knees. Why couldn't he have been born Gilbert Heublein instead of Christian Graves? What had he done to deserve this fate?

Two hawks spiraled outward, stealthily spying from a distance where prey could never spot them.

He watched the hawks for some minutes then stood. He could spy from a distance, just like a hawk. As long as he didn't linger, as long as he just swept by the lake every now and then to ensure Elizabeth was safe, he could watch her without being fingered by Giltine's spies.

Decision made, Christian loped back down the mountain. Darkness had enveloped the lakeside house by the time he reached his hidey-tree. It didn't matter. Highlighted by the full moon, Elizabeth sat cross-legged on the dock, nibbling animal crackers as she watched the water lick the pilings.

The rumbling of the car announced its arrival seconds before headlights targeted her and then blinked out. Picking up her box, she strolled down the dock with slouched shoulders, her bare feet slapping the wooden planks. Renkin met her halfway.

"Hello, Mr. Renkin."

"Hello, there, Izzy." He tweaked her braid.

She jerked her head back.

A faint glow pinpointed the shadows when he sucked on his cigar. "Your daddy home?" He didn't survey the yard or the house, as though he already knew the answer.

"He's at work."

"I need to speak with him."

She edged past him. "I'll tell him you stopped by."

"Wait." His glance roamed the yard. "You're all alone?"

She stalled at the end of the dock and took one slow step back. "Yes."

Christian gripped his elbows and tucked his chin to his chest.

"How old are you?" Renkin asked. "Seventeen?"

"Sixteen."

"A young dame shouldn't be alone at night with no man to protect her."

"Daddy will be home soon." Her tiny voice exposed her fear.

Christian held his breath until his body calmed, and then slowly released the air with a low hiss.

"I worry about you, Izzy. You're too trusting. One day one of those hoboes you're fond of coddling is going to demand more than a few table scraps."

She took another step back. "Daddy will be home any minute."

"Is that so?" He waved his cigar toward the lake. "Been swimming lately?"

She shook her head.

"Your sister liked to swim, didn't she? Alone at night. She was inviting trouble, you see, kissing boys and picking up strays. See what happened to her?"

Her sharp intake of breath ricocheted through the darkness. "What do you mean?"

Christian tried to stay as still and unemotional as a corpse.

"That crumb, Christian. He shows up and Mary drowned. Coincidence?"

"Yes," she whispered.

Renkin fingered her collar. "Come on, doll. Go for quick dip. I'll watch, make sure no one bothers you."

Her frantic heart pounded a distress signal. "I don't think so, Mr. Renkin."

The taste of the man's lust took a sharp bite out of Christian's tongue. Grinding his teeth, he let his anger uproot him from his hiding spot.

Renkin was a dead man.

Chapter 14

Present Time

Brooke stopped for breath next to her car. The walk from Panera Bread hadn't been far, but reapers were F-bomb everywhere, and the chill from brushing against them made her hold her breath until she was light-headed. Add to that the adrenaline rush from meeting a cold-voiced near-demon who made her heart slam, and the energy-drain from her fancy mouth-work to steer Abby away from William without spilling her whole I-can-see-reapers thing, all made her feel as if she'd sprung a leak in her muscles.

Brooke settled in the driver's seat and leaned back against the headrest. She tapped her fingers on the steering wheel. Glancing in her rearview mirror, she gasped at a reaper wiggling his tongue at her through the back window.

She twisted in her seat and gave him the finger. "Piss off!"

The reaper hissed but moved away. Sighing, Brooke faced forward once more. The woman who'd overheard Abby's virginity question inside Panera Bread was approaching Brooke's car, but swerved to give her a wide berth, clutching her boy to her side as though Brooke was a raging nymphomaniac escaped from the nearest halfway house for sex addicts.

Two reapers leaned on the hood of her car. One grinned at her while the other licked his lips. Fingers trembling, it took her two tries before she got her key in the ignition and the car started. She was going home. Going home and into bed and staying there for the rest of spring break. She was done with the whole epic mess.

Car idling, she watched Abby smoking outside Panera Bread. She leaned against the wall and studied her cigarette. A reaper sniffed her hair, making her friend shiver and glance over her shoulder.

"Oh, crap."

She couldn't bail on Abby. Brooke had to watch over her, protect her from whatever game almost-reaper William was playing. She'd seen the games reapers played—they stole souls—and she couldn't let that happen to Abby. As much as Brooke wanted to jet home and hide like a coward, she had to face her demons . . . literally.

Abby jammed her cigarette in the outside ashtray then strode back inside the coffee shop. Brooke bit her lip. She would watch over Abby. She would not bolt. But first, she had to face her demons. No more agoraphobia, no more feeling sorry for herself, and no more taking any shit from almost-reapers.

Decision made, she put the car into drive, stepped on the gas, and shot through the reapers standing in front of it. She knew exactly where to go to get herself level.

Hiking the Heublein Tower's pitted and rocky trail with a notebook clutched to Brooke's chest made for an awkward climb. Gaze rooted to the ground, she refused to slow down or look up, afraid to see if reapers were tailing her.

Despite her burning legs and lungs working overtime, she didn't stop to catch her breath or enjoy the view once she reached the mountain's edge. She continued on the path to the left, keeping pace until she stopped at the Hang Glider Overlook, a large clearing cut out of the trees and butting up against the edge of the cliff. The sun baked the dead pine needles that carpeted the ground, and she inhaled the tangy scent.

While she peeled off her hoodie, she made sure to keep several feet away from the edge; standing too close to the drop always made her bladder feel like jelly. Tying the hoodie around her waist, she studied the view, tossing words in her head for the latest poem she was writing.

Behind her, a vernal pool harbored frogs which emitted a continuous chorus of cheeps. The *pop, pop!* from a firing range at the base of the mountain mingled with birdcalls and squirrel chatter. She shifted her gaze right toward the horse farm; a horse-and-rider team popping over fences like a jumping bean. Around and around the jumping bean circled the arena, and Brooke watched until, finally, the rider led the horse into the barn.

A breeze cut across her sweat-cooled shoulders, and she shivered. Holding her notebook between her knees, she shoved her arms through the sleeves of her hoodie and yanked it back on, but her head got caught somewhere in the middle and wouldn't pop through.

"What the hell?" She clawed at the cloth.

"I think you have it on backwards," murmured a low voice.

She froze for an eternity, and then scrambled into her hoodie and whirled, the notebook plunking onto her toes. The sight of Christian standing less than three feet away immobilized her blood, her heart, and her body.

She blurted, "What are you doing here?"

"Enjoying the view."

He stared at her when he spoke. Had he intended the double meaning? She didn't like the way the gray shards in his eyes glinted when her heartbeat jacked up.

She pointed to her left. "The view's over there."

A smile slid through his lips, and two dimples popped out in his cheeks. Her heart did a double take. Holy . . . holy . . . something. She couldn't think of a word worthy enough to attach to the holy part; she couldn't *think*.

She closed her eyes. *Not boss, not boss, not boss.*

"Not that view," he said.

Her eyes snapped open. "I'm not a view, or viewable, so stop viewing."

"You can't stop a guy from looking, Brooke, especially when the view's so," he paused to sweep her with a gaze, "enjoyable."

Heat shot to her face, and she crossed her arms over his *view*. "Go enjoy someone else's view."

"I think I'll stay and enjoy this one for a while."

Her stomach fluttered and her heart. She had to get out of there, and fast, before she started falling for his corny lines. "Fine. Then I'll leave."

Brooke pivoted. A hand clamped on her arm, stalling her escape.

"Are you going to dis me twice in one day?" he asked. "You're starting to hurt my feelings."

A jolt sheared through her body like an electric knife. Lazy warmth trickled through her veins, rising until her cheeks burned. She snatched her arm away before he could feel the tremble building through her body.

"Are you all right?" he asked.

Brooke, who'd been staring at her arm, nodded. After a prolonged silence, she looked up. A breeze brushed his dark hair across his blue-silver eyes. He had the same high cheekbones and full lips as William.

"You look kind of like William."

"William?" Christian's mouth tightened and his fingers flexed as though he considered punching someone.

She edged sideways from him, afraid that someone would be her. "Do you know him?"

His cheek rippled from clenching his teeth. "He's my uncle."

He stepped forward so suddenly Brooke faltered. Flirty Christian had morphed into frigid Christian.

"How do you know him?"

"Panera Bread. He told me not to talk to any other almost-reapers."

"Hmm," he murmured, some of the aloofness sliding away. "So, you know what I am."

"Yes."

"And that's your name for my kind?"

"Yes."

"How does it feel, always having to tell the truth?"

"It sucks."

"Why'd he tell you not talk to me?"

She dug her fingernails into her palms. She'd been so caught up in his cuteness she'd forgotten about the death threat, and she certainly didn't want to admit to him she knew, not out loud, not there at the edge of a cliff.

"Well?"

"He said you want to kill me," she whispered.

"He told you?" The words fell from Christian's mouth like chunks of concrete.

He didn't even try to deny it. The dick!

Her heart hammered, and she couldn't help glancing at the distance between her feet and the edge of the cliff, which seemed too damned close. One push from him and she'd be sailing. They stared at each other, and he was oddly still, yet tense. The air between them seemed to drop ten degrees. She pulled her hands into her sleeves.

"You dropped this," he said as though they hadn't just been discussing her death, and bent to pick up her notebook.

As she took a moment to register the change in topic, his eyes moved back and forth while he read.

She snatched the notebook. "That's private."

"You're writing about death?" he snapped.

"No."

"This poem's about killing yourself."

She glanced at the title on the open page: *Goodbye*. "'It's about saying goodbye, dumbass."

"Because you're going to die."

Icy fear crawled over her heart at the winter sea look in his eyes, and she backed away. A nano-second of stomach-dropping fear rolled through her when her heels left solid ground. She choked back a scream, and he grabbed her arm. The book slid from her fingers. Eyes widening, she hovered over the endless depths of air that crept up her spine. Clutching at his sleeve with both hands, her nails dug through the cloth. Her bladder clenched then loosened, a sharp taste of metal stinging her dry tongue.

In one smooth movement, he yanked her against his chest. He wrapped his arms around her, and she trembled against him. He pressed his cheek to her head, running a hand down her hair. He smelled of grapes and rich leather and spice, and it was an oddly seductive mix of scents. The panicked intensity of her beating heart slowed.

"Are you suicidal, Brooke?"

"N-no."

A violent vibration gripped her entire body. Every breath she took turned colder, colder, but then her stomach flamed white-hot, digging deep inside her.

With another massive shudder, she tore herself away from him. Her heart slammed and her stomach was caught in a never-ending free-fall.

Her brain blinked fuzzily as she pressed her palms to her temples and focused on regaining some sort of thought function. Shaking her head, she dropped her hands to her sides.

Instead of thanking him, she asked, "What was that?"

"It's called saving someone's life."

"Not that," she snapped. "The other thing."

He lowered his lashes over the frightening gleam in his eyes and shoved his hands in his pockets. "I don't know what you mean."

He could play dumbass all he wanted. She knew what it meant. He'd wanted to rip her soul out, kill her, just like William had warned.

Her upper lip curled. "I know what you were doing."

Ice seemed to have gripped Christian's face muscles as he studied her.

"I've seen you things steal souls before."

"I'm not a thing." The words ground between his clenched teeth.

"I saw one of you things steal my brother's soul."

"How do you know it was stolen?"

"I know about the mark, and you're only supposed to mess with the people who've got it, because the ones who mess with the unmarked stink." She wrinkled her nose, exaggeratedly, because though he did smell of Aeu de Rogue, it was kind of faint. "Literally stink, Reaper Boy."

"You know about Giltine's mark?"

Brooke hesitated, having no clue who Giltine was. "You bet your reaping ass I do." She tapped her cheek. "And Ryan had nothing. Nothing!"

Christian's cheek muscles rippled from grinding his teeth. He stepped toward her. "Then you should have done something to stop it, Watcher Girl."

"You know what else I know? I felt you . . . touching . . . my soul." Irritation spit like an angry cat trapped in her chest. "You dick," she added, not knowing what else to say.

His eyes glittered dangerously as they narrowed.

"Just piss off." She didn't wait for him to respond. Scooping her notebook off the ground, she bolted.

Chapter 15

1938

Another set of sweeping headlights swept over the dock, highlighting Elizabeth and Renkin facing off in the yard, and snapping Christian back before he could rip the man's head off his neck for threatening her. She jerked toward the light. Renkin lodged his cigar between his teeth, and then faced her father exiting the passenger side of a rusty truck.

Her fear and Renkin's lust battled on Christian's tongue, and he swallowed, trying to erase the taste.

"Thanks for the lift, Joe," Mr. Vincent mumbled in a flat tone, and the truck rumbled off with a loud belch.

Her father shuffled toward the porch, his head tilted awkwardly. He paused at the steps. "Izzy? That you?"

Giving Renkin a wide birth, she moved toward him with rapid steps. "Hi, Daddy. You're home early. Oh! What happened?"

He touched the bandage over his right eye. "Lathe machine accident. Chip caught my eye."

"Are you in pain?" She guided him up the steps. "I'll get some aspirin and water."

He rattled a bottle. "The doc fixed me up."

"Are you blind?"

"Naw."

"What about work?"

He brushed her hair. "Don't worry. I'll be back at work in a day or two."

Mr. Vincent's lifeless tone made shivers scuttle over Christian's skin.

"Evening, John," Renkin said, placing one foot on the bottom step.

She flinched. His cigar glowed, and Christian wanted to shove it up the man's nose. It wasn't that he liked her—he would feel obligated to protect any dame from a leech like Renkin.

Her father twitched a curt nod. "Ray. What brings you here so late?"

"Just came to look in on Izzy while you worked your night shift. I was just leaving."

Christian waited for the girl to rat him out as a liar, but she focused on her toes.

Mr. Vincent's tone was frigid. "Thanks, Ray, but I can tend to my own." He paused. "Was there something else?"

"Ah, it can wait. I see you have more pressing matters." Renkin dipped his head. "If you need anything, just holler."

He sauntered to his car. Elizabeth helped her father to the door.

"Why are you trembling?"

"Mr. Renkin just gave me a fright, is all." She patted his back. "I was sitting in the dark and didn't hear him come up behind me."

They slipped into the house. Christian scraped his tongue against the roof of his mouth then spit out the taste of his own disgust.

"Come with me," a reaper's voice commanded in a dead tone.

Startled, he whirled to face her. Despite the stark contrast between the dark hair and silver eyes, her features contained no animation. She assessed him with indifference.

"Why?"

"The girl."

His lips tingled as though the blood had just leeched out and then rushed back in. "What about her?"

The reaper remained silent. Christian froze. Was Forrest right about Giltine taking vengeance by bringing Elizabeth to the Other World?

He grabbed the reaper's coat. "Tell me, you soulless son of a dog!"

The reaper jabbed him in the chest with her palm. His head cracked against the tree, and he crumpled. He gasped for air, his lungs feeling as though they'd collapsed, and he vaguely wondered if the reaper was grinding her heel into his skull.

The reaper hauled him to his feet. "Come with me."

Christian couldn't disobey, only panted and tried to focus past the pain while they de-fragmented into the darkness. He gasped when the Void slapped him, and he hit the tunnel floor on his knees. The reaper wrenched him upright, and then dragged him up the mountain. Her vice-like grip, he was sure, would leave finger-shaped bruises on his arm.

The reaper pushed him through the Other World wall, and once again his knees connected with the ground. A sandaled foot with black toenails tapped the dead grass in front of his nose. He sat on his heels and gazed at Giltine while he massaged feeling back into his arm. Though his lungs still ached, the worst of the pain in his head receded, only to be replaced by cold sweat sticking to his skin.

"You pathetic fool," Giltine said.

He started to rise.

"On your knees, secucro," the reaper snarled.

She jammed her boot between his shoulder blades and shoved him back down. He sprawled facedown in the dirt, agony flaring down his spine. Groaning, he curled his fingers into the ground.

"Enough," Giltine ordered. "Leave us."

The reaper scuffled away.

He staggered to his feet, wiped dirt from his mouth with the back of his hand, and focused on Giltine's crown instead of vomiting.

"Once again you have flaunted my laws." A long, black fingernail clicked against the snake's head on her ring.

"I didn't."

"Interacting with humans is forbidden."

"I didn't even talk to her."

"Moot." Giltine steepled her fingers. "You are meddling in human affairs and that, my dear Christian, simply will not do."

"Why does it matter anyway?"

"Lust leads secucron to seek freedom from my domain. Most die, very few succeed. Regardless, I lose my chil . . . valuable slaves."

He gripped the back of his neck. "But there's no law against bargaining."

Giltine stood immobile for a long time. "The price is steep."

"A life?" He said it half-aloud, wondering why he would say such a thing, knowing he could never bargain such a thing.

She chuckled, slowly and darkly. "The price to surviving the bargain is a price you will never pay, my dear, ethical Christian. I have no doubt you will remain a secucro until the day I mark you, which I hope not to do for a very, very long time."

He held still, every molecule within his body simmering with hatred.

"I have a new rule, just for you." She placed a finger beneath his chin, digging her nail into his skin. "Stay away from the girl. No speaking, no spying, no protecting."

His swallow juggled his Adam's apple in his throat. "But . . . "

Giltine seemed to grow to a great height as she glared down the length of her nose. "If you wish to be close to your darling human, I could summon her to reside in the Other World, with you. Is that what you desire?"

His heart froze. He didn't care about Elizabeth, but she was innocent, young, and alive; the Other World darkness would extinguish the light from her life. His heart lifted as he saw the light of redemption. He wouldn't doom her to that fate. Saving Elizabeth from Giltine's wrath might well free him from guilt from his soul-stealing past.

"I thought not." She waved a hand. "Now be gone, before I change my mind and punish you for displeasing me."

He couldn't protect Elizabeth from Renkin; Christian had to protect her from Giltine, his world, and himself.

Eyes burning, he dusted the Other World as quickly as he could. He'd just sealed the girl's fate with Renkin, but that was by far the lesser of two evils.

Chapter 16

Present Time

After almost falling off a cliff and being saved by Christian who'd then turned around and violated her soul, Brooke's brain was mush. Her muscles trembled one moment and tensed the next, and her heart beat as if she'd just run a 20K marathon at a jackrabbit sprint. What was his game? One minute he was saving her ass, and the next he'd practically admitted he wanted to kill her.

It didn't make sense . . . unless he was a sociopath.

She sat in her car for twenty minutes before her hands were steady enough to drive home. She spent the afternoon watching music videos on TV. The leather couch seemed to suck the chill from the air and transfer it to her butt. Brooke clutched a blanket to her chin, tensing her muscles against the shivers.

Television wasn't enough of a distraction, though, and Christian's words slunk through her mind.

Then you should have done something to stop it, Watcher Girl.

What could she have done to stop the reaper from killing Ryan? The guy was seriously whacked, because all she ever wanted to do when she saw a reaper was pee her pants.

Brooke gave up on the TV, settled into bed with her laptop, and started a search. "Gilteenay."

Google came back with, "Did you mean Giltine?"

"No clue." She clicked on it.

Lithuanian goddess of death. Giltine collects poison from graveyards on her tongue, marking those whose death is imminent by licking their faces.

"Gross."

Brooke wiped her forehead with her palm. The people with silver streaks on their cheeks . . . that must be the Giltine lick mark. Both William and Christian mentioned that Brooke was a descendant of these watchers, but she still couldn't find a connection to reapers. They were maneuvering her like a pawn in a twisted, Other World game of chess.

She slapped her laptop closed. The whole deal was slanted, and she wanted no part of it, yet she couldn't stop from getting dragged into it. Those almost-reapers were stalking her, and now Abby was involved.

Brooke thought about how her body tingled when she touched Christian's hand. He seemed unfeeling, yet an occasional flicker of warmth would light his eyes. At times he was personable and charming, and others he was distant and dangerous.

She cleaned the dust from her laptop with her thumb, thinking how Abby was drawn to the bad boys. Brooke had sensed the danger, too. It was slowly sucking her in, and the thought of unlocking the mysteries of the dangerous reaper boy was very seductive.

She shuddered.

She was completely bat-shit.

"What have you been doing this week?" Brooke's mom asked at dinner.

Brooke smooshed a pea with her fork. She wasn't in the mood for chicken and peas, unless it was served on a greasy crust with extra cheese. She should have stopped for pizza on the way home from Heublein.

She answered her mom. "I've been to Heublein."

"When?" her dad asked.

"I don't know, over the last couple of days." Her parents exchanged one of those our-poor-pathetic-daughter looks. "Oh, I get it. The thing with Bekka the other day."

Her mom moved her coffee cup in front of her face, as though hiding behind it. Her mom liked to hide from awkward subjects, at least around her. She thought Brooke would shatter, or break, or start ranting like she had after Ryan died. They thought she'd gone insane until she convinced them she knew reapers didn't exist, and she'd just been having nightmares that seemed kind of real. Maybe she had gone off her nut. Maybe her whole life was one epic hallucination; one epic, living, F-bomb nightmare.

"Did you see it?" her mom asked.

"Yes, but I'm good. There were other people there, and I got someone to call 9-1-1." And I kept a reaper from stealing her soul, she added to herself.

Smiling slightly, she lifted her chin.

"That's good, kiddo," her father said.

Her mom peeked over the cup and stared at her, and she hated the pity she saw in that gaze. She squirmed in her seat. That itchy, belly-button burn ignited her gut again.

Watch.

Brooke dropped her fork. "Do you mind if I go out for a while?"

Her mom eyed Brooke's plate with a frown. "You haven't eaten much."

"Sure," her dad said in an overly loud voice, as if speaking loudly would smother the tension. "Plans?"

"I thought I'd see if Abby wanted to catch a movie or something."

"Do you need money?" Without waiting for an answer, he fished his wallet out of his back pocket and handed her more than enough bills. "Have fun."

"Thanks, Dad."

She scraped her plate and loaded it into the dishwasher. Collecting her keys and purse, she made for the door, calling over her shoulder, "'Bye, Mom. Love you guys."

"Love you, too," her mom said.

Once in her car, she eased onto Route 202 and headed toward Canton. Like her reaper radar, she had the feeling this belly-burn thing was a signal. Every time she felt it, dread weighed on her mind like thick sludge, a feeling she had to watch someone, and her mind would whisper to her. It seemed odd to her that this new radar—or whatever it was— started when William and Christian barged into her life.

She shivered slightly at the thought of Christian. What was he doing now? Where did he live? How did he get those scars? There was so much she didn't know about him, and what she did know both scared her and lured her.

Wincing, she undug her fingers from her stomach. Why couldn't she stop thinking about him? Because he was cute, and a mystery.

If Christian wanted her dead, he could have just let it happen. He could have stolen her soul or let her fall to her death. It didn't make sense for him to save her life. Unless William lied.

She scrunched her shoulders against a tremor. Then again, Christian never denied that he wanted to kill her. Maybe he was just playing a demon version of a cat-and-mouse game, rocking on the edge of insanity. Bat-shit crazy.

She clenched the wheel. It was time to get level, time to stop thinking about these almost-reapers. It was time to ignore the tingles every time she thought of him.

Crunching thoughts of him under a mental heel, she pulled into the strip mall. She hurried toward Panera Bread, ignoring the usual onslaught of demon shadows.

Her almost-reaper radar buzzed between her eardrums, and she slowed. Someone stood in front of the coffee shop, his face shadowed by his hood, staring inside. It was creepy in a stalker sort of way. She was still twenty feet away when he glanced at her.

Christian.

She stopped, her breath catching. He wore the usual hoodie beneath his leather jacket, and when he slipped his hood off, his hair swept back then forward across his face. She clutched her stomach, which not only burned and itched, but swooped.

Lifting her chin she continued on, stopping a few feet from him. "I think we need to settle some things."

"Like what?"

"I know what you are, and you seem to know things about me."

He leaned against the window. "How do you know?"

"Because of what you said earlier."

"What did I say that has your panties in a twist?"

Heat flamed her cheeks. "You know nothing about my panties."

He raised his eyebrows, one side of his mouth lifting. "Not yet."

She clenched her fists to keep from slapping that smirk, at the same time she was horrified at the warmth blooming in her gut and radiating downward.

She ignored his comment. "You said something about stopping my brother's death."

"You don't know?"

"Obviously not, if I'm asking."

Christian moved into her space, and she pressed back against the window. His gaze ran down her body, then back up again. One long, deliciously warm shiver slid through her.

"You have got serious issues with personal space." Her voice sounded breathy.

"Oh, I have no issues with the amount of space between us."

Brooke took a deep breath and tried to ignore the hard

muscles in his chest, so close to her beating heart. "So, about my brother?"

"What do you want to know?"

"What I am."

His gaze slowly worked over face, lingering for a long moment on her lips. "I don't think so."

Brooke opened her mouth, closed it, then blurted, "Why not?"

He dipped his head, his breath skimming her ear and scattering goose bumps over her skin. "Maybe we can make a deal."

Her back muscles tightened. "What kind of deal?"

"Don't make promises to William, and I'll tell you."

"Why not?"

A flash passed through his eyes, then died. "Promises have a way of binding you. Yes?"

"Yes."

Christian backed up. "If you agree not to make any promises to my lying, rat-bastard uncle, I'll tell you everything. Trust me, I'm doing you a favor. You don't want to be bound to him for the rest of your life."

She ran her tongue over her teeth. "If I agree, then is that like making a promise to you?"

"Hmmm." The sound was like a low purr coming from his chest. "It's a fine point, but maybe. I don't know." He shrugged slightly.

The warmth she'd been feeling morphed into an itchy burn, and sweat prickled her forehead. "In that case, forget it. I don't want to make any promises to your kind. Period."

Christian smoothed the tension from his mouth before saying, "It was nice seeing you again, Brooke."

He stepped off the sidewalk. A flash of headlights swept his face.

"Watch out!"

She grabbed his hood and yanked him back. He stumbled on the curb, catching her arm to maintain his balance. The car honked its horn as it sped past.

He stared at her, then whispered, "Why'd you do that?"

Panting, she brushed hair from her face. "So you wouldn't get hurt."

He studied her for a long moment, his face immobile. "Are you my guardian angel?"

She snorted. "No."

"Brooke . . . "

His face softened, his lids lowered, his thumb gently traced her lower lip. Heart slamming, she swayed as if he was a riptide, slowly sucking her toward him. The silver in his eyes flashed and then, suddenly, he tensed.

Without a word, he pivoted and strode down the sidewalk. She stumbled slightly, blinking as she righted herself.

"You're welcome," she shouted at his back, and then added softly, "dumbass."

He melted into the darkness, and she puffed out a loud breath. She unclenched her trembling fingers. She'd just saved the guy who supposedly wanted to kill her. She should have let him die. Instead, she'd leaned in for a kiss!

What a dork she was. She closed her eyes and ran a hand through her hair. Since when was it okay to let someone die? When was it okay to kiss a demon? What the hell was wrong with her?

She looked at the empty corner where he disappeared. She was thinking that she was attracted to him, and that was very, very bad.

She needed some serious girl-time with Abby, fast, before she did something totally stupid, like kiss the soul-stealing half-demon. Turning, she peeked inside Panera Bread, and then pressed her palms against the window to keep from sliding to the ground.

Abby stood behind the counter while William leaned against it. Abby's mouth gaped, and William's eyes had narrowed to slits. Both of them stared through the window, directly at Brooke.

Chapter 17

1938

For three days, Giltine's threat about claiming Elizabeth for the Other World haunted Christian. He hunkered down at an abandoned farm he discovered on the outskirts of New Hartford; another failure due to the depression and the new industrial era. Farm equipment sat stale and unused, coated with rust and dust and bird shit. Doors swung open on vacant stalls, letting loose the earthy stench of decaying hay and manure.

He leaped over the loft railing and landed on the barn's dirt floor. A fluttering of wings broadcast the birds' exit through broken windows. Dust swam in the sunbeams filtering through the cracks in the roof, making him sneeze.

He tried not to think about Elizabeth, but he couldn't seem to stop.

What if Renkin returned during the past three days and attacked her? She'd saved Christian's life . . . how could he leave her to face that horror?

He ran a hand through his hair. Was her fate with the old man better than residing in the Other World's barren wasteland, living a life of wretched heat and eating rats?

He paced. He wasn't sure Giltine could bring a living person to the Other World without the person first being judged by the Goddess of Life. Yet he didn't know the limits of Giltine's power. Perhaps it could be done.

Or perhaps she was bluffing.

A bird perched on a windowsill and studied him. Apparently deciding Christian wasn't a threat, it flew to the safety of its nest cradled between two crossbeams.

Safety. He wanted her to be safe, to save her life as she saved his. He wanted to protect her forever, be with her for a lifetime. He couldn't do those things while enslaved to Giltine; he'd never survive a lifetime of punishment for disobeying her. He needed his freedom, but refused to sacrifice a child's life for his. He could think of only one other way to free himself without hurting anyone but himself.

Abstaining.

He would kick the habit. He simply wouldn't take a soul-hit until he no longer craved the poison, until he no longer needed the poison, until he no longer felt he'd die without the poison.

He would hide from Giltine and her reaper spies for the rest of his life if he had to; as long as he was with Elizabeth he could endure. He wouldn't let Giltine drag him back to her sordid world. He would be free. He would be a man. He would be a *free* man.

He stroked his chin. He'd broken his addiction to stolen souls, but he used copious amounts of Giltine's poison to do it. He would have no such fallback when abstaining from her poison. How could he succeed?

Unfastening the top three buttons of his shirt, Christian studied the purple bruise left by the reaper who'd punched him in the chest, now a blend of faded greens and yellows. The poison from the two souls he ushered had sped his healing.

He flexed his fingers, feeling the strength. Picking up a rusty pitchfork, he ran his fingers along the wooden handle, and then snapped it in half. He wouldn't have been able to break the pitchfork before he'd taken those hits of poison.

Perhaps his approach toward abstaining had been wrong. He needed strength; the strength that came from Giltine's poison. He needed enough soul-hits to fortify him for the length of time required to break his reliance on poison, and then he'd succeed. He wouldn't be reaper-strong, but he'd be secucron-strong, and that was strong enough.

Two souls weren't nearly enough. Brushing hay from his hair and coat, he marched from the barn.

A couple of days later, Christian's veins flowed with poison and his senses were saw-blade sharp. He strode down the road with whisper-quiet steps, as though he walked on bubbles instead of packed dirt. His mind was focused and clear. Giltine had been bullshitting; there was no way the Goddess of Life would let Giltine bypass her judgment and bring Elizabeth to the Other World.

Forrest was wrong. Giltine was bluffing. Christian was in control.

He'd ushered seven souls, and he'd become strong, powerful, invincible. For once in his life he was going to do what he wanted. Not his father, not Giltine, not William . . . him.

High on death, he strolled into Bakerville. A car spewed dust into his face before pulling into the gas station. Whistling, he swung past the schoolhouse with its summer-vacant look, and the church resting in a tranquil mid-week stupor. The road wound sharply downhill, past a gristmill perched on a rocky foundation above a rumbling brook.

A bell tinkled behind him and a voice shouted, "Look out below! Coming through!"

Christian darted off the road. Elizabeth blurred past him on a bicycle, braid flapping, her legs spread out like wings, and a delighted screech riding the dust behind her. She braked to a stop, and then twisted around to laugh at him. He jogged up to her.

"Sorry." Despite the dark circles beneath her eyes, her cheeks were rose-burnt and her smile shone like a sunbeam.

He held the handlebars and tried not to ogle her tanned gams; the expanse of bare skin extending below her flower-print shorts jingle-brained his senses. He smiled. Yes, he was going to do what he wanted, and he wanted Elizabeth. Giltine was all bluff, and she couldn't take the girl from him. He was sure of that. If the goddess found out, the worst she could do was punish him, and he would endure a lifetime of punishment to be with her.

Feeling quite lit, he said, "You don't seem very sorry."

Elizabeth's laughter resounded like notes from a heavenly harp. "Maybe not."

"Do you make a habit of running people over?"

"I didn't run you over."

"Because I jumped out of the way."

"Hmm, quick reflexes. Very rugged."

He inhaled her lilac scent. So good.

"So." She buffed a rusty spot on the bell. "Where you headed?"

"The lake."

Her eyes widened. "But you don't swim."

He shrugged and smiled.

"Where's your bicycle?"

"I don't own one."

She bit her lip.

"You ride ahead. I'll meet up with you."

She rolled her eyes. "I have to push my bicycle up these hills anyway. Let's walk together."

"Allow me." He took her bicycle and pushed it.

Corn thrust its immature stalks through the rocky soil. Crows pecked the ground, their black feathers harsh against the young, green shoots. They strolled in a silence filled with heady anticipation and, as they struggled up a steep hill, labored breathing.

When they reached the crest, Elizabeth gasped and held up a hand. "Stop."

She leaned an elbow against the seat and panted. His gaze wandered from her flushed face to the hand molding her blouse against her chest. Warmth trickled through him until his lower body tensed. He cleared his throat.

"Well," she said between breaths. "How is it you're not winded?"

He shrugged.

"I wondered if Mr. Renkin had scared you away, and if I would see you again."

"You were thinking about me?"

"You're cute as a bug's ear and so shy. I couldn't stop thinking about you. Which is more than a good girl should admit to, I suppose."

She certainly had no qualms about expressing herself. Christian liked that about her . . . especially what she said.

"Oh, I've offended you," she said behind her fingers.

"No."

"Daddy says I should take care to control my tongue."

"Perhaps I've been thinking about you more than a good boy should."

Elizabeth grinned and moved on. "To answer your question, I don't normally run people down with my bicycle. I'm normally quite cautious."

"Why were you being reckless?"

"I don't know. Maybe I wanted to escape."

"On the lam, are you?"

"No. I just needed to escape my house and my life, and I see Mary everywhere. And Daddy." She swallowed. "He's just a shell now; first my mother then Mary. Haven't you ever just longed to be free from everything? To just end it?"

Christian knew too well how it felt to long for death rather than endure a life filled with pain. "Yes."

"So you understand."

"I feel we're very alike."

"I feel it too."

A tremble skittered up his legs, then his spine, and settled on the back of his neck. He was falling in love with her. No, not falling.

Crashing.

He tore his gaze away from her to the hill flowing downward at their feet.

"Thank God," she said. "We can finally ride."

"We only have one bicycle."

"You steer, and I'll ride on the handlebars."

He ignored the uncertainty tapping his head. He hadn't ridden a bicycle in years, and certainly never with a curvy dame perched on the handlebars.

"You do know how to ride a bicycle, don't you?" she asked.

"Of course."

"Well, then, what's the story, morning glory?"

"No story." He straddled the seat and flashed what he hoped was a confident grin.

Elizabeth giggled and hopped onto the handlebars. He averted his gaze from her bottom and peered around her so he could see the road. He pushed off with his foot. They wobbled while he searched for his center of gravity.

"Careful," she said.

His palms sweated against the handlebars. He attempted to steer, but she threw off his equilibrium. Gravity had no care for his unsteadiness, and they gained momentum. He gripped tighter and focused on aligning his weight with hers.

Faster, faster, they sped downhill. Her braid nipped at his cheek, the wind clouding his vision. Her joyful shriek buoyed his self-assurance, and Christian allowed a small smile. Trees blurred past them. Air moaned around his ears like a hollow train.

"Middle of the road!" she cried.

"What?"

"Turn! Turn!"

He saw the hole just as the front wheel clipped it. The front tire bounced once. The back tire lifted before slamming back down. The jolt snapped his head back, pressing the air from his lungs with a grunt. He fought to straighten the bicycle, over-corrected, and it wrenched sideways. Elizabeth soared into the air, her scream chasing her. With a lurch, the bicycle pitched off the road. Shielding his face with his arms, Christian saw the stone wall just before he smashed into it.

Chapter 18

Present Time

Brooke tried to stare down a smirking William through the window of Panera Bread until, as though trying to instigate a reaction from her, he reached across the counter, took Abby's hand, and sucked her index finger. It worked. Brooke's teeth clenched, and her body exploded with renewed energy.

She flung open the door and stomped inside. "Hey, guys."

"Hey," Abby said, her voice about as animated as earwax. "Hi, Brooke."

She flicked a glance at William but ignored him. He chuckled.

"Was that Christian's ass you just saved?" Abby asked.

"Yes."

"Does she do that kind of thing a lot?"

"All the time," her friend answered William. "She's got a bit of an angel complex."

He laughed. "Does she now."

Abby yawned before speaking again. "I can't believe you actually did it. How far have you two gone?"

She rolled her eyes. "We haven't *gone* anywhere."

"Hunh." Abby had laced her eyes with heavy eyeliner, giving her a haunted look. Her mouth muscles were slack and her eyelids drooped over glassy eyes. Even the diamond in her nostril seemed dull.

Brooke glanced over her shoulder, searching for Matt.

He must have given her some kick-ass drugs, because this wasn't a weed-induced stupor.

"Seen Matt today?"

Abby blinked, slowly, as if she'd forgotten how to operate her eyelids. "No."

"Fine. Can I get a coffee?"

She blinked a couple of times before saying, "Oh, sure." Sliding a cup across the counter, she yawned again.

She was so stoned she could barely function. Brooke was seriously going to kick Matt's ass. Two ladies approached the counter and started placing their orders. Abby stared at them as though they honked like geese.

Brooke moved to the self-service station to fill her cup, watching Abby from the corner of her eye. William followed.

She wrinkled her nose and stepped sideways. "I thought I told you to stay away from Abby."

"And I thought I told you not to talk to any other almost-reapers but me."

"I don't have to listen to you."

"Ditto."

Huffing, she dumped sugar in her coffee.

"You were looking pretty chummy with that guy out there," he said. "Who is he?"

"Christian, and you know who he is, *Uncle* William."

"So he told you. What else did he say?"

She ground her teeth, tired of these almost-reapers grilling her as if she was a baby-back rib on a barbecue. "That you're a lying rat-bastard."

He lounged against the counter. "And you believe him?"

"As much as I believe you."

His laugh was melodic with a hard edge, like techno music. She glanced at Abby who was staring slack-jawed at them; but she didn't appear jealous or pissed Brooke and William were talking. The life and laughter usually sparking from Abby's eyes had vanished, leaving behind orbs empty of feeling.

"You two are polar opposites," William said. "Kind of an odd couple."

"We've been best friends since the fifth grade, and she's stuck with me through some hard times, even when things got . . . weird." Brooke paused. "She's never judged me."

"Of course you don't judge her. Right?"

She started to agree, but stopped. While she accepted Abby's inner weirdness, she did give her a hard time about her self-medicating habits. Oh, crap. Brooke *was* judgmental. She jerked her stir stick and sloshed coffee over the top of her cup. Swearing softly, she grabbed napkins to clean the mess.

"I see how it is," he said.

"You don't see anything," she snapped.

Abby cleaned the glass window-case with a rag.

"Christian try to kill you yet?"

Brooke flinched. "No. In fact, he saved my life yesterday." She raised her eyebrows, daring William to rectify his lie.

"Is that why you saved his ass? Returning the favor?"

"No, that was a reflex. You know what they say, do unto others."

"I don't say that."

"I'm not surprised."

He snorted. "Don't buy into his Boy Scout sham. He's playing you."

A tingle of doubt crept up her scalp. "Speaking of shams, why are you interested in Abby?"

"She's fun, and cute." When Brooke twisted her lips, he asked, "You don't think I can be attracted to her?"

"No."

"Does she know you have such a low opinion of her?"

"I don't, it's just that you're not exactly human."

"I'm half human, and I still want what any guy wants."

"That's gross." She pointed her stir stick at him. "I don't

like it, I don't like you, and I don't think it's a good idea for her to hook up with some almost-reaper."

"Aren't you Little Miss Hypocrite."

"What's that supposed to mean?"

"You're falling for Christian. Talk about unhealthy. The guy wants you dead, genius."

She gulped her coffee, burning her tongue and making her eyes water. "You can't possibly know that, or anything about me."

"Want to bet?"

"Yeah." Brooke closed her eyes. "I take that back."

"Too late."

Oh, *crap*. She didn't know if making a bet was the same as making a promise, but the way her chest constricted around her ribs when William smiled, slowly, as though he cornered the most elusive prey of his life, she had a feeling it would be impossible to back out.

He sipped his coffee while he studied her. "Right now, you're scared that you took on a bet, and you're confused, wondering if it's binding on you."

She shivered as though a clammy finger drifted up her spine.

"Now you're worried because I've guessed right."

Her lips parted but she couldn't breathe. "How do you know that?"

William leaned close. "I can taste everything about you, Brooke."

Her heart fainted then sputtered to life as though it had been doused with icy water.

"Now you're turned on," he added with a curl to his lips.

"Am not, you ass."

He laughed. "Now it's time to collect my winnings."

Her eyebrows snapped to her hairline, and she flashed a look at Abby, rearranging goodies in the glass case.

"Get your mind out of the gutter. I hardly have to win bets to get girls." He threw his cup in the garbage. "Ever hear of the Bakerville Cemetery?"

She nodded. The cemetery was practically in her front yard.

"There's a grave there for Elizabeth Vincent. Go check it out; the sooner the better. Go tonight, in fact."

"Why?"

"Because," he said. "Christian killed her, just like he's going to kill you."

Chapter 19

1938

Christian's head ached and drifted as though he was a boozehound who dipped one too many bills. He lay on the ground. The bicycle laid beside him, one wheel twisted toward the sky like the frozen limb of a corpse. Elizabeth leaned over him, a shaft of sunlight lighting her head with a halo. She looked like an angel. His angel.

He brushed his thumb along the dirt smudged on her cheek. "Are you all right?"

"I'm fine."

Her braid had loosened, and hair fell forward and tickled his chin. Her body pressed against his, and it was soft and warm. His heart *pounded*. He forgot about his headache.

"How about you?" she asked.

"Dizzy."

Her fingertips searched his hair, sending goose bumps spreading along his scalp. His muscles tensed, and he resisted the urge to haul her against him.

"I don't see any blood."

"Not from the fall," he said.

Hand freezing in his hair, their gazes linked. Christian broke the connection to let his gaze wander to her mouth. Would she let him kiss her? Her lips parted, and he could just see the tip of her pink tongue. A spasm tightened his stomach, then drifted lower.

"You have a twig in your hair."

She freed the twig and tossed it. "I must look a fright."

"You're beautiful."

"Oh." She giggled and ducked her head. "Really?"

He nodded.

"I mean . . . " She bit her lip. "Mary's always been the beautiful one. I've always been Mary's younger sister, or the Vincents' youngest, or childish Izzy. No one ever really sees me."

"I do."

"Were you in love with Mary?"

"No."

"Half the boys in town were."

He could taste Elizabeth's confusion; the love for her sister was stained by the guilt she carried over her jealousy.

"Then they are blind," he said.

Her heart's tempo quickened. He wondered if she was aware that her hand, resting on his thigh, seared him with warmth that trailed upward. Suddenly, she pressed her lips against his. Her mouth was warm and soft, and tasted good, like strawberries.

Heat deepened the color in her cheeks. "I shouldn't have done that. I'm too bold. I'm sorry."

His body burned, his blood pulsed. Her lilac scent made him drip with desire. He wanted her. Her body. Her heart. Her soul.

She blurted, "No, I'm not."

She kissed him again.

With a quick movement, he had her pinned beneath him. He covered her mouth with his, pushing his tongue past her lips. When their tongues met, she flushed against him, her heat rising by degrees. He licked her tongue, savoring the warmth.

So, so warm.

He spun into a cozy, dark hole he never wanted to leave. Her heat was so good; his head swam, the frigid holes in his soul melting. And she tasted sweeter than honey. Deeper, deeper, he drifted into that dark, inviting place until he thought his head would float from his body.

Beneath him, Elizabeth shivered as though she lay on snow-covered ground. Christian froze.

Gods! What was he doing?

He rolled off her, panting and running his hands through his hair. Was William right? Once a rogue, always a rogue? Sitting up, Elizabeth stared at her lap, blinking rapidly.

"Oh, dear," she whispered and shivered again. "I've never felt anything like that."

He staggered to his feet and paced off a few steps. Breathing deeply, he beat back the demon longings he knew gleamed silver through his eyes. He pressed a palm to the goose egg on his head, hard, forcing his headache back with potent reality.

A car horn wheezed. Maintaining a shivery control over his body, he studied a man with a dirty cap glaring at him through the open window of a rattling truck.

"You all right?" the man asked Elizabeth. He stepped on the gas, and the truck growled a warning. "That fellow bothering you?"

She shook her head as though clearing it. Christian offered her his hand. She took it, and he helped her to her feet, the damp cold seeping from her trembling fingers into his. She swayed, pressing her hands against his chest.

"No," she said slowly, as though trying to remember where they were. "We took a fall on our bicycle."

"Hey," the man said. "You're the Vincents' youngest, aren't you?"

She sighed. "Yes, Mr. Phillips."

"Take care that you get yourself home and cleaned up." He hung his arm out the window and rested his clenched fist against the truck. "Give your father my regards."

"I will."

The truck bounced down the road. They stood immobile. Did she regret kissing him? Did she know the vague, cold she experienced was due to Christian tasting her soul? Rubbing his thumbs along his pants' seams, his shoulders slumping, he waited.

She studied the road. "You must think I'm terribly bold."

She was completely unaware of what he'd done to her. He turned his head, unable to face her.

"Oh, God. I should have waited for you to kiss me." Her eyes widened. "I mean, if you wanted to kiss me. I mean, I think you wanted to kiss me." She covered her face with her hands and moaned.

"I did."

She peeked at him through her fingers. "Mary had a reputation for kissing a boy or two, but I don't skate around."

He nodded.

"Did you feel it too? That kiss was surreal."

Closing his eyes, he nodded again.

She brushed her blouse. "Anyway, Mr. Phillips is right. I should get cleaned up."

He rolled the bicycle, and the wheel screeched against metal. "No more riding."

"Daddy's going to be mad. It's the only one we own."

"I can fix it."

"Aces!" She hesitated. "Are you feeling well enough to walk?"

"Yes."

They walked on, each lost in their thoughts; Christian's filled with soft lips and a heady, lilac fragrance, shadowed by guilt that when he kissed her he'd lost control and dabbled with her soul. It had been so *good*. He startled when Elizabeth clutched his arm.

"What's that?"

She darted off the road and peeked through a sea of ferns.

When she stood, she was clutching a calico kitten, which promptly extended its claws into her blouse and meowed.

"Poor thing. I can feel her ribs. I'm taking her home."

"Your father won't mind?"

"Of course not." She tickled the kitten's chin. "Aren't you a bonnie little lass? I shall name you Bonnie."

Later, when they arrived at her house, she pried the kitten from her blouse and kissed its nose. "Now it's time to feed you, my Bonnie." She ran up the steps, and then turned at the door. "Coming?"

He hesitated at the foot of the porch. "I'll wait here."

"Why?"

"It wouldn't be proper."

"I've already kissed you. Twice. What could be more improper?"

"You don't know me. I could be a junkie, or a grifter, like Renkin said." The problem was, he *was* a junkie . . . a soul junkie.

"I don't think so."

"What would the neighbors think?"

"I don't care. I can't face that empty house alone. Please?" Elizabeth pouted.

He wanted to kiss her again. His gaze licked her from head to toe. He wanted to do more than kiss her. Inhaling, her lilac scent shot like a fireball into his lungs. Yes, he would follow her inside and kiss her and . . .

"Am I interrupting?"

The familiar voice froze his foot in mid-step. Moving as though Father Time himself had seized his limbs, Christian set his foot down and turned.

"William."

Chapter 20

Present Time

He'd killed another girl. Christian had killed another girl.

Brooke sat in her car outside Panera Bread, numb, her chest cold, her heart heavy. She couldn't bring herself to move, or think. Her mind and body seemed encased in ice.

And yet, part of her refused to believe what William said was true. Christian was dark and mysterious, but dangerous? A killer? He was too cute, too charming, too *appealing*.

She checked herself. He was half-demon with soul-stealing residue. It wasn't a far stretch to imagine he'd killed someone.

She bit her thumbnail. If ever she needed pizza—and lots of it—it was now. Putting her car in gear, she jetted the parking lot and drove a couple miles down the road to an out-of-the-way pizza place. It was small, and a dive, but had the best pizza ever.

She pushed through the heavy front door, needing to throw her weight behind it. A TV on the wall overlooked the only three booths, and in the dim light she could see two of the booths were occupied. The minute she breathed in the scent of grease and cheese, the tightness between her shoulder blades loosened, then re-tightened at the giggles emanating from one of the booths. She didn't need to look; she knew the owner of that high, nasal laugh belonged to Tara, one of the popular elite who had it in for Brooke ever since she'd gone to the spring dance with Paul.

She strode to the counter and ordered a small pepperoni pizza, extra cheese, thick crust, and a root beer. Taking her soda, she moved toward the empty booth behind Tara.

"Lesbo," she said as Brooke walked past her table.

She missed a step and stumbled, soda sloshing over her fingers. Tara and her blonde friend, another clueless clone from the popular crowd, laughed. Brooke's lips tightened.

"Aren't giraffes supposed to be kind of graceful?" Tara asked.

"No, all those long legs make them look like a *big* joke," the other girl said.

Brooke's face flamed as she slid into the empty booth, the girls' laughter invading her gloomy space. Wiping her hand with a napkin, she endured a few more flip comments until Tara said, "Holy hell. Who's *that*?"

Looking up, Brooke spotted Christian leaning against the counter. He gave her a half-smile. Her body went cold, and then warmed.

"He just smiled at me," Tara stage-whispered.

"His scars are so boss," her friend added.

"Dark and sexy," Tara agreed.

Was Christian a killer? Was she on his hit list? Brooke wanted to look away, and yet she couldn't. She wanted to bolt, and yet she didn't. She could only stare at him as he strolled toward her with a cup of coffee.

"May I join you?" he asked.

"No."

"It's the only available seat. Are you going to make me eat my pizza standing up?"

"You can sit with us," Tara offered.

Christian eyed her.

Dipping her chin, she gave him a you-can-have-me-any-way-you-want-me smile.

"No, thanks." Focusing on Brooke, he asked, "Please don't leave me hanging."

She wanted to believe he was a killer, and yet she didn't. She couldn't, because if he was that meant she was bat-shit crazy for even thinking about sitting with him or talking to him or kissing him . . .

She stopped herself right there. She peeked up at him through her bangs. Bad-ass move. The riptide power of his eyes made all brain function go haywire, putting the wrong word on her tongue.

"Okay."

He folded himself into the seat across the table from her. "So."

"So." A few awkward moments ticked by. She broke the silence. "Coffee and pizza?"

"Coffee goes with everything."

"Not pizza."

"Okay, then. Let's just say pizza goes with everything."

"Not coffee."

"I call this an impasse."

"I call that coffee addiction."

"You can say that."

"I think there's help for that."

Tara sashayed to their table, interrupting their conversation as she leaned toward Christian. The neckline of her sweater dipped, her push-up bra producing an eye-jutting boob crack. Her nearly naked legs stretched below her very short skirt. She was giving him a perfect view of a lot of cleavage and a lot of skin which, Brooke was sure, was exactly what the girl intended.

Brooke knew how much the guy liked his views.

"Hey, there," Tara said on a wisp of breath.

He raised an eyebrow.

"I was wondering." She paused to glance at her giggling friend and giggled herself. "My *friend* was wondering if you wanted to eat us." Another giggle. "I mean eat *with* us."

"That's a very . . . " His glance slid to her chest, "attractive offer."

"I know. Right?" She licked her lips. "We saw you sitting here, and I thought, *we* thought, that someone so, well, like you, shouldn't sit alone."

"Sorry." He smiled smoothly. "No can do."

"Oh?" She straightened, red-glossed lips puckering into a seductive pout.

"I'm not alone, as you well know."

She squinted down her nose at Brooke. "Why sit with *her* when you can eat with me?" Tara laid a hand on his shoulder, licked her lips again, and murmured, "Food optional, of course."

He jerked away from her.

Tara narrowed her eyes. "You'd rather sit with the lesbo?"

He stood. "What did you call her?"

"Lesbo. Lesbian. Dyke."

At each word, Brooke flinched.

She transferred a frosty look to Brooke. "Paul told me all about your spring dance fiasco. The hottest guy in school, and you wouldn't even kiss him."

"Couldn't," she corrected. "Big difference."

"Not if you're a lesbo."

Christian bent toward Tara, forcing her to lean back. "I assure you, Brooke is far from any of those things."

"How would you know?"

His lids closed halfway, a slight smile sliding through his lips. "I've tasted her."

Brooke choked on her root beer. What the *hell*?

"Oh, please." Tara snorted. "Look at her hair, and those clothes. She doesn't even wear make-up! Everything about her screams butch."

He ran his fingertips up Tara's arm. She shivered, her

mouth parting. Then he pushed her away from their table. "Take your fake breasts back to your own table."

She blinked, stumbled back a step. "What?"

"Get. Lost."

Face flashing red, she muttered at Brooke, "Bitch." Then shot toward the door, calling over her shoulder, "Come *on*, Lindsey."

Lindsey rushed through the door behind her friend.

Sitting again, he sipped his coffee. "So."

He gazed at Brooke with those amazing eyes, what might be described as cold-gray flecks on an ice-blue horizon on anyone else's face, but not his, not with the light of laughter sparking the gray, not with the curl to his lips.

She couldn't rip her gaze away. He lowered his lids, his gaze trailed down her face, lingered on her mouth. Her toes curled.

She cleared her throat. "What was that tasting remark all about?"

"I think Tara's imagination will do more damage than anything I had to say, don't you?"

Grinning, she shook her head and then said, "Fake? Seriously?"

"We can always tell. It's a guy thing."

She was still chuckling when their pizza was delivered to the table, her pepperoni and his topped with everything. She grabbed a slice, not bothering with a plate, and bit into it. Greasy cheese exploded in her mouth. She closed her eyes and sighed.

"Enjoy pizza much?"

"Oh, yeah. It's my favorite."

He slid a slice onto his plate, then used his knife and fork to cut a piece and pop it into his mouth.

Her mouth dropped open. "What the hell are you doing?"

"Eating my pizza."

"No, the silverware; that's blasphemy." She snatched the silverware from his fingers. "Eat with your fingers like a normal human. You have to enjoy the experience."

Smiling, he picked up his pizza and took a bite.

"Doesn't it taste better?"

"Absolutely liberating."

"You know what they say, live every day like it's your last."

"You don't seem the type to live life on the edge."

"You're right, that's more Abby's thing. But I'm thinking I should, you know, take more chances. Life's for the living, after all." She licked her fingers.

He froze, the smile slipping from his face. She swallowed, feeling warmth hit the back of her neck. Jeesh, they were only greasy fingers, not a death warrant. He still hadn't moved. Heat from her neck flared to her face. Silver tracked through his eyes, and his gaze fell to her mouth.

"I have to go," he said suddenly.

Without another word, he was gone. Mouth gaping, she twisted around to stare at the door.

What the *hell*?

Later that night, Brooke stood in her front yard, embraced by a darkness that seemed to press the air out of her lungs. Christian's sudden departure from the pizza place had her brain whirling. She tried not to be hurt, but her chest tightened at the memory. Fine. He'd actually done her a favor by leaving. She shouldn't be hanging around with him anyway; he was a demon, had all but admitted he wanted her dead, and William told her he'd already killed a girl.

She was a dumbass for forgetting any of that.

Her sigh condensed in front of her. The setting sun brought in chilly air, reviving the aroma of dirt and damp leaves. Clouds shadowed the moon like a coating of fine dust, and a barn owl screeched with an intensity that coaxed chills along her spine. Shivering, she flashed her light into the trees; something skittered away, snapping sticks and rustling dead leaves.

She tried to turn back toward her house, but her feet moved forward instead. She kicked a stone across the driveway. These stupid promises and bets and reapers! It seemed she'd be forced to see the grave marker of Elizabeth Vincent whether she wanted to or not.

Tossing a look at the warm lights seeping through the windows of her brick house, she strode out of the yard and along the side of the road. Was it her imagination, or did the few neighboring houses seem dark and empty? Were the trees larger? Was the night darker?

The barn owl shrilled again, making goose bumps dance over her skin. The bushes rustled to her left; she gripped her light and jerked it in that direction. Leaves crunched behind her; she whirled, tracking her light along the edge of the woods, spotting a raccoon before it dove into the underbrush. She walked backward a couple of steps before turning to continue up the road.

Her gaze darted left then right then left as she walked, reaching an area where there were no houses. Trees were rooted so close to the road she could reach out and touch their trunks. A pack of coyotes bayed in the darkness. Brooke tightened her neck muscles, resisting the urge to look over her shoulder.

One big-ass hill later, the road left its steep incline and rolled gently upward. Panting, she paused, giving her burning leg muscles a break. A few houses were scattered through the trees, porch lights not quite reaching the road. The red stoplight at the end of the street throbbed against the dark-windowed library, which had once been the Bakerville school. Next to the school sat a church foundation, the church having burned years ago.

She regarded the one-lane, dirt road that squeezed between the two buildings. Weak moonlight crept through the trees, and then disappeared into darkness. She directed her light ahead, but the shadows sucked the beam like a vacuum. Taking a deep breath, she plunged forward.

Within a minute, the trees choked what little moonlight kept her company. The road was lumpy and uneven, and Brooke stumbled repeatedly. A bird shot out of a tree, its wings whistling in the dark, and she flung her hands over her head. The flashlight slipped from her trembling fingers, making a half-spin before reflecting off a pair of eyes. She snatched her light off the ground and aimed it at the woods. With a screech, a cat sped away.

"Friggin' F-bomb frig!" Brooke blurted, slapping a hand to her chest.

She squinted. Was that a shadow slinking in the distance?

"Hello?"

Empty darkness answered. Chills licked her neck with an icy tongue. She inched forward, paused. The air dripped in dark silence. Goose bumps rippled her hair, and the chill drained her courage. A dog barked from the house next door.

With a yelp, she ran like a stumbling drunk down the road.

Breaking from the woods, she stopped and let out her hoarded breath. Fog swept the ground, and gray-shadowed gravestones rose in the smoky moonlight. Clenching her flashlight, she pushed open the gate to the cemetery, the hinges moaning. The back of her neck prickled. The shriek of an owl made her intestines curl like gnarled fingers.

"I really hate reapers, especially the almost ones."

Brooke paused, passing her light over cracked and eroded headstones, reading the faded names of people long dead. A twig snapped behind her, and she whirled.

"Who's there?" Her voice cracked, and she swallowed.

Silence. Swallowing again, she tried to ignore how her

light trembled through the chain link fence surrounding the cemetery. She breathed deep, and her breath shook in her lungs.

She should just go home. This night hike was stupid, and her shoes were seriously wet from the dew-drenched grass. Her feet were freezing, and her heart was going to hammer itself to death. William was no doubt lying about the headstone and was probably laughing his ass off at her gullibility.

"Screw you, William."

As she turned to leave, she cracked her knee against a headstone. Swearing, she jerked her light over the non-descript grave marker.

"Oh, crap."

Squatting, she traced Elizabeth's name, and her blood stopped flowing, turning the rest of her body as cold as her feet.

"1938?"

Brooke swore at the night. She'd been totally played. Christian told her William was a lying rat-bastard, and there was the proof. There was no way Christian had known Elizabeth, let alone killed her.

"What are you doing?"

Brooke gasped. Her feet slipped in the wet grass, and she toppled backward. Massaging her wrist, she stared up at Christian, who glared at her like an ice god ready to freeze her with a look.

"Looking at headstones. What are you doing?"

He caressed Elizabeth's name with his fingertips. The hard-ass look melted, and his face softened. Brooke got to her feet, beamed her flashlight in his face, and pretended her ass wasn't wet.

Wait. He acted as if he knew this girl. Intimately. No. No, no, no. There was no way he was alive in the 1930s. William and Christian were in on it together. They were both lying rat-bastards.

"Who told you about this?" That cold look snapped back onto his face.

"William."

He swore. "Stay away from here."

"You're not the boss of me."

"And stay away from William."

"What the hell's your problem?"

"My problem?"

"One minute you're almost nice, and the next you're a complete dick."

He closed his eyes for a second. When he spoke, his voice lost its sharp intensity. "He's playing you."

She crossed her arms over her chest. "And you're not?"

"Tell me you didn't promise him anything."

"I don't have to tell you a damn thing."

"Hmm." Christian leaned against a headstone. "Did you promise him anything?"

"No, but I made a stupid remark about betting, and," she swept her flashlight across the cemetery, "here I am, checking out Elizabeth Vincent's grave in the middle of the damn night arguing with a psychotic ass-hat."

"You think I'm psychotic?"

"It's crossed my mind."

"Why did he tell you about Elizabeth?"

"Don't know. You don't honestly expect me to believe you were alive back then." Brooke paused. "Do you?"

He held her gaze, and then went back to studying the headstone.

She rubbed the corners of her mouth. Were almost-reapers immortal? That couldn't be right . . . they were half human, and humans got old, then died. Did reapers die? Probably not. Maybe it wasn't a stretch to believe almost-reapers were immortal.

The soft look in Christian's eyes melted her from the

inside. She clenched her fists and lifted her chin. "What happened to her?"

"She died."

"No shit, Sherlock."

When he didn't respond, she said, "You didn't answer my question."

"I did."

"Can you be more specific?"

"No."

"Why not?"

"What's in it for me?"

"Nothing."

"There's your answer."

She bit her lip, played her flashlight over Elizabeth's headstone, then back to his face. A slight breeze brushed his hair from his eyes, gleaming with hints of haunted silver. Brooke's heart fluttered like butterfly wings, and heat danced through her veins. She gripped her flashlight until her fingers ached.

"Did you know her?"

"Yes," he murmured.

Her chest muscles squeezed the breath from her lungs. She didn't care if he'd been into some random girl; he was a demon. Right?

Pissed at her own damn self for going soft, she blurted, "Almost-reapers are immortal?"

"No, they age; just much slower than humans."

"How slow? You don't look older than nineteen."

His cheek rippled from his teeth clenching. "*I'm* immortal."

"Why?"

He studied Elizabeth's headstone.

Brooke refused to be put off. "Did you kill her?"

He didn't look at her, though his jaw hardened.

"William said you killed her."

Christian's chest expanded with the depth of his breath, and then it hissed through his teeth. "Another man was sentenced for her death."

Relief tangled with fear; relief that he hadn't killed Elizabeth, and fear that he was lying. "Why would William lie about it?"

"To hurt me."

"What does all this have to do with me?"

Christian gave her a long look. "It has everything to do with you."

Brooke swallowed.

He stepped toward her, breaching her personal space. She tilted her head back. His faint grape-leather-spice scent tickled her nose. She stopped breathing when he played with a lock of her hair.

"Why did you try to save me from being hit by that car?" he asked softly. "Knowing what I am, and what William told you?"

"Because I might be falling in love with you."

She gasped at her own revelation, which sunk into her heart like a brand. His hand froze in her hair as he stared at her.

When it was obvious he wasn't going to return the sentiment, she quickly added, "Besides, I would have done the same for anyone . . . no matter how much of a dick they are."

"You really think I'm a dick?"

"Sometimes."

"And other times?"

"Not so much." She was hyper-aware of his hands in her hair, sliding it through his fingers. "Sometimes you're colder than a witch's tit, and other times . . . "

His fingers grazed her scalp. "Um . . . " Her head tingled, distracting her. Swallowing, she said, "You're, um, not."

"Are you afraid to trust me?"

She nodded, her heart fluttering to the point where she thought she might start hyperventilating.

"Let me prove I'm not a dick. Will you let me do that?"

"Okay." She was finally able to breathe when he let go of her hair.

He half-smiled. "I'll tell you about the watchers, free and clear, no promises. Okay?"

She studied her feet, sucking her lips between her teeth. "I don't know."

He lifted his hands. "No games. I promise."

She peeked at him through her lashes.

"Come on. Meet me tomorrow."

She tried not to gulp, failed. By the way he was ogling Elizabeth's headstone, he was just a sad, lonely guy. And she wanted to find out more; about him, about herself, about what kind of insanity she descended from.

She nodded. "Okay."

"Your house?"

Heat crept up the back of her neck. "My house?"

"It's private."

Her almost-reaper radar buzzed a get-the-hell-away signal, but her head told the signal to get the hell away. She swallowed.

"Where do you live?"

She jerked her thumb over her shoulder. "Down the road, like you don't already know. I saw you drive by my house the other night."

Christian gave her a lopsided smile. "Busted."

His fingers lightly touched her cheek. He brushed her lower lip with his thumb, breathed deeply, and then pulled away. Tingles raced along her skin in the wake of his touch, and her gut exploded in warmth. She wondered if he had the same tingles, but his face remained stoic and unreadable—except for the silver in his eyes that flashed for a moment before dying.

"See you tomorrow," he said and strolled out of the cemetery.

Brooke collapsed against a headstone. She snagged a quivery breath, ran shaky fingers through her hair, then staggered after him.

Chapter 21

1938

Christian's head buzzed and he stood very still, his desire for Elizabeth freezing under William's stare. Why had he come to her house? It couldn't bode well. The floor creaked when she stepped back. His great uncle's casual stance, leaning against the porch with crossed arms and tilted head, belied the intensity of his fingers gripping his biceps. Bonnie mewed softly.

"You have an appointment," he said.

Christian's teeth clenched.

"Christian? Do you know this man?"

His mind mumbled thoughts of dread; he should have known he'd be caught. His heart took off at a gallop.

Brushing past him, William took the steps two at a time and extended his hand. "I'm William, Christian's uncle."

"Elizabeth," she said, taking his hand.

Christian concentrated on regaining the poison-induced confidence that had propelled him throughout the day, and his heart settled to a lazy trot.

William hadn't released her. Christian's breath came hard as he studied their clasped hands.

"Is it your head?" She extricated her hand from William's grip and touched Christian's arm. "He hit his head earlier," she explained.

"I'm all right," he said.

"We should go." William gave an easy smile, as though he invited him to play lawn darts. "You know Giltine hates to be kept waiting."

"Giltine?"

"Our boss."

"No," Christian said.

"I'm sure she'll understand you have to leave."

"Christian, if you need to go . . . "

He cut her off. "I don't."

"May we have a moment alone?" Instead of waiting for an answer William grabbed Christian's arm and hauled him toward the lake.

He wrenched free from his grip.

William gave him the once-over. "So gowed-up on poison you've become a palooka, have you?"

"Not your business."

"Fun's over. It's time to go."

"No."

"The dame's not worth getting ringed by Giltine. Don't ignore her, or you'll wish you were dead when she's done."

The flicker of apprehension in Christian's chest quickly vanished, absorbed by the poison racing through his veins.

William frowned. "Why would you act so reckless over some dame?"

"She saved my life."

"So? She'd pull any drowning boob out of that lake. I know the type. She's a sap, just like you."

"I don't care. I want to be with her."

William smacked his forehead. "Your life consists of duty and family. Reaping is your duty, and I'm your family. Not her. Forget her."

Christian crossed his arms over his chest.

"I can't let that dame ruin your life, Thomas."

He flinched. "I'm not Thomas."

The other man closed his eyes and rubbed his temples with his fingertips. "If you try to bargain with Giltine, you'll die. I won't let that happen, not over some stupid dame."

Christian glanced at Elizabeth, setting out a bowl of milk for the kitten. When she knelt, her hair sifted over her shoulder like silk.

"Don't call her that," he said in an undertone.

With swiftness that paralleled an igniting match, the mask returned to his great uncle's face. "You're a rube. You deserve what you get."

Spinning, he stomped across the yard. Elizabeth rose, but he ignored her. Christian leaped onto the porch with what he hoped was a carefree grin.

She scooped Bonnie from the floor. "Are you in trouble?"

"No."

"Imagine! A woman for a boss. Though William seems young to be your uncle."

Christian couldn't tell her Giltine's poison slowed the aging process, or that William was really his great-uncle, or that William, who looked no more than twenty-two, was really seventy-two.

After doing some quick math in his head, Christian said, "His father married late to a younger woman, so he was born not long before I was."

"What is it about old men and young women?" she murmured.

Old men like Renkin, and young women like her. A queasy feeling rolled through Christian, not only from disgust. He needed another soul-hit. He swallowed the bitterness of failure. No, he was abstaining. No more poison. He could do this.

She set a wiggling Bonnie down, and the kitten wobbled toward the bowl of milk. "So, you mentioned you could fix my bicycle?"

The afternoon waned while Christian worked. The fading of the poison chilled him, and he had to clench his hands to hide their shaking. Fevered sweat crawled along his scalp and the backs of his knees.

Damnation!

Instead of needing less poison, it seemed he needed more to maintain his high. He wasn't stronger, he was weaker. He rubbed his eyes, his shirt clinging to his back and sweat dripping down his face.

"Thank you." She rested the bicycle against the shed and wiped her forehead with her arm. "I wish you knew how to swim. I could sure use a dip right now."

He waved a hand toward the lake. "By all means, don't let me stop you."

Hands on her hips, she said, "How'd you go swimming with Mary if you can't swim?"

"I watched."

"Would you like to watch me?"

"Yes." His voice dropped an octave.

She bit her lip before her smile fully formed. "Race you!"

She streaked across the small yard and pounded down the dock. She launched herself off the edge—clothes and all—and molded her body into a perfect dive, her slim body slicing the water with a small splash.

He raced after her.

Elizabeth's head bobbed in the water, her face shiny-wet, her saturated braids darkening to a burnt-gold sunset. Her legs beckoned below the surface. "Oh! You have no idea how good this feels."

He smiled. He knew how good it looked.

She swam out a hundred yards, dove, then swam back. Her tanned arms cut through the water with an easy rhythm, and she lifted her face every four strokes for breath. The sun tilted toward the horizon, setting the water aflame and silhouetting her sleek form. When she returned, he pulled her onto the dock.

His breath snapped like a sail caught in a sudden wind. The white fabric of her clothes had become transparent, the blue flowers seemingly tattooed to her skin. Her wet blouse clung to her body, revealing the outline of her bra. When he managed to move his attention from her body to her face, her lips parted.

Christian's heart slammed. His blood pounded between his ears. Every nerve came alive, and his body reacted with swelling desire, burning every inch of him.

Her fingers tightened in his. "I can teach you to swim."

His gaze wandered the length of her body once more. "I like watching," he murmured. "Do you often swim in your clothes?"

"I do now." She smiled. Slowly. "Tonight I just might try swimming without them."

Blood rushed to his head. "Reckless, are we?"

"I've seen too much death. Life is for the living, don't you think?"

"Yes." His head dipped toward hers, desire pulsing through his body.

"What's going on here?" Renkin demanded from the end of the dock.

She gasped and took a quick step back. The corner of Christian's mouth twitched before he turned to face the old man marching down the dock and hoisting his walking stick like a sword.

"M . . . Mr. Renkin."

She hugged herself, and Christian shifted to block Renkin's view. Cold trembled through his body. Not the cold from poison withdrawal, but the cold hatred of the vile dog lusting over Elizabeth.

His Elizabeth.

Thunking his walking stick on the dock, Renkin growled, "Ed Phillips told me you were trouncing around with a vagrant, so I thought to make sure you were home safe, and by God, it's a good thing I did. Now, what's going on here?"

She peered over Christian's shoulder. "I was only swimming."

"Where's your bathing suit? By God, you're indecent!"

"I'll go change." Brushing past them, she ran for the house.

Renkin's face mottled like a rotten tomato. Christian wanted to crush the man's head between his hands and watch it explode. They glared at each other while Renkin tapped his walking stick, the hollow thumps punctuating the silence like a countdown to battle.

"I thought I told you to take a powder, boy."

He ground his teeth and held Renkin's gaze, hoping he wouldn't get pushed into the lake again. Elizabeth wasn't there to save Christian this time. His neck throbbed as though his heart had moved up and taken residence there.

The man rapped Christian's shin. "Folks around here listen when I tell them something."

He didn't flinch from the sharp sting. "I'm not from around here."

Renkin grabbed the front of his shirt, his knuckles boring into Christian's chest. Despite the sickening withdrawal, with his feet planted firmly on dry ground and not the bottom of the lake, he thought he could take him.

He dipped into the dark well of secucron essence he used to journey to the Other World. He embraced it, but held back enough so he wouldn't slide into the Void and bring Renkin with him. He only wanted the sight of his silver-gleamed eyes to haunt the man.

He hoped his slow smile was as sinister as his voice. "Don't mess with me, Renkin."

His grip loosened and his mouth went slack. "What the . . . "

Christian's smile deepened. Warmth from Renkin's soul slid through his skin. The heat rushed to his head, clouding his senses and filling him with longing brought on by his dark need.

He closed his eyes.

"Break it up!"

Elizabeth's voice, sharp with alarm, sliced through the fog in Christian's brain. Biting his lip hard, he let go of the black need. Renkin shivered, shook his head, and then staggered down the dock. He took several deep breaths to calm his breathing and settle back into his humanity. Shuddering once, he joined them.

She'd changed into a plain, brown dress that swept past her knees. Her feet were still bare, and her hair wet and tangled. Her lips were rosy from chewing on them.

Christian looked away, swallowing the desire to kiss her. He counted to ten before facing her once again.

Puckering his mouth, Renkin rocked on his toes, his shifting gaze taking in everything but him. His uncertainty was satisfying, yet disquieting. Christian thought of a cornered dog, prepared to attack in defense of its bone.

"I thought you couldn't swim." The man's voice cracked, and he cleared his throat.

"He can't. That's why he was watching."

He squinted at Christian, a calculated squint that made unease ripple between his shoulder blades.

"I suppose you just watched Mary, too?"

Christian's unease settled in his chest like a corpse in a coffin.

Renkin let the silence hang for an eternity before asking, "Did she know?"

Ice constricted his heart, freezing it to a dead stop.

"Mr. Renkin, Christian's not a pervert."

"Says who? Mary?" Renkin twirled his stick. "This here grifter waltzed into our town right about the time your poor Mary drowned. By his own admission he went swimming with Mary, but he can't swim. What else has he lied about?"

A lash from Lucifer's flaming whip wouldn't have been enough to unfreeze Christian's tongue. Doubt brought her eyebrows together.

Renkin went on. "When did you go swimming with Mary? The night she died?"

Christian could almost hear the shattering of his lies. He looked to the trees as though an answer would fall from the leaves.

"Eh? You just tipped your mitt, pally."

"It's not what you think," he said.

"Here's what I think. You spied on Mary swimming naked."

Christian opened his mouth with a ready denial, but snapped it closed on the lie.

"Did she scream when she saw you?"

"No."

"Were you the one who tore that dress off her?"

"No."

"Did you bump her off?"

"No!"

"Oh, my God." Elizabeth's gaze moved to the lake, then to Christian, then to Renkin, back to the lake.

"Let me explain." Christian held out his hand, but she shrank away. "I did meet Mary the night she died. I spoke to her after she, ah, went swimming."

"Impossible," Renkin screamed. "After she went swimming she was dead!"

Christian focused on Elizabeth. "She asked me to watch out for you."

Renkin swore. "That's bunk."

"How did you know Mary wasn't clothed, or that her dress was torn?" she asked Renkin.

He wet his lips. "Your father."

The seconds passed. Hesitantly, she dropped her hand from her throat, then pressed her hands against her stomach. "I don't believe Christian would hurt anyone, and certainly not Mary."

Renkin smacked his stick against the ground, making her jump. "Izzy Vincent, you're a sucker."

She didn't respond.

"He's stringing you along," he said, then slashed Christian with a dark look when she shook her head.

"Give him the gate, Izzy."

"No."

"Then by God, I will." Renkin marched to his car, throwing over his shoulder, "Don't blame me if you end up on ice." He sped off, his tires spitting dirt and gravel.

"Oh, my God," she whispered.

Christian studied the settling dust from Renkin's departure. The salty taste of his slyness briefly brushed Christian's tongue, mixing with the man's twisted lust. And something else was there, too; a sharp and bitter secret. His mind rolled back to the cloudy chaos of Mary's crossing, and her words reached him from the Void.

That pill, Renkin, will come after her next.

Next. Was Renkin connected to Mary's death? Had he been infatuated with her as he now was with Elizabeth? Christian feared she would, indeed, end up on ice like her sister. He bowed his head, linking his hands behind his back.

There was no other choice for him now. He loved her and had to save her. He had to free himself from Giltine. He had to bargain.

"About the things he said." She gnawed her lip. "There's more to your relationship with Mary than you've told me. Did you lie to me?"

He shuddered at his escalating nausea. "Yes."

She scooped up Bonnie and pressed the kitten to her throat. She didn't look at him. "Did you . . . kiss her too?"

"No."

Dizziness overwhelmed him. He leaned against the railing. He would need at least three hits of poison to cure his sickness. This had all gone wrong.

She looked at him, then away. "Are you all right? You look ill."

He could taste the sweetness of her blush, could hear the pulse throbbing in her neck, could feel the heat radiating from her skin. He sucked in a quick breath.

The lightness in his head was unsettling, and his voice shook when he spoke. "I just need to go and rest. I'd like to see you tomorrow, if you'd allow me, and we'll talk." He held his breath; hoping she'd say yes, and afraid she'd say yes.

He gripped the railing behind him. He lowered his gaze when she took a subtle step toward the front door, but then she nodded once.

"Good night, Elizabeth."

He waited for her to slip into the house before he sought the darkness of the woods. Dropping to his knees, he vomited.

Chapter 22

Present Time

Brooke waited for the demon to come to her house. Her parents were at work, and wouldn't be home for hours. Was she stupid? A little. Pathetic? Probably. Bat-shit crazy? Definitely. Yeah, he was kind of a dick, and he could piss her off in a heartbeat, and there was that whole death-threat thing, but he had his chance to kill her at the cliff's edge, and he hadn't done the deed.

Yes, she'd fallen for him, and she'd give him every chance to redeem himself. She was sure he wouldn't hurt her, even though he hadn't returned her sentiment.

On one level, her feelings for Christian were visceral, a chemical reaction to his epic cuteness. She also suspected there was an emotional level he kept buried beneath his icy exterior. The way he'd touched her face, and spoken her name . . . no one could fake that level of fondness.

Brooke sighed. She was beyond bat-shit. She was certifiable.

She checked herself in the mirror. Ryan's t-shirt made her look like she was twelve years old. Damn Abby for being right. Brooke stripped off the shirt and flung it over a bedpost; it missed and dropped to the floor. She chose a pale-green shirt that set off her hazel eyes and was fitted enough to highlight her chest. Should she brush her hair? No—she didn't want it to look like she cared, just in case Christian didn't.

She rushed to the kitchen and studied the stuff in the

fridge. Should she eat? She didn't want her stomach to growl in front of him, but eating something might make it gurgle.

Settling on a cup of coffee, she waited at the butcher-block kitchen table. Was she making an epic mistake? Her intestines felt like jellyfish, wiggling around and zapping her insides.

When the doorbell rang, she made herself walk, not run, to the foyer and open the door. "Hey," she said.

"Hello, Brooke," Christian said.

The silver in his eyes was muted, and there were dark circles edging the skin beneath his lashes. The scars on his face melted into his skin like pale threads.

She cleared her throat. "Do I have to, like, invite you in?"

He half-smiled. "I'm not a vampire."

"Oh, right." She giggled, a little too loudly, and waved him in.

He slipped his boots off before following her into the kitchen.

"Drink?"

"Coffee's good."

"Right, how could I forget? How do you like it?"

"Black; lots of sugar." A pause. "Are you nervous?"

She tried to laugh, but it came out more as a squeak. Lola waddled into the kitchen, winding around Christian's legs.

Scooping up the cat, she said, "Meet Lola. I rescued her from a kill shelter on her last day of life. She was pathetic, and scrawny, and it was love at first sight."

His gaze was intense enough to make her shiver. He stiffened, his gaze sliding to Lola.

"I'm sorry, are you allergic?"

"No," he whispered.

"Then why do you look like I just told you I torture kittens for a living?"

He blinked and shook his head. "It's nothing."

Brooke snuggled Lola to her chin. "I have a thing for strays."

Lola wiggled, and she let her jump free. The cat hit the floor with a solid thump.

"Not so scrawny now." His gaze trailed after Lola as she strolled out of the kitchen.

"She constantly cons me into giving her treats. I'm a sucker for a pretty face."

"Me too."

Brooke grabbed a mug from the cabinet.

"Do you make a habit of picking up strays?" he asked.

"Well, everyone roots for the underdog."

"Or undercat."

Smiling, she filled a cup with coffee. When she turned, Christian was gone. She set the mug on the table and wandered into the foyer. He stood at the bottom of the stairs. He had one hand on the rail, one foot on the bottom step.

"Christian?"

He didn't answer. He crept up the steps, his hand caressing the dark banister, his socked feet making no sound on the navy-blue runner. Every other step creaked under his weight.

"Christian."

He didn't acknowledge her. Icy centipedes skittered over her back. He paused at the top of the stairs. She wiped her mouth across her shoulder, and then ran up the steps after him. He stared at the closed door to Ryan's old room, stroking it with his fingertips.

"What are you doing?" she whispered.

Christian slid his fingers down the wood and rested them on the doorknob. He closed his eyes, breathed deeply, and slowly, slowly, turned the knob. The latch clicked, loud in the eerie quiet. The door creaked open.

She locked her knees to keep from collapsing. Haunted dreams made her skin clammy: a decaying Ryan sat on his bed, stretched a rotting hand towards her, called her name, a grape smell clogging her nose, a shadowed figure hovering behind the bed, bending closer, closer, before pausing to look up at her.

"Brooke."

She screamed, staggered back across the hallway, and slammed into the wall, positive her heart had just exploded. Clutching her throat, she stared into the stale and unused room.

Ryan wasn't there; it was just a ghostly memory calling her name.

Christian tilted his head as he watched her, the silver in his eyes swirling. She pushed off the wall and inched her way into the room. Dust motes churned in the murky light sifting through the dull-blue curtains. Her brother's lifeless lava lamp rested on his grimy nightstand, its yellow-jellied center sitting at the bottom like a dead lump. The docking station for his iPod sat like a dusty headstone, forever silenced. She stopped by the bed and studied the carpet, trembling as a chill nipped the backs of her knees.

Christian said, "He died here."

Brooke sagged onto the bed. Opening her mouth she then closed it. What could she say to that? When she couldn't breathe, she opened her mouth again.

He licked his lips.

There was a quick flash of silver before he lowered his lids. She swallowed and pressed her thighs together, her stomach igniting. He knew Ryan had died in there; he was getting *off* on it. Wrinkling her nose, her upper lip curled as she squeezed her eyes shut, trying to remember the shadowy figure that had stolen Ryan's soul. Had it been someone more human? Someone like Christian? While he was tainted, he didn't reek; not like William, or the reaper who'd taken Ryan.

Her stomach burned. Her fingers itched.

Watch.

She stilled at the voice in her head, and then darted a look into the hall. Is that why William said Christian wanted to kill her? She could smell him; smell that sweet, soul-stealing, reaper residue. Her stomach flamed, her fingers itched.

Oh, *crap*.

Brooke leaped up and shoved him. "Get out!"

She pushed past him, stumbled down the stairs, slid on her socked feet into the foyer, and fell.

Christian drifted down the stairs.

"Get out!" She crab-walked backward into the wall, wishing she could close her eyes and he'd be gone.

He grabbed her arms. "Stop it."

"You liar! You're a soul stealing thief, aren't you?"

"I never said I was a saint."

One look at the silver in his eyes, and she erupted with an anger that burned her from the inside. She hauled back her arm to slap him. He caught her wrist and pinned it against the wall.

Silver danced along the blue horizon of his eyes. Breathing hard, he said, "Calm down before you get hurt."

"You're the one about to be hurt."

"I didn't kill Ryan. Okay? It wasn't me."

She glared at him, her hand growing cold, the numbing sensation riding along her wrist and up her arm.

"I'm begging you, please calm down. I don't want to hurt you."

Before she could respond, he leaped up. Studying her from the far side of the kitchen, he leaned against the counter, gripping the edge until his knuckles turned white.

Feeling started to return to her fingers. Chafing her hands, she paused a moment before speaking. "Have you stolen souls before?"

"Yes."

"But not his?"

"No."

"When's the last time you've stolen one?"

"Decades ago."

"Do you want to kill me?"

"No."

Her heart resumed a normal pace, the heat of her anger receding. Christian's shoulders relaxed, and the silver in his eyes faded to slate gray.

She massaged the finger marks he left on her skin. "Why should I believe you?"

"Why would I lie?"

"To trick me?"

"Into doing what, exactly?"

Good question. "I don't know."

"I don't want you to be afraid of me."

Light leaped into his eyes, a flash of sun on an angry sea. The trembling fear and anger morphed into a liquid heat. He looked oh-so-cute with his hair tousling around his cheeks. She tasted her lips, breathed in a fairly fresh breath of air, and then swallowed.

He'd saved her life. He said he didn't kill Ryan. And he said he didn't want to kill her. She loved him, believed him.

Christian said, "I've done things I would change if I could. Things I regret deeply. Haven't you ever done something you wish you could do over?"

"Of course."

"I'd like to prove I'm not such a dick. I'd like a second chance with you."

Her muscles relaxed a fraction. Everyone had good and bad sides. Everyone deserved a second chance. Everyone should be allowed to fix the mistakes of their past.

She took a breath. Another. "Okay, I think I'm done tweaking out."

Holding out his hand, he said, "Shall we talk?"

Brooke hesitated, then took his hand.

Chapter 23

1938

With coyotes yipping in the darkness, Christian rested on his hands and knees in the woods outside Elizabeth's house. Sticks punctured his palms, and the smell of decayed leaves and his vomit made his stomach roll again. He spit out the acrid taste of bile, then wiped his mouth on his shirt. He wanted to keep watch over her in case Renkin returned, but her father was with her now.

Abstaining was no longer an option. It was time to bargain with Giltine, and he needed to prepare. The way to do that was with poison, and lots of it. West of Bakerville was Torrington. Filled with factories and laborers who churned into the night, he thought he might find a soul or ten to usher.

Loping through the woods, he nearly collided with the reaper who stepped from behind a tree. Christian veered right. A second reaper materialized. He changed course to the right once more, only to encounter a third reaper.

He headed for the middle reaper. She stretched her hands toward him. At the last moment, he pivoted hard on his toes. Her hand skimmed his back, and his muscles tightened. Breaking free from their circle, he ran a few strides, and then splashed into a creek.

The snowmelt cold bit into his body, making him gasp. He sloshed to the opposite bank, then turned and studied the distance, hoping the creek was too wide for the pacing reapers to jump. He chafed his arms while his teeth chattered.

"I have a message for Giltine," he called.

The snarling reapers paused, their stares as icy as the water. "Tell Giltine I want to bargain."

One reaper chuckled. More ice dripped along his spine.

The she-reaper said, "I will relay your message to Giltine, secucron scum, and then I will laugh as I watch you die."

The reapers melted into the night. His whole body shook. Christian tucked his hands into his armpits. Spying a beam of light piercing the darkness ahead, he staggered through the woods on numb feet. His body ached, his legs became stiff and heavy. Hitting the road, he dropped to his knees, too exhausted to hold up his hands as the light stopped several feet away.

Blood pounded between his ears, competing with the rumbling motor of the truck. The truck coughed and sputtered and sounded as wretched as he felt. A door creaked open.

"Gods of the Other World," Forrest muttered. "You look half-dead."

"I am."

"Bunk."

The man hauled Christian up by the armpits and deposited him in the passenger seat. He revved the motor once, then gunned it.

"You're getting my seat wet," he said.

"C-creek."

"You fool." Keeping one hand on the wheel, he reached under the seat for a wool blanket and tossed it at Christian's head.

Teeth chattering, he wrapped himself in the blanket. He thought he might need four or five hits to relieve the ache in his bones.

"Will you take me to Torrington?"

Forrest grunted. Christian concentrated on a crack in the windshield, trying to ignore the draft seeping through the holes in the floor and creeping under his wet clothes like frost.

"T-turn on the heat."

"I didn't buy the heater unit."

Groaning, Christian pulled the blanket over his chin. He'd wager his life Renkin's luxury car had a very good heater. "What brings you here?"

"William told me you were going off the rails for a dame, and that you ignored Giltine's summons. He wanted me to talk some sense into that fool head of yours."

"The rat."

"He's your great uncle. He cares about you."

"I'm not the one going off the rails. He keeps calling me Thomas."

"You do look remarkably like your grandfather."

"No. It's as if he thinks I *am* Thomas and he's going to save me from dying."

"Oh. That." Forrest's glance shifted toward him before lighting on the road again.

"What happened?"

He cleared his throat. "Thomas was William's twin, and they were closer than fleas on a dog. You know how twins are, joined at the hip, finishing each other's thoughts. That is, until they turned fourteen."

"And William was taken by Giltine."

"Right. Their daddy was a reaper, but their mama was an austere, rigidly religious woman. William and Thomas were brought up to believe anything or anyone outside the church was an abomination and damned to eternal Hell. No joy, no games, no laughter, and no sparing the rod . . . just school, church, and praying for salvation."

Despite the chill and his wet clothes, sweat clamped between Christian's shoulder blades. "Did she know what her husband was?"

"Not until the big day. William was the eldest by a couple of minutes so he was the one taken by Giltine."

"Then what happened?" he asked when it seemed as though Forrest wouldn't continue.

"Thomas and his mama knelt over their Bible and prayed for deliverance from their demon family. They damned William and their daddy; 'Satan spawn' they called them. They fasted for two weeks and cut their names from the family Bible, their lives, and their past. Thomas and his mama took back her maiden name."

"What happened to their father?"

"He wandered, alone, became a bum who caught sick and died. William despised his mother immensely, but still loved Thomas."

They'd reached Torrington. Forrest parked on the side of the road, and then twisted in the seat to face him. "Their mama died, Thomas married, and your mama was born. William begged Thomas to let him re-connect with his family. William was even willing to bargain for his freedom for the chance to be with them. Thomas rejected him."

His great-grandmother had cut her husband and son out of her life. Christian's grandfather had cut his twin brother out of his life. His own mother had been so ashamed of him that she killed herself when he was taken by Giltine. If family couldn't accept what they were, how could Elizabeth accept him?

His heart sluggishly sank.

"William went goofy," Forrest murmured. "He really gave Thomas the Broderick."

"He beat grandfather to death?" Christian could barely get the words out of his dry mouth.

Forrest traced a stain on his trousers. "William stole your grandfather's soul. The guilt pushed William off the tracks, and he went rogue after that. He watched your mama grow up, watched her marry, but never tried to contact her; didn't want to stain her life with knowledge of the Other World and his existence. He couldn't face rejection again, I think."

Christian snorted. "William had a heart?"

"At one time. He waited a long time for you to join him in the Other World, to be family."

Christian tried to swallow. Couldn't. He leaped out of the truck, leaned over a stone wall, and vomited. Slumping onto the wall, he drew in a breath of smoky air, tinged with the scent of Giltine's poison.

"You all right, boy?"

"I need a soul-hit."

"Let me go with you. We'll find a number and get you feeling right as rain, and then you come back to the house and get warm and dry."

Christian made a vow when he was fourteen to never step foot in that house again. "I'll be fine. Just go home."

The older man hesitated, but then said, "Don't over-do it, you hear?"

"I won't."

Forrest jutted his chin toward the city. "I heard on the radio some houses caught fire. There were deaths."

He nodded. "Thanks."

"Don't be a stranger. Stop by once in a while and give me the rumble on what you're up to."

"I will." Christian slammed the door shut.

Forrest turned the truck, and Christian watched until the taillights blinked out of sight. He stumbled toward the beckoning fire. Smoke ballooned above the skeletal remains of the buildings, eager tongues of flame licking the broken windows and holes in the roofs. Reapers roved among the crowd, and he drew to a halt. The heat warmed his skin, and the cloying scent of Giltine's poison sent a shudder between his shoulder blades.

One of the houses collapsed, sending flames and sparks and smoke billowing into the air. People screamed, cops yelled at gawkers to stand back, medics bellowed orders, and firefighters shouted to be heard over the ruckus. A half-dozen bodies covered with sheets lined the street.

He leaned against a lamppost. Several souls stared at the swathed bundles on the ground, while others watched the commotion with furrowed brows and narrowed gazes.

Christian licked his lips, wanting, needing. He couldn't usher a soul out in the open, though. Someone might see him dissolve. He had to entice a soul to a place where his vanishing act would be hidden.

Not an efficient way to operate, but such was the life of a secucro. It was truly a game of Hide and Reap.

"Excuse me, but have you seen my Phil?"

Christian jumped at the elderly voice. With Giltine's mark shining on her cheek, the woman's ethereal glow made her white hair shine, smoothing the lines in her face. Bushy, gray eyebrows scrunched together while she stared at him, a mole with a single hair sprouting from her quivering chin.

Giltine's poison wafted from her like a seductive spirit, its sweetness intensifying his need. His mouth bled dry so he couldn't swallow.

"He was here a moment ago," the old woman said.

"What happened?" he whispered, rubbing his thumbs along his pants' seams. He glanced behind him, searching for a place to reap.

"Well, let's see." She grabbed her right elbow and circled her index finger over her mole. "I was fixing tea for my Phil when there was a loud explosion." She tapped her ear. "My hearing ails me, but I swear it was loud enough to wake the dead."

He focused on the woman to ascertain her identity. "I'm sure it was, Gladys."

"Have we met?" Gladys didn't pause for a response. "Then I was lying on the street." Straightening her sooty nightdress, which had been eaten by burn holes, she leaned closer. "In my nightclothes. It was a bolt from the blue!"

He nodded, eyes nearly rolling back in his head at the scent of poison.

"Then some frightful man wrapped me in a blanket. I gave him a piece of my mind, yessiree." Her glare softened, and she furrowed her forehead. "I don't think he heard me, though."

"He couldn't."

The woman didn't seem to hear him. "I saw Phil then, talking to one of those gents clad in black; not too fashionable if you ask me." She paused. "No offense."

"None taken."

"Then Phil was gone. I just couldn't odds it. So I asked another gent to help me, but he paid me no mind." That look of bewilderment stole over her face again. "It was as though he couldn't see me."

"He couldn't."

Her gaze sharpened. "What's that?"

He waved a hand toward the sheet-wrapped bodies. "I think you know."

Gripping her elbow again, she gazed at her blackened house. "Why," she said, "I think I may be dead."

"Yes."

"Bugger." Her chin quivered. "I want to see my Phil."

"He's moved on, but I can take you to him."

"Oh, you're such a nice young man."

He wanted to smile, but his need was too great, and he couldn't get his facial muscles to cooperate. He waved her toward the city. "This way."

The old woman's stride was swift, and he forced his weak legs to keep pace. He led her into a deserted alley where the streetlamps were out. Littered with papers and a stench of urine, the alley trailed into darkness.

Ducking into a doorway, he ordered, "Take my hand. Phil's waiting."

Her hesitation seemed an eternal torture, and then their fingers connected, and the delightful warmth tugged at his center. A voice shouted at the end of the alley, and his heart tripped.

Poisoned heat lured him into its embrace just as Renkin's voice darted into his head.

"He went this way! Find him!"

There was no stopping. Christian faded into the darkness.

Chapter 24

Present Time

Brooke and Christian sat at the kitchen table, each clutching a cup of coffee; hers very blonde and his black, though even she was amazed at the amount of sugar he dumped in his. The black cat clock on the wall ticked in the silence, its eyes and tail swishing from side to side. Christian's slight, grapey scent mixed with the coffee aroma.

"How did you know Ryan died here?" She spoke to the table.

"I can taste the rogue. Its scent lingers."

"Rogues are reapers who steal souls?"

"Yes."

She glanced at him. "They smell like sweet grapes."

He gazed at the ceiling where a spider's web, empty of food but bloated with dust, linked the corners of the walls together. "Yes."

Just like you.

She tensed, and then shifted and tucked one foot under her leg.

"When did Ryan die?"

"One year and seven months ago."

"How much do you know about the Other World?"

"Giltine's death lick. Reapers. Watchers." She shrugged. "Just the basics, what I got off the Internet."

He gripped his coffee mug as though channeling its clay-baked strength. "Giltine resides over death and the eternally condemned. Laima resides over the living and the afterlife."

"Laima?"

"Some religions recognize Laima as God."

Brooke snorted.

"People used to believe in the goddesses, until they were substituted with male deities. Those deities were forgotten when the Christian faith emerged. People simply switched their pagan rituals with Christian rituals; they exchanged the old gods for new gods."

"You believe in the old gods?"

"Yes."

"Have you seen this Laima god?"

Christian hesitated. "No."

"Have you ever seen God?"

He hesitated even longer. "No."

"Then how do you know Laima isn't really God?"

"How do you know God isn't really Laima?"

"Everyone knows that pagan stuff isn't real religion."

"Says who?"

She pinched her bottom lip between two fingers. She wasn't going to get into a religious debate—she honestly didn't have an epic background on the subject—but she thought he was completely off his nut.

"I've seen Giltine," he said.

It was her turn to shrug.

"Giltine and Laima are sisters," he said.

"Is Giltine Satan?"

He half-smiled. "I've called her worse."

Brooke rolled her eyes. "Seriously."

"No, Lucifer's a fallen angel. He doesn't rule the Other World; Giltine does."

"Then what are angels?"

"Lesser gods. Spiritual beings. There are many." He sipped his coffee. "It defied the gods' law for angels to interact with humans. A cast of angels, called watchers, were sent to watch over humanity. But when the watchers started having kids with humans, their offspring weren't . . . normal. The watchers were imprisoned."

"By who?"

"God/Laima."

Brooke lowered her brows. "What do you mean, not normal?"

"Some called the Nephilim monsters, but I think they were just giants."

She glanced down at her legs; her very long legs.

"I guess that's why you're so tall."

"Go on."

"Giltine's law forbids reapers from taking the soul of any person not marked for death, but rogues were growing in numbers. At her request, Lai . . . God released the watchers from prison and sent them to watch the reapers."

"She did this out of the kindness of her heart?"

"No. If there's one thing the goddesses love to do, its bargain."

"What did Giltine have to give up?"

"Her beauty."

"Oh. So she gave up her beauty . . . why?"

"Rogues were stealing souls by the thousands, and Giltine was losing her authority. She may be Goddess of Death, but she couldn't be everywhere all the time. The watchers became her personal army, and she used them to keep the reapers in line."

She drummed her fingertips on her mug, then asked, "Why do rogues kill people?"

He toyed with his mug. "When a reaper ushers a soul, it feels good."

"Like sex?" Her face heated.

He watched her for a long moment before answering. "It's like a drug. It's Giltine's poison."

"So this poison is just so reapers can get high?"

"It feels good, but reapers need the poison to sustain their existence in the Other World. It's like eating your favorite food; you need food to live, but it's nicer when you enjoy it."

"Why steal souls if there's no poison?"

He looked at her then away. "It's different then. When Giltine marks someone, her poison prepares the soul for crossing over; it's neutralized, so to speak. Without it." He shrugged. "An unmarked soul is pure, unadulterated heat. It's not just powerful, it's addictive."

"Oh, I see." Her fingers tightened around her cup.

"There are three things about reapers: they hate water, they detest the cold, and they crave sweets. Giltine's poison is sweet, and souls are warm."

"And if a watcher saw a rogue?"

"The watcher killed him."

She dug her nails into her legs. "If I see a rogue stealing a soul, I could kill him?"

"I think so."

"Can I kill any reaper, or just rogues?"

"Any reaper, I guess."

Her belly button burned; her fingers itched. When she glanced at Christian, his eyes glowed like melted silver.

"Do I get a sword or a knife or something?"

One side of his mouth lifted. "No; you're not an angel, avenging or otherwise. You're a descendant—a long, long-lost descendant—of one of the Nephilim."

"Oh."

"But," he continued. "As a descendant of a Naphil you're hotter than most humans. Your power is inside you."

The heat from Brooke's fingers flashed up her arms, then her neck, then her face. His gaze wandered down her body, back up.

"Your touch is destructive."

She sagged back in her chair as though her spine dissolved. She was a living, breathing weapon. She could tell any reaper or almost-reaper to back off. She could tell William to stay away from Abby or she'd kill him . . . once she figured out how to do it.

But did she want to kill anyone? *Could* she kill anyone? Even if they were demonic dicks?

Yes.

Finding the reaper who killed her brother and killing *him*, would be her ticket to avenging Ryan's death. "How does it work?"

"William told me it comes from an emotional level, like anger. I've felt your heat when you're angry. Do you realize how hot you are?"

She squirmed, her body heat rising again, so she changed the subject before her flushed cheeks signaled him that her heart had just gone loopy. "Where are the watchers now?"

"No one knows."

"Who took care of the kids when the watchers went to jail?"

"They were killed by the goddesses. Apparently, one got away," he said softly.

"From what I've heard, God doesn't make mistakes."

"No."

He grazed a finger along her cheek. She couldn't stop the jolt of warmth that slid through her skin and into her soul.

"Isn't it funny, how this all played out?" he murmured. "I've been searching for someone like you for years, an impossibility, and yet here you are. My own fallen angel."

She thought his eyes had the power to pick her up off her feet and toss her across the room. The way the room spun, she almost thought they had.

"It's as if the gods planned this meeting thousands of years ago."

"You think God missed killing one of the kids just so we could meet?" she asked. "Not buying it."

"You know what they say. There's a reason for everything."

"How do you fit into all of this?"

He blinked, and the corners of his mouth twitched downward. "Giltine's been looking for a mate so she can have a child. She bargains with reapers, offering them souls, hoping they'll become her mate."

After a lengthy pause, she prodded. "Go on."

"It never quite works out for her, but she keeps trying. One day she chose my father."

"Giltine's your mother?"

"No. My father fell in love with a human."

Brooke leaned forward, elbows on the table.

"My father begged Giltine to free him from the Other World, let him live a human life and marry. Giltine agreed, though not before forcing a price to be paid for granting his wish."

"What?"

"He promised his children to her."

Brooke gasped. "You?"

"Me."

Chapter 25

1938

With the meager warmth of Gladys's crossing flickering in his veins, Christian flew through the darkness, his molecules re-arranging, solidifying and hardening until he materialized in the doorway of the urine-scented alley in Torrington. Despite the sultry air, the door was cool against his damp clothes, and that single hit of poison wasn't nearly enough to take the chill from his body, or the queasiness from his belly.

Nearby, Renkin was having a tense, whispered argument. His cigar competed with the acrid smell of the fire. The smoke scraped the back of Christian's throat and made his lungs ache.

Renkin cursed. Christian leaned against the wood, trying not to swallow too loudly. He tightened his muscles and leveled his breathing.

"Where'd the kid go? He was right here."

A gravelly voice answered. "I don't know. Didn't see him."

"You sure you ain't imagining things, Renkin?" asked a third man.

Renkin snorted. "Don't be a bunny. You saw him."

"Not me," said Gravelly Voice.

Christian clenched his teeth, trying to keep himself pressed in the doorway, trying not to think how much he wanted to lie down. A thunking sound pulsed a rhythm against the ground.

A fourth man spoke with a tenor-pitched voice. "Maybe you saw a ghost."

Laughter followed.

"Not a ghost, but there's something odd about that kid," Renkin said. "He's got witching eyes."

Tenor said, "A witch? Now who's being a bunny."

"The kid must have given us the slip," said Gravelly Voice.

"Did you check all the doors?" Renkin asked.

"Yeah, and they're all locked. Let's scram."

Heavy footfalls tread closer. The doorway was small, and Christian wasn't. He melted into the shadows, clenching his muscles to keep from shivering and his teeth from chattering. Cigar smoke wafted into his alcove as Renkin came abreast of him. His nose itched as he passed, followed by three men. They'd just cleared the doorway when Christian sneezed.

"Son of a bitch!"

Renkin exploded into Christian's space, grabbed the front of his shirt, dragged him out of the doorway, and slammed him against the brick building. Air shot out of his lungs.

Renkin wobbled the cigar from one side of his mouth to the other. "So you thought you could give me the slip, did you?"

The three men behind him sniggered. One of them, a broad-shouldered thug, thumped a baseball bat against the ground. Renkin's forearm bore down on Christian's throat. He could wheeze just enough air into his lungs to keep from passing out.

"Not so rugged now, are you, boy?" He slapped Christian's wet shirt. "So Izzy went swimming with you even after all of your lies, the dumb broad."

His wet clothes were the result of splashing through the creek to get away from the reapers, but he let the old man believe the lie.

"Stay away from Izzy; she's mine." Renkin licked his

lips. "I hope she puts up a fight. I like a doll who squirms when I got her under me."

Fury burst behind Christian's eyes. "I'll kill you first."

He jabbed his palm into Renkin's nose and was rewarded with a spurt of blood. When the man's arm loosened, he tackled him, and they slammed onto the ground. Before Christian could sock him again, he was dragged to his feet. Two thugs twisted Christian's arms behind his back while a sniggering bat-boy swung his bat.

Renkin wiped blood from his nose with the back of his sleeve before retrieving his cigar from the ground. "Give this punk some chin music, boys."

Bat-boy smiled, launching the bat at Christian's midriff. Agony bit into his ribs, and he doubled over. The bat connected with his side, then his other side, and then his middle once again. The shattering pain ripped a scream from him before his legs buckled.

Renkin lifted his head off his chest by the hair. "You listen to me and you listen good. I told you to take a powder, and I don't like repeating myself."

"Then don't," Christian whispered between shots of breath.

"So you're a wise-head now, eh?" Renkin drew on his cigar until the end glowed red. "Maybe you need help remembering what I tell you."

He pressed the cigar into Christian's cheek. Pain seared into his skin. He jerked against the thugs holding his arms, tearing the muscles in his sockets. He squeezed his eyes shut, clenched his jaw, and hissed air through his teeth.

"I'd let him go if I were you."

His eyes snapped open, staring wide-eyed over Renkin's shoulder at William.

"Beat it, boy. I got no kick with you."

"But that's my nephew you're holding there."

"Give him the gate, Leroy."

Bat-boy smacked the bat into his palm. Linking his fingers, William stretched his arms then leaped into the air. One foot snapped the bat from the man's hands, and his other foot cracked against his chin. Leroy hit the ground on his back, his head smashing the cement stoop with a sharp *crack*. His great uncle landed lightly in a crouch, the bat rolling to a stop against Christian's foot.

William grinned. "Who's next?"

"Get him!" Renkin screamed, the cigar falling out of his mouth.

The thugs released Christian and he dropped to his knees. William stooped in a fighter's stance, throwing a left jab at the larger attacker. His head snapped back, spraying blood. He kicked the second thug in his kneecap, and he dropped with a loud cry. The first attacker threw a punch; William ducked then caught the guy's chin with an upper cut, and the man staggered back, shaking his head. The guy on the ground made an attempt to rise, so he kicked him in the temple. The man sprawled on his back, twitched once, then stilled.

His great uncle spun, fists flying, until the second guy joined his pally on the ground. The men lay as crumpled and still as Leroy. Renkin scurried down the alley without looking back, his forgotten cigar smoldering on the pavement.

William laughed, and then blew on his knuckles. "What a bunch of rubes."

"What are you doing here?" Christian winced. It hurt to talk. And breathe.

"Saving your ass, you ungrateful pisser."

He scooted against the wall, watching William admire his flexed arms.

"Are you going to tell me why those goons were bracing you?"

"Elizabeth."

William cracked his knuckles. "Giltine's out for your blood, reapers are hunting you, and those goons just gave you the Broderick. All of this over a dame?"

When Christian didn't respond, he said, "You look like shit."

A reaper drifted past the alley, followed by another. They returned a moment later and coasted toward them. Swearing, Christian struggled to his feet. The pain tearing his ribs hunched him over like a man ten times his age.

"Don't let them take me." He hated having to ask William for help, but he had no other options. "I can't face Giltine like this."

"Sure thing." William planted his feet in a wide stance and crossed his arms over his chest.

"Give us the secucro," one reaper said.

"Um." He looked up as though considering their request. "No."

The reaper hissed. "He's been summoned by Giltine."

"He needs bracing first, but I'll make sure he sees her when he's ready."

The reapers veered their malevolent gazes to Christian.

William flicked his fingers at them. "Shoo. Before I get angry. And you know what happens when I get angry."

One reaper bared his teeth like a rabid fox. Then he glanced at the other before they spun and, coats billowing, marched back down the alley.

Christian rubbed his side. "Why are they afraid of you?"

"Because, my naïve nephew, I have a deal with a watcher."

"They don't exist."

"They did."

"Where are they then?"

"Some say they died. Some say they got tossed back into prison. Some say they're hiding."

"And you're telling me you know where they are."

"Not an actual watcher, but I found a descendant of a Naphil. He had enough juice to get the job done."

He drew his knees to his chest. "Liar."

William studied his nails. "If I tell you about it, can we be family again? Can we go back to the way it was in the beginning and stick together?"

Christian's mind hunted through possibilities like a rat through a maze. He'd seen Giltine's agitation with regard to her slipping control over rogues. Could he trade a watcher for his freedom? Surely obtaining that knowledge was equal to the price of cruising with William, of making a promise he couldn't keep, of lying to his great uncle.

His back muscles tightened, because once he was free, he wouldn't stay in the Other World; he was sure William would get over it.

"Deal." Christian slid to the ground and stretched his legs. The toe of his boot rocked the bat.

William sat next to him. "A few decades ago, I came upon the soul of a very young prostitute who died in a very indecent position with a highly respected political figure who was also a watcher."

"How'd you know he was a watcher?"

"Three things. First, there was the heat. A watcher's soul burns hotter than other humans. Best advice I can give you is never piss off a watcher, because they're deadly."

When his great uncle didn't say anything for a few moments, he said, "We had a deal. Keep going."

"Fine. Second, this egg could see the reaper who also happened upon the very young prostitute's soul, and third, this egg dusted the reaper in seconds."

"How?"

"The rogue moved in for some tasty soul-snatching—probably didn't know what he was dealing with, to be honest—and the watcher melted the demon's face with his hands. Nothing but dust."

Gods below, it was true! Christian's heart slammed. Giltine would surely pay any price—including his freedom—to have a watcher within her control. He poked the bat with his boot, and it rolled across the ground, coming to rest against Leroy's limp leg.

"Anyway," William continued. "After I ushered the whore's soul, I tracked down my new found friend, and we came to an arrangement. I became his button man."

"Who'd you kill?"

"Politicians who stood in the watcher's way to success."

"And you got what in return?"

"If a reaper gave me some chin music, I'd tote my watcher to the Other World—did you know a watcher can cross into the Other World without getting bumped off?—and he'd turn the reaper into dust. Reapers learned to leave me alone or pay the price. You can't imagine how powerful it feels to control those blackhearts."

Christian had to bury his excitement when he spoke, though some trembled through his words. "Where's your watcher now?"

"Dead. The reapers don't know that, though, since none have been sucker enough to bother me in decades. It was tricky crossing his soul over; good thing reapers are such patsies."

"Any descendants?"

"Nope."

Crap. Christian's billowing hope deflated. He resumed thinking about the bleak prospect of bargaining with Giltine. His heart hammered at a sudden thought. Why couldn't he just bargain then renege on the deal? What if he bargained his firstborn then never had children? What could Giltine possibly do to him that she hadn't done already?

William cracked his knuckles. "You look like you could use a couple of hits."

Holding his side, he muttered, "Or three."

"Spoken like a true junkie. Get up." William hoisted him to his feet and clapped him on the shoulder. "I don't think poison will do you. You need an unmarked soul."

"No."

"Come on; then you'll be so rugged your punishment will be duck soup."

They stepped over the thugs—William catching his boot heel on Leroy's long nose—and made their way down the alley.

Christian limped alongside the whistling man. "Wait. What did you say?"

"Gods, Christian. You've poached souls before. Have you forgotten how invincible you are afterward? You're almost as strong as a full-blood reaper."

His brain suddenly clicked.

When his father bargained with Giltine, he'd offered Christian to the Goddess of Death. Taking his child from him was her ultimate revenge, because for all Giltine's own bargaining, she remained mate-less and child-less.

He stumbled, and William steadied him.

Christian's blood froze. What he was required to offer as part of the bargain was only half of his problem. Giltine hadn't said the price to bargaining with her was too steep . . . she said the price to *surviving* was too steep, and that he was too ethical to pay the price.

There was only one way a secucro could gather the strength needed to bargain, and it wasn't from Giltine's poison. In order to save the life of the girl who saved his life, he'd have to steal a soul. Something he'd sworn never to do again . . . the bitter guilt of the deed was a shoulder-crushing burden. What if he started down that road again? Would he lose himself to the darkness forever? Would Elizabeth ever truly be safe with him?

Once a rogue, always a rogue.

Shit, shit, *shit*.

Chapter 26

Present Time

Brooke watched a robin snack at the bird feeder outside the un-curtained kitchen window. Christian had been quiet for what seemed a very long time, the hollow plunks of the dripping faucet the only sound to break the silence.

"Your father sold you into slavery? That's totally slanted."

When he spoke again, his voice was as lifeless as his face. "I lived as a human for fourteen years. Then I was ripped from my family and my home, and brought to the Other World where I became Giltine's slave." He laughed; a sound as hard as peanut brittle. "Only she calls us her children, as though we're one big, happy family. Because I'm half human and have a soul, my transition to the Other World was brutal. I could feel pain and loss and fear as I was forced to usher souls. All so my father could be free from Giltine."

Brooke studied his tortured face, the way he massaged his temple with one hand and rubbed a thumb along his pants' seam with the other. She wanted to wrap her arms around him. Instead, she pressed her hands between her knees.

"What happened to your parents?"

The muscles around his right eye ticked. He plucked the seam of his jeans with his thumbnail. "My mother didn't know about my father's heritage." His thumbnail plucked faster as he spoke. "My mother screamed and cried and begged my father to stop Giltine." He moved to scrub his face, but his hand stopped and covered his eyes. "I told my father I hated him, cursed him, wished he was dead."

She gave him a minute to recover, then prompted, "And?"

"My mother killed herself. Out of grief, for her I assume and not for me, my father took his own life as well."

Brooke gasped and laid her hand on his arm. "I'm so sorry."

Christian gazed at her hand, then shot from the chair and paced to the other end of the kitchen. "It wasn't until years later I finally understood why my father did what he did."

"You fell in love?"

"Yes." His laugh was over-loud and over-long. "Like father like son; I fell in love with a girl and was cursed by Giltine."

Her eyes widened. "You're *married*?"

"Gods, no." His lips barely moved when he spoke. "I walked away from the Other World and Giltine."

"Can you break the curse?"

He sighed, staring at his feet then raising his gaze to study her. Their gazes locked and, as though she was a puppet on a string, she stood. Striding toward her, he lowered his head, and his gaze slid down her face. His dark hair swung across his cheek, and she followed the curve of his jaw to his lips. His incredibly delicious-looking lips.

Heat flashed over her skin. His breath brushed her lips. Christian trailed his fingers down her arms, and a shudder vibrated through her body.

"A kiss from an angel," he whispered.

Her stomach swooped. Her lids were suddenly heavy, and she could barely keep them open. "Me?"

His gaze flicked from her eyes to her mouth. He dipped his head toward her, then gazed into her eyes again. "Don't you see? It's part of the gods' plan. It meshes. It's cohesive. Who are we to say no to that?"

He trailed the back of his index finger along her jaw,

over her lips. They trembled under his touch, throbbing with heat. She swayed toward him.

He stared at her lips, then at her eyes. "Brooke, there's something else I have to tell you first."

The front door rattled, and they jerked apart. Her dad froze in the doorway, his gaze probing Christian's face like a poisoned needle. Her father set down his briefcase, spread his legs, folded his arms across his chest, and blocked the door.

She swallowed. "Hey, Dad. You're home early."

"Who's this?"

"Christian."

"Nice to meet you, sir." Christian held out his hand.

After a moment that was longer than polite, her father shook it. He peered over his glasses at her. "What's going on here?"

"We were just talking."

Christian said, "Sorry, but I was just leaving."

Her father grunted and, keeping his arms crossed, shuffled sideways just enough for Christian to slide past.

"Maybe I'll see you tomorrow," he said to her and, "Nice meeting you," to her father. Stepping into his boots, he slipped out the door.

"Where'd he come from?" her dad demanded.

"I met him at Panera Bread."

He grabbed a bottle of water from the fridge. "I recall laying down a specific rule against bringing strange boys into this house when we're not home."

"He's not strange."

"There's something off about that guy."

Could her dad smell Christian's reaper residue? No, impossible. He couldn't see reapers. "What do you mean?"

He pointed his water at her. "I know what boys want, and it's not talk."

Her muscles relaxed upon hearing that her father was

worried about sex, and not soul-sucking shadows from Hell. "That has nothing to do with anything."

"I don't know him."

"I told you, his name's Christian. And he was polite."

"Biggest red flag in the father handbook. Ever hear of Eddie Haskell?"

"No."

"Doesn't matter. You can't trust boys; not even the polite ones."

"That's not exactly fair."

"Are you planning on seeing this boy again?"

She lifted one shoulder and studied her toes. "Maybe."

"No more boys in this house when your mother and I aren't home. You hear?"

"I hear, but that's not fair. I'm nineteen, Dad."

"My house, my rules. Got it?"

"Got it."

Her dad smiled. "Whew. Glad that's over. Any plans with Abby?"

"Not tonight."

She planted a kiss on his cheek, and then trailed up the stairs. She launched herself across her room to the window, but Christian's motorcycle was nowhere in sight. She pivoted and paced back to the door. She repeated the maneuver over and over, her mind trapped by thoughts of death and almost-reapers playing her.

William said Christian wanted to kill her.

Christian wanted to kiss her.

Which one was the player?

Chapter 27

1938

It was early morning, and a defiant mist swept over the lake, resisting the sun's attempts to banish it. Birds swooped from the trees to skim the dew-drenched grass, and then returned to their perches to bathe. A soft breeze tickled the leaves and brought with it the scent of damp earth. Christian imagined Elizabeth sleeping inside her house, innocent and unprotected.

Beside him, William shifted from one foot to the other. "Why are we here? Gods high and above, this lake isn't going anywhere."

Christian rubbed his thumbs along his pants' seams. He was going somewhere . . . to Hell. This would most likely be the last time he saw this lake, but he had to try to win his freedom for Elizabeth's sake. He wished he could see her one last time.

William said, "Let's just get this punishment over with, shall we?"

They strode into the woods, halting beside a copse of low-arching mountain laurel.

"Last night was aces." He linked his hands behind his head. "My head's humming."

Christian clenched his teeth.

His great uncle's grin was both cruel and content. "You're such a sap. You picked through souls like a gaycat choosing a tramp. I thought you'd never decide."

Christian ran his tongue over his teeth. He'd chosen a soul so vile his actions in life would have condemned him to an eternity in Giltine's third level. Still, the bitterness of what he'd done gnawed at him, but not because he'd stolen the soul.

It was because the rush of pure heat was so potent, so fulfilling, he hadn't been able to stop at just one.

He'd stolen three.

"I have to admit, I'm impressed," William said. "Didn't take you long to get back into the swing of it, eh?"

He swallowed the intense memory of the stolen souls and rode the breeze to the Other World without answering. They climbed the mountain, avoiding the lost souls lounging in miserable repose and the impatient reapers. At the top he drew a deep breath, then stepped through the wall.

William surveyed the dead field, his gaze sweeping past curious secucron and souls with their haunted faces. "Where's Giltine?"

The first part of the bargaining process was the slow, murderous trek to the third level. Christian said, "I'll go find her."

His great uncle's eyes narrowed. "I'll come with you."

Crap.

The hiked together until they reached the wall barring their way to the second level. He paused, unbothered by the heat or flies, though his heart thrashed against his ribs.

"Something's up," William said.

Ignoring him, Christian pushed through the gate and faced a set of uneven, wooden stairs descending into swirling darkness. The smell of rotting wood made him think of worms and bugs and dead things. Chest tight, he rested one hand on the cracked railing and took one step. The stair creaked under his weight.

"What are you doing?" William asked. "Just wait here. Giltine doesn't expect you to go past the first level for your punishment."

"I'm going to look for her. You can stay here if you want."

William raised an eyebrow. "We're family now, remember? I better tag along in case you get into trouble."

Pushing his tongue against his teeth, Christian tested each step before putting his weight on it, causing them to screech as though in pain. The stairs groaned behind him as William followed. The staircase shot downward at a steep pitch, and they descended for what seemed an eternity. The backs of Christian's legs burned with the strain, and splinters needled his hand.

Fingers of wintry air swept across his face before he hit the bottom step. The second level of the Other World's stark landscape froze beneath an icy sun. Drifts of snow climbed the horizon like small mountains. He gasped, and frigid air encased his lungs, his lips instantly numbing and his skin tightening on his cheeks.

Souls held metal shovels with their bare hands, raw and bleeding, digging holes to nowhere that filled as quickly as they'd been dug. In the distance, bonfires crackled, flames pale against the stark whiteness, smoke licking the skyline like lazy tongues. Giltine's black-hooded disciples held flaming leashes connected to rust-furred hellhounds that stood as high as a man's shoulders. Their fangs were razor-sharp, dripping with drool and blood, and the droplets froze when they hit the ground.

A soul tossed his shovel and sped for the nearest bonfire. A hellhound tore after him so fast its red eyes became two bloody streaks across the snow. Barking fire, it pounced on the soul and they rolled, showering the air with flames, snow, and blood.

Christian turned from the carnage. The sound of the crackling fires was torture. Teeth chattering, lips cracking, he chafed his numb hands together in a weak attempt to get the blood flowing again. His feet ached inside his boots.

Christian had no idea how long they walked. It could have been minutes, hours, days. His muscles throbbed, his skin froze, and his eyes burned from the blinding sun reflecting off the snow. Snow filled his shoes and numbed his feet. Dull pain buzzed inside his head, but the unmarked souls he'd absorbed kept his body from collapsing. The rhythm of his steps became a mantra: E-li-za-beth. E-li-za-beth.

They limped to the next wall. The red gate rose twenty feet high. Burn barrels melted snow, thick smoke spiraling upward. Two hellhounds narrowed their blood-red eyes, ears laid back as they snarled. Their breath fanned his face, rank with sulfur. He tried to swallow past his dry throat.

A cherubic-looking man sat atop the wall and swung his feet, clicking his boot heels against the bricks and whistling a lively tune. He had an unlined, round face and white-blond hair that cascaded past a pair of dark sunglasses. His white fur coat glowed in the sun, a fluffy, pink scarf curled around his neck.

He leaped to the ground, patted a hellhound on the head with a black-gloved hand, then smiled benignly, as a grandfather might when greeting his grandchildren. "Christian! William! Welcome!"

"Lucifer." William's voice scratched like dead leaves across a tin roof.

Grinning, the man studied a clipboard. "Christian has business with Giltine, yes?"

Shivering, Christian hugged himself, trying to chafe warmth into his arms. "Yes."

Lucifer peered at William over his sunglasses. "What are you doing here?"

He glared at Christian. "I'm starting to have an idea."

"Hmm." Lucifer consulted his clipboard. "Giltine requires payment, of course." He exchanged the clipboard for a black whip. He flicked his wrist and orange flames consumed its long length.

Christian's heart crashed. He wanted to run; run back to the lake where the air was fresh and clean, run back to Elizabeth who was soft and warm.

"Only five lashes," Lucifer said to him. "Giltine is a generous goddess, isn't she? Are you willing to pay?"

Christian clung to thoughts of Elizabeth. If he turned back now, what would he find? Would he find her squirming beneath Renkin's cruelty? Would she be beyond his help, meeting the same fate as her sister at the bottom of the lake? His gaze shifted from Lucifer to the whip to William. His great uncle tightened his lips, which were blue and split, his face cracked and peeling, his eyebrows lowered over bloodshot eyes, his cheek muscles clenching.

Lucifer again peered over his sunglasses, and Christian returned the man's dead gaze.

"Yes, she's very generous."

"What's going on?" William asked.

"Business." Lucifer chuckled. "If Giltine made it easy to bargain, every secucro in the Other World would be free, and she hates losing her *precious* children."

"Blast the gods," William snapped at Christian. "I knew it! What are you bargaining for?"

Lucifer's white locks took on a shimmering, honey gleam, his features softened.

"Elizabeth," Christian whispered.

She smiled. "I love you."

William's voice was tight. "You're going to bargain for that useless broad?"

"Do you love me?" she asked.

"Yes."

"You lied to me!" William socked him in the arm.

Elizabeth disappeared. Lucifer's white eyebrows peeked over his sunglasses.

"Why didn't you tell me?" William asked.

"Because you'd try to stop me."

"Damn right."

Lucifer's eyebrows arched even higher. "Oh, dear. Is there a problem?"

William's jaw tensed. "Thomas, how could you lie to me? How can you leave me?"

"I'm not Thomas."

"If you choose her over me, you're dead to me. Do you hear? Dead!"

Lucifer draped an arm over William's shoulders. "The cruelty of family never ceases to amaze me. Trust me, I know. How do you think I ended up here?"

Christian glared at him.

"Now, William, why don't you want him to bargain with Giltine?"

"Because he'll die."

He gasped, clapping his hand to his chest and *tsking*. "And yet he chooses to go through with a bargain he has little chance of surviving. He doesn't care about you. He doesn't care about family. He only cares about himself."

"No!" His great uncle clenched his fists. "I won't let you do it. I won't let you get bumped over some stupid dame. Thomas, we have to stay together. We're all the family we have left, all the family we need. You don't need her!"

"I'm not Thomas!" Christian squeezed his aching head between his palms. "I'm not going to die."

"Oh, well, we all die sometime," Lucifer murmured.

William's face crumpled. He dropped to his knees and clutched the hem of Christian's coat. "Thomas, it was an accident. I'm sorry. Please don't leave me." His voice was small, like a child begging his mother to check the closet one more time for monsters.

The sight of him with his head full of bees, thinking Christian was William's dead brother, crushed Christian's heart. It beat wildly, not willing to make a choice. He closed his eyes.

"Maybe I can be of assistance," Lucifer said. "If Christian chooses to go with William, he may lose his dear Elizabeth. And if he chooses to bargain with Giltine, he'll lose William and probably his life. Do I have that right?"

William nodded, his bloodshot eyes glistening.

"I'm sorry, William, but I can't live as a slave any longer."

Lucifer snorted and rolled his eyes. "Complain, complain, complain."

Christian swung toward the devil with clenched his fists. The hellhounds rose to their feet, growling low. One chuffed, and smoke puffed from its nose. He counted until the urge to sock Lucifer on the chin passed.

"I can't believe you lied to me." William's voice was devoid of emotion.

Christian's shoulders sagged as he watched the man, still on his knees. He appeared smaller now, as though the life that had animated his body had died, leaving a crumpled shell behind. Christian laid on hand on his great uncle's shoulder.

Lucifer wagged his finger at him. "You naughty boy. Christian isn't the only one who's lied, is he?"

William's Adam's apple jiggled when he swallowed.

Christian tensed. "What's that supposed to mean?"

"Giltine knows William's gone rogue. Goodness, even the dead could smell the stench rolling off you, boy." Lucifer caressed his whip. "But, generous goddess that she is, she overlooked his indiscretion so long as he spied on and harassed you. A few lost souls were worth the price of your life being made even more miserable than it already is."

Nostrils flaring, he narrowed his eyes at his great uncle, digging his fingers into the man's shoulders. "There never was a watcher, was there?"

"Of course there was."

"You used me, and lied to me, just so you could get stoned without getting punished."

"I only made the deal with Giltine after my watcher died and reapers started giving me chin music. Besides, you made promises too. You said we'd be family again."

Christian released William's shoulder, but not before pushing him first. "I don't think we ever were."

William's gaze emptied as though all emotion slid from his body. He leaped to his feet and stomped across the snow.

"I think he's angry." Lucifer clucked his tongue.

Christian crossed his arms over his chest. Jutting his chin, he glared at Lucifer. One of the hellhounds shifted from paw to paw, licking its lips. It panted, shooting bursts of flame in Christian's direction. He forced himself to relax and let his arms drop to this sides.

"Funny thing, family." Lucifer inspected him with a small smile. "Such a shame you can't choose your family. But then we'd all choose the wealthy families, the stable families." He leaned close and whispered, "Did you ever wonder what it would have been like to have been born Gilbert Heublein instead of Christian Graves?"

Christian's body simmered and seethed. He blinked repeatedly, trying to swallow his anger. He stared at Lucifer's neck, pictured wrapping his own whip around it, squeezing, squeezing.

The other man chuckled. "You can only choose how to treat your family, right?"

"I've never deceived anyone."

Lucifer pushed his sunglasses on top of his head, and his eyes flickered with angry light. "You pecksniff. You didn't con William into telling you about the watchers? You didn't betray Giltine? Do you think I don't know what you did to make it this far?"

Christian's face cooled as the blood drained from it. The other man flicked the whip, and sparks bit at his face. He jerked back.

"Are we ready?" Lucifer asked.

"Do it."

Spinning, Christian gripped the gate. The whip cracked. He clenched his teeth, unable to hold back a groan. Every inch of the blazing trail melted his coat and shirt into his skin. The whip seared him a second time. His knees buckled, and he locked them so he wouldn't fall. He choked on the smell of burnt cloth and flesh. The hellhounds' snapping teeth and loud barks pushed into his eardrums as he struggled to stay upright.

He sucked in frozen air that did nothing to ease his pain as the whip lashed a third time. He dropped to his hands and knees, pressing his forehead into the snow; the pain in his back slicing through skin and flesh and muscle all the way to his spine. Again the whip lashed, and again. Groaning, his breath rasped as he focused on the gate spinning in front of him. Sweat dripped a stinging drop into his eye.

"That wasn't so bad now, was it?" Lucifer coiled his whip, the flames now dead. He inclined his head toward the gate, which swung open. "Go on. Forget about your great uncle, you selfish maggot. I just hope your whore doesn't reject you like you rejected your own family."

Hoping the souls he'd stolen were enough to sustain him in the last level of the Other World, Christian crawled through the gate and entered the bowels of Giltine's domain, the hellhounds biting his heels.

Chapter 28

Present Time

Brooke woke with a start, her laptop sliding off her lap and onto her bed. Lola lay like a beached whale on the pillow next to her head. Purring, the cat stretched without ever opening her eyes, then curled into a ball.

The itchy shove-a-hot-curling-iron-in-her-gut feeling flamed, and Brooke's brain waves tried to cut through the sludgy feeling in order to form a coherent thought. Her hair stuck to her sweaty forehead. She kicked off her socks, rolled onto her side and checked her clock. Eight thirty.

Scratching Lola's ears, she watched the glowing numbers on the clock change minute by minute. Every time she'd had the sizzling belly-button feeling, William had been around, and he wore the sweet rogue scent like bad cologne. Was her flaming tummy a signal a rogue was hunting for a soul? Great, first reaper radar, and now rogue detector. Next, she'd see a Batman signal lighting the sky. Brooke slipped out of bed, her thoughts chasing her to the window.

A flat-black motorcycle rolled down the street. Heart racing, she sucked in her breath and backed away from the window.

Christian.

She couldn't let him see her with major bed-head. Smoothing her hair, she searched the floor for her jeans, then froze. Wait. She thought back, and numbness climbed her legs like a cat clawing its way up a curtain. Correction.

Every time she'd had her belly-buzz, William *or* Christian had been nearby. Had he lied? Was Christian still rogue?

She squeezed her itching fingers. No, maybe the old Christian had been rogue, but the new Christian wouldn't hurt her or anyone. William was the one who smelled like a neglected winery. William was the one who couldn't be trusted.

Her stomach flamed, and her fingers itched, and she wanted to get out of the house. Now. Her mind whispered to her.

Watch.

Without taking time to think, she called Abby.

"Stilts, what's up?"

"You at work?"

"Yup. Closing, then hanging with Billy."

Brooke's hand puked sweat all over her cell phone. "Mind if I stop by for a sec?"

"A quick sec, because I've got some boss lips to lock."

She rolled her eyes. "Okay." Yanking on her sneakers, she yelled, "Mom! I'm going to see Abby for a quick sec!"

She jetted outside and steered her car onto Route 202. The activity in the strip mall had pretty much died out; most shops in the process of closing for the night. From her car, she watched Abby wiping down tables. Brooke chewed a fingernail, wincing when William peered through the window and twitched his fingers at her in a mocking wave.

Pressing her lips together, Brooke got out of her car and headed for the sidewalk, trying to avoid all the reapers emitting low hisses like they'd sprung leaks.

A man with a torn army jacket, a dirty baseball cap, and a scraggly, white beard held out his hand. A silver streak lined his gaunt cheeks, the skin wrinkled and sagging beneath his watery eyes.

"Spare some change for a hot meal?" he asked.

She studied the silver mark, knowing this would be his last meal. She dug into her purse and handed him ten dollars.

He grinned, revealing missing teeth, and shook her hand. "Bless you, miss." He limped down the sidewalk, and her heart clenched at the reaper that followed.

"Hey, Brooke."

She spun, clapping her hand to her chest. Christian straddled his motorcycle, having obviously morphed from a reaper boy to a stalker boy.

"What the hell?" she snapped. "You can't sneak up on someone like that. I could have had a heart attack."

He gave her a slow smile. "I hardly think a bike like this could be considered sneaky and besides, you're not marked so I think your heart's safe with me."

Her eyes widened before she worked up a very un-cool sounding snort. Scratching her cheek, she turned her attention to his motorcycle. The bike looked like it came out of an old black-and-white movie, all rounded edges with flat-black paint. "You sure that thing's trustworthy?"

"I'll have you know that this is a 1964 Harley Davidson."

She stared at him.

"You're supposed to be impressed."

"Got it."

"You don't look impressed."

"That's because it's all rusty and old."

He smiled, and his dimples winked at her. She parted her lips, her heart swooping aimlessly like a bat with kinked radar. Those stupid-hot dimples almost made her believe he was harmless, but he looked kind of dangerous on that bike, and he *was* a demon. Well, half a demon anyway.

She would *not* think about the subtle warmth radiating through her body.

No, that feeling was her rogue detector burning in her belly. She twisted her head; nothing but a few shadowy reapers floating aimlessly through the dark, and William and Abby having a major make-out session . . . nothing that resembled soul-snatching, though a chill snaked up her spine at the thought of Abby kissing an almost-reaper.

"What are you up to?" Christian gazed down the sidewalk, his mouth softening. "Besides saving kittens and feeding the homeless."

"I'm waiting for Abby to get off work. You?"

He blinked and straightened. "No plans. Can I hang with you for a while?"

She glanced at Abby sucking face with William. "Um, let's wait outside."

Christian leaned against the wall. Brooke studied the half-dozen reapers pacing the parking lot and sneering while they ogled her. Tension mingled with the belly-buzz until she thought she'd implode.

"What's up with all these reapers? There seem to be more than usual."

"Being near you warms their cold bones."

"Well, that's not at all creepy."

"You're an anomaly to them. The stuff made of legends, something they haven't seen in generations. They're curious, not sure if they should be afraid, yet wanting to be near you. Most reapers are smart enough to keep their distance, knowing what you are and what you can do. I expect there are rogues who won't be able to resist you, though."

"Great."

The silence droned for an eternity, and her palms started to sweat under his continuous stare even though, thankfully, his eyes glittered blue and not silver. She checked her watch. Abby should be ready to leave soon.

Her belly was really burning now, and her fingers itched. Brooke squeezed her fingers, dug her nails into her palms, and shifted from one foot to the other. Apprehension tightened her chest like a bra one size too small, biting into her skin, constricting her breath.

Watch, watch, watch.

Her inner voice pounded the word between her ears. A rogue was near. She searched the parking lot, her gaze coming back to Christian leaning on the wall next to her.

He smiled. Slowly.

Him? Was Christian the rogue she was supposed to watch? Despite her internal warning, the look he gave her made her toes curl and her heart clutch. She looked over her shoulder again.

He moved suddenly, pivoting her and pushing her against the wall. He leaned his forearms on either side of her head, his face just inches from hers. He lowered his lids, letting his gaze trail down her face and linger on her mouth. Heat exploded in the pit of her stomach.

God, how she wanted to melt into him.

He bent closer. His mouth was as close to hers as he could get without touching. His legs pressed against hers, long, strong, and lean. She closed her eyes and concentrated on breathing; his leather-sweet-spicy scent was very, very distracting.

"Do you have any idea how much I want to kiss you?" he murmured against her lips.

Her breath hitched. She wanted him to kiss her. God help her, she did, but he was all wrong and she shouldn't be doing this but she knew she would. She was in too deep.

"Some."

He brushed his lips along her throat. He moved to her ear, his breath tickling the skin on her neck. Her heart fluttered, her body trembling with wicked warmth. She licked her lips, wanting to do the same to his. He sighed, and his breath swept her lips. Warmth erupted through her chest and flooded her head. Her thighs trembled.

"So why don't you?" she asked.

He pulled away in order to gaze into her eyes. "I can't."

"Why not?"

"I haven't been honest with you."

Her head was floating in a sleepy fog. One corner of her mind resisted the dreamy warmth, the bottom dropping from her stomach as his words sunk in. Brooke wasn't sure if she was standing or falling or breathing. The only thing she was sure of was how the nippy air brushed her flaming skin, how her stomach was on fire; burning, burning, burning.

Watch.

Gasping, understanding clicked with the suddenness of a dead-bolt being shot home.

Brooke slammed her palms into Christian's chest, and he jerked back.

"It's William."

He wasn't just kissing Abby. How could she have been so stupid?

She raced toward Panera Bread, crashed into the door because she hadn't thought to slow down and open it, flung herself through it, and gasped for breath as the grape smell knocked her back. Her nostrils flared, and her mouth twisted.

"Get the hell away from her," she snapped.

Chapter 29

1938

Once Christian crawled through the gate to the third level of the Other World, he found himself kneeling before another set of stairs that stretched into the bowels of the Earth. Heat and sulfur rose to greet him, instantly thawing his frozen skin, making it itch and ache. The lashes on his back burned as they oozed blood, warm trails that collected at the waist of his pants.

Peering below, tension knotted his thighs. Through the stifling darkness, red reigned, and a relentless rumbling shook the stairs so they rattled and groaned and emitted puffs of dust. Grabbing the railing, he stood and descended the rickety stairs.

The steps wobbled, leaned, creaked. He stopped time after time, waiting for them to crumble beneath his feet and pitch him into the flaming darkness. Each time the stairs held, he'd shuffle downward, his snail's pace seeming to take a lifetime. His mind was blank and his body devoid of moisture by the time he reached the bottom. His legs buckled, and he dropped to his knees.

Mountains of black rock stretched as far as he could see. Lava bubbled in lakes and rivers. Clouds of sulfuric ash hung like a low, gray sky. Souls were chained to wooden poles at the bottom of a small mountain near a lava pool. A waterfall of molten rock cascaded into the pool, the spray showering souls with skin-melting drops, the posts flaring into flames. The screams were endless.

Pits of lava were circled by flaming crosses, upon which hung souls strung up with barbed wire. Occasionally the pits erupted and burned already blackened skin. Hellhounds slashed flesh, worms burrowed into open crevices, rats chewed exposed limbs, and a constant stream of blood blended with the boiling fire. Disciples hovered, their instruments of torture dripping blood. The screaming and heat and sulfur-drenched air made Christian's head ache and his stomach spasm.

Drawing a shaky breath, he lurched forward. Jagged rocks tore through the soles of his boots. His ripped shirt stuck to the congealed blood on his back, and blood from his cracked lips was the only moisture to touch his dry mouth. His skin reddened, blistered, and then peeled, exposing raw flesh. Then, as though by magic, his skin would heal and the process would begin again.

The sustenance from his stolen souls evaporated. His muscles gave out, and he dropped to his knees. He knelt, panting, groaning, and wishing he was dead. He couldn't go on; he was slowly burning to death.

Blinking rapidly, he raised his head, clenching his fists. Without him to save her, Elizabeth would die under Renkin's hands. Christian had to survive.

So he crawled.

He climbed one mountain, then another, then a third. His hands and knees were raw. His clothes were shredded from the rock and eroded from the heat.

He pulled himself along until he reached Giltine's throne. His eyeballs had dried in his sockets so he could no longer blink. Sulfur burned his nose, stung his tongue, but he couldn't swallow or spit or sweat . . . he had nothing left to give the molten atmosphere.

Orange light seeped from the lava pit behind her black, granite throne and mingled with the blinding darkness, an odd, orange glow that highlighted the emaciated soul chained to the rock. The soul's bones protruded from skin covered in blisters, his silver eyes were hollow and haunted. All the hair had been burned from his body.

"Son," it rasped.

Christian stared at his father. Despite the pain that encased his body like melting plastic, a tendril of pity encircled his heart. He stretched out a hand toward the man.

"How droll," Giltine drawled.

He dropped his arm to his side. The glow gouged shadows into her face, and accentuated her bottomless eyes, gazing at him as a child might study an ant she was about to squash. Her virginal dress blazed against the black backdrop of her throne.

"The apple doesn't fall far. Does your father's fate alarm you? Are you still willing to play the game?"

"Don't," his father said. The word sounded as though it'd been ground out between cinder blocks.

Giltine peered at Christian over her steepled fingers, and her gold ring glowed in the lava light. "You see what happens to those who break their promise to me."

He desperately wished he could swallow. He touched his swollen tongue to his bloody lips, his father's fate a monument to bargains gone badly. He needed to rethink his strategy of reneging on his deal with her, unsure whether he could endure an eternity of torture such as his father suffered. Christian's brain froze into immobility.

"Will you offer what I desire?" Her darkness faded, replaced by glimmering youth and fearful, green eyes.

"I'm afraid," Elizabeth said. "Is Mr. Renkin going to hurt me?"

"Yes," he said.

"Why should I trust you?"

"Son!"

His father pawed Christian's coat. He blinked, and Elizabeth's beauty faded. Giltine twisted the ring on her finger.

"I have served faithfully," he rasped.

Her bored tone took on an edge of malice. "Not so faithfully, if you've made it this far."

She knew about the stolen souls. He opened his mouth, snapped it closed.

"And there is still your father's betrayal to reckon with."

His eyes widened, the movement making his blistered skin sting.

"No," his father said. "Hasn't my suffering been payment enough?"

Giltine held up a finger to halt his words, and then said to Christian, "You would promise your first- and secondborn to serve me, as did your father?"

No, anything but that, he thought.

Her face softened, hardened, softened. Her hair brightened to gold, and Elizabeth lifted her hands. "Don't you love me?"

He spoke past his blistered throat. "Yes." He extended his hand toward Elizabeth, only to drop his arm back to his side when he discovered it was Giltine within reach.

"My dear Christian, how I feel your pain." Her fingers lifted his face by the chin, a frozen grip that sucked the breath from his lungs in a wispy fog.

"I know you do not appreciate the gift I've given you, to become my child. You feel condemned, enslaved, and you do not wish that for your own children. Is that not true?"

He nodded.

Her smile was vacant, like a jack-o-lantern leer. "I would not force such an abhorrent bargain upon you."

Hope glimmered weakly in the darkness of his heart. The burden of enslaving his children to Giltine lifted from his shoulders. He couldn't think of a worse punishment.

"Am I not a gracious goddess?"

His father clutched his arm. Christian stared at the man's

rotting, hairless face. No, not a gracious goddess; a vindictive goddess. Doubt flickered at the back of his mind.

She snapped her fingers. With shaking hands, his father handed her a sheet of silky paper, leaving it marked with his bloody fingerprints. She rolled the paper into a cylindrical shape, blew on it, and then slid it through her ring where it promptly burst into flames. She offered the flaming paper to Christian. The flames died and morphed into charred words when his fingers touched it.

"Kiss my ring," she demanded.

"Christian, don't. It's a trick."

Uncertainty descended like darkness. Christian backed away.

Giltine's hand snapped out and seized his hair. "You have stolen souls. You will finish what you have begun."

She raised her free hand. As her icy ring neared him, ice collected on his eye lashes. His sinuses ached. His head ached. Even his hair ached. Straining against her grip, neck muscles popping, he couldn't stop her ring from pressing against his lips.

Mouth and jaw flashing with agony, he cried out, expecting his teeth to shatter. Pain exploded inside his head, veins flooded with icy fire. He convulsed like a convict strapped to an electric chair.

He couldn't move. Couldn't blink.

Couldn't even scream.

He could only wish for death as pain consumed his body. Christian crumpled to the ground, his screams lost inside his head.

The ground scorched Christian's back. The stench of sulfur made his mouth spasm with the need to vomit, body aching as though broken, like an ice sculpture that had been tossed to the ground.

"Jeremiah Close," Giltine said.

He opened his eyes, head resting on his father's lap, nose and eyes stinging with the smell of decayed flesh. Giltine lounged upon her throne. A drum-shaped, glass jar sat by her side, and black-streaked fog swirled inside. She reached inside for a slip of paper.

"Allison Tenney." Flicking the paper into the pile collected at her feet, she selected another. "Kenneth Zweig."

A disciple stood at a podium, writing the names into a large, leather-bound ledger. Christian had only heard rumors of the Jar of Souls and the Ledger of the Dead. Little did Jeremiah, Allison, and Kenneth know, but they would be dead inside a day.

Giltine waved her hand. "That is all for today." She spit on the papers and they disintegrated under a burst of flame. She nudged the pile of ash with a toe.

The disciple bowed—Christian caught a glimpse of shadows upon shadows under the hood—and shuffled off.

Drumming her fingers, she observed him with one arched brow. "So, the bargain is sealed."

"I'm free?" His voice sounded shriveled and old.

She nodded toward the paper that lay by his boot. "Read it." She smiled a closed-lipped smile, as if opening her mouth might let him see inside, revealing secrets better left hidden.

He scanned the words. "What does this mean?"

"It means you are more like my child now than ever before. You have my greatest gift, the ability to mark people for death."

He studied her, then the paper. "That's all?"

"That is all."

"Christian, my son, have you any idea what you've done?" Bloody tears streaked his father's face.

"I know I didn't trade my son for my own. I found another way."

"I'm sorry. If I'd known . . . if I'd only known . . . please forgive me."

The euphoric feeling of being free, combined with his father's pitiful condition, overcame Christian's hatred. He reached out to touch his father's cheek, but stopped short of making contact with the blistered skin. "I do."

His father covered his face in his hands and laid his forehead against the ground. Christian staggered to his feet. Giltine and his father and the flames of Hell spun before him.

"Christian," his father screamed.

Pitching forward, Christian saw the steaming ground for a mere second before his face smashed into it.

Chapter 30

Present Time

Brooke stood inside Panera Bread, fury starting from her feet, snaking around her ankles, and creeping up her legs, her back, her neck. Sweating, she crossed her arms and gripped her biceps. A breeze cut across her shoulders when the door opened and Christian entered.

"Abby!" she snapped.

Abby sighed, and her body deflated against the wall. Every muscle in her face seemed to have lost its fight with gravity as she stared at Brooke.

William's beautiful lips pulled back to show his beautiful teeth, a bruise circling one beautiful, blue-silver eye. "Hey, Brooke."

Ignoring him, she went to Abby, who stared at the ceiling with a small smile.

"Abby."

The girl's glassy eyes rolled around until they were able to focus on Brooke. Shadows hung under Abby's eyes, and Brooke wondered how late Abby had been staying up, or how much weed she'd been smoking, or if she was doing something more than weed. She pushed off the wall and careened into Brooke, knocking her against a table.

"S'sorry," Abby slurred.

Brooke used two hands to hold her steady. "Don't worry about it."

"Really, really sorry." Abby stepped toward her, then veered off to the side and bumped into another table. "S'sorry."

She turned to William. "What did you give her?"

"Nothing." He lounged against the glass counter.

Christian tilted his head. "He's been taking hits off her soul."

Her body became sumo-wrestler heavy, but somehow she turned toward William. "You what?"

He lifted his hands. "I just licked it a little."

Heart crashing like a meteor, she struggled for breath as anger constricted her throat.

"Besides, she likes it," he added.

Abby swayed in her chair. "Fabulous kisser."

"You dick!" Brooke gripped a chair, afraid she'd chuck it at the bastard's head. "It's not permanent, is it?" She prayed the answer would be no, but she thought there had to be some lasting effect of losing bits of your soul.

He shrugged. "I left her soul intact. She'll be fine. For now."

Her stomach burned. She dug her nails into her palms "You're using my best friend to get your rocks off, you perv? All that crap about not talking to any almost-reapers, you just didn't want Christian to tell me what you were doing to her. You freaking liar!"

"*I'm* the liar?" He jutted his chin at Christian. "I'm not the one who's been lying to you."

Christian went a shade whiter than chalk.

"You be nice to Stilts or I'll ass your kick." Abby tried to glare at him, but the glare morphed into a grin. "What did I just say?"

"I want you to stay away from Abby, you soul-sucking thief."

"Hey, don't talk to Billy that way." Her friend's hand wavered as she tried to point at Brooke.

She jerked her head in Abby's direction. "Why not?"

Abby wobbled to a standing position. "Boyfriend."

There was a roaring sound in Brooke's ears, an explosion of emotional pain behind her eyes. Her mouth hung open like an escape hatch, but no words escaped.

William went to Abby's side. "Yeah, we're an item, so leave us alone. But listen, all you have to do is ask Christian one thing, and then come talk to me. I think we can strike some sort of deal."

Brooke stopped grinding her teeth long enough to form one word. "What?"

"Ask him how to break his curse. Then you'll know he's always been a liar and a jackass, and always will be."

He winked at Christian, and then draped his arm around Abby's shoulders. She snuggled against him.

Brooke folded her arms across her chest and shoved her fists under her armpits. Her face went numb. How much color was left in it?

She glared at Christian. "Got something you want to tell me, Reaper Boy?"

Chapter 31

1938

A mourning dove's low-throated tones chimed in the distance, followed by the rapping alarm of a woodpecker. Opening his eyes, Christian blinked against the muted rays of sunlight that worked through the trees. A wisp of cool air brushed through his hair. His muscles were fatigued, as though he'd just recovered from a long illness, and his eyes had the grainy feel of Other World sand. He ran his parched tongue over his dry lips and contemplated the twisted mountain laurel.

His heart spasmed with an itch he couldn't scratch. His father's eternity was one of torture and misery . . . was that a fair fate for what he'd done to Christian, and what he would have done to Henry had he lived? Christian thought of his mother and then Elizabeth, and could understand why his father had done it. But Christian was smarter, he'd found another way.

He may be a maggot, but he was no longer a monster. His heart paced. He'd bartered for his freedom without condemning his future children to Giltine. He could love Elizabeth without fear or guilt or misgivings.

Laughing out loud, he rolled onto his hands and knees, and then winced. He sat back on his heels, flexing his fingers, then his arms and shoulders. He removed his tattered coat and kicked off his sole-less boots.

His buoyancy deflated. Had Renkin returned for her?

Was she safe? He shouldn't linger. Christian unbent like a man five times his age.

His heart pounded with each step through the woods, each step that brought him closer to the rest of his life. The lake wavered dark blue below the sky stretching above him like a clean slate. He knelt and studied his reflection in the water.

Either he'd been lying dormant for a very long time or Giltine had healed him before he'd come topside. His lips were dry but not bleeding, the skin on his face tight but not burnt. Even Renkin's cigar burn had healed, leaving Christian with a purplish-red scar.

His eyes were still a marbled silver-blue. He may be a free secucro, but he was still demon. Bargaining with Giltine hadn't changed who he was inside.

He no longer cared.

He drank from the lake, then hastened toward the lakehouse. The creak of a rocking chair came from the shadowy porch, accompanied by Bonnie's soft purr. The smell of lilac shampoo reached him even from a distance.

His feet flew across the grass, and he stopped at the bottom of the stairs. The creaking halted. Elizabeth sat immobile in the rocker, the shadows unable to dilute the brightness of her hair.

His chest filled with elation, ready to burst from joy. He could barely speak past his wide smile. "Elizabeth."

Face set like stone, she stared at her clenched fingers. His gaze didn't stray from her tight expression, even when Bonnie leaped from her lap and, tail in the air, scampered across the porch.

Legs trembling, he rested one foot on the bottom step. "Elizabeth?"

"Don't come near me," she whispered.

His grip tightened on the railing. "What's wrong?"

She pushed herself from the rocker. A metallic taste tingled his tongue. She feared him.

"Mr. Renkin was right all along, wasn't he? He always thought there was something hinky about you."

Christian pushed his palm against his chest as if he could get his heart pumping again.

She swallowed. "You're a monster."

Gods below. All feeling sank away from his limbs. She squinted at his eyes, at the sign of his demon. He averted his head.

"Was William here?" he asked.

When she didn't answer, he knew with certainty his great uncle had been there before him and betrayed him. "You can't believe everything he told you."

"Leave." She turned toward the door.

"Wait." He leaped up the steps.

Eyes wide, she backed against the house. Her fear froze him.

"I don't know what he told you . . . " he started.

"He told me that you . . . " Her lower lip trembled. She sucked it between her teeth.

"What did he tell you?"

She darted a look toward the side, then dashed toward the door.

He got there first, slamming his hand against it and blocking her path. "What did he tell you?"

She flinched then blurted, "You killed my sister!"

His mouth dropped open. "What?"

Her eyes glittered, whether from anger or unshed tears he wasn't certain. Her teeth ground beneath her accusing gaze. "I saw you! You hid behind the tree, watching us look for Mary. I convinced myself I was mistaken, but I wasn't, was I? It was you all along."

His arm dropped to his side. "I was there."

She sagged against the house. "Oh, my God."

"I didn't kill her."

"Liar! William told me." She scooped up Bonnie and hugged her.

"Elizabeth, if you'll just let me explain."

"No. I trusted you. I saved you. I *kissed* you." She paused to wipe her mouth with the back of her hand. "And you lied to me."

"I can explain."

"Stop it! I hate you! Go away and don't come back!"

She dove into the house and slammed the door. The door blocked her from view but was unable to block the sound of her sobbing. Christian ran his hand down his face. The door wasn't the barrier. It was his lineage. She hated him. She rejected him. Head hanging, his shoulders slouched. He could barely lift his feet as he lurched down the steps.

But he didn't leave.

This wasn't the end of it. One way or another, Elizabeth would be his. Forever.

Chapter 32

Present Time

Abby took off with William, leaving Brooke and Christian glaring at each other on the sidewalk outside of Panera Bread. Her heart pumped too much blood to her head, and it throbbed. Maybe his lies wouldn't be as bad as her heart was telling her they were; maybe he wasn't planning on killing her. And maybe there was no good left inside him.

He yanked a piece of paper out of his pocket and held it out.

"What's that?"

"Read it."

She plucked it with her fingertips, cleared her throat, and then read out loud:

"With poisoned tongue, the gift of death.

Marking souls for one last breath.

'Till angel's kiss lent from the heart,

Breaks the spell, and you depart."

Her gaze roved the paper, again, again. Her fingers shook, her face deadened. Every strangled breath she took rattled like death.

She raised her gaze. "This is your curse from Giltine?"

"Yes."

"This is why you're immortal?"

"Yes."

She blinked, rapidly. "You have a poisoned *tongue*?"

"Yes."

His answer sank into her heart like a scar.

"I can explain," he said.

"Explain what? Explain how you were playing me? Explain how you lied to me? What the hell does this mean?"

He hesitated. "Giltine truly made me her child. Like her, I can mark people for death."

"And?"

"And it's not something I can turn on or off. Even a kiss from me will mark someone."

Her mouth went dry. "A kiss of death."

He bowed his head.

"The angel part?"

"Would break the curse."

"That's why you wanted to kiss me." He'd never said he loved her. Now she knew why; he didn't. Her heart shattered; shards plunged through her, shredded everything inside.

"I tried telling you."

"Oh, my God, I'm an idiot. You made me fall in love with you, and when I kissed you, the curse would be broken." Pain roared in her head, making her sway. "You never cared about me."

He held her gaze. "That's not true."

"And because your Giltine's son, I was going to die." She lifted her hands and dropped them to her sides. "William was telling the truth. You were going to kiss me dead."

"I'd never let you die."

"I'm supposed to believe you . . . why?"

"Because I love you."

Too little, too late. How could she believe him now? "How many girls have you killed trying to break the curse?"

"One, but I wasn't trying to break the curse. I loved her."

"You loved her," she repeated like a robot running out of batteries. Did he always kill the ones he loved?

A car horn blasted from Route 44. Brooke jumped like a startled cat. The paper slid through her fingers and floated to the ground. She stepped on it when she stomped toward her car.

"You lying *dick*," she called over her shoulder. "Stay the hell away from me."

Brooke sat in her car at the trail to Heublein Tower. She glanced up and down the vacant road as she tapped her fingers on the wheel. Outside her window, frogs cheeped in the woods and a mourning dove cooed to the dawn. She'd tossed and turned all night and, unable to take the suffocating confines of her bedroom, finally left a note for her parents and jetted. It was ironic. A week ago she couldn't leave her house; now her house strangled her like a cage. She needed to burn off energy and think, and maybe even do a little screaming.

She jiggled her leg while she waited for the sun to rise. Reapers hovered by the gate. Her rogue detector buzzed, and her head hummed. Even though the grape smell was absent, her inner voice chimed in.

Watch.

She breathed again, deeply, but scented nothing. These reapers weren't rogues. Who was she supposed to watch?

She flung open her door. After grabbing her flashlight from the glove compartment, she darted across the street. One of the reapers made kissing noises. Who knew they could be such dicks.

"Piss off," she yelled.

They scattered.

The distant drone of a motorcycle rumbled in the dark. Brooke jerked toward the sound, thinking it might be Christian, but the noise faded into the distance. It was just as well, because right now she didn't believe his bullshit story. How far would he have gone? Would he have told her the truth, or would he have let her kiss him?

She glanced once more down the street, then flicked on her light and attacked the trail.

Darkness overwhelmed her light. She shook it, rattling the batteries, and it resumed its battle against the dark, barely able to capture the ground in its beam. She plowed up the trail until her lungs burned and her leg muscles trembled. She paused, listening to her panting and her buzzing reaper radar. A glance over her shoulder caught the silvery-eyed gleam of at least six reapers. She shivered.

Scuffling, grunts, and hisses broke through the wall of buzzing. She smelled a rogue.

Watch.

Her gaze roved the dark, stared blindly into the shadows. She tucked her chin to her neck and sucked her lips between her teeth. Her heart seemed to explode and fire ignited in her gut. Ignoring the clamminess on her hands and back, she moved up the trail until she reached the Hang Glider Overlook.

Moonlight bathed the reaper using Christian as a punching bag. She opened her mouth to tell the reaper to stop, but fear jerked the words back inside. Christian grunted with every punch. He swayed, the reaper catching him as he collapsed. He held Christian at arm's length before punching his jaw. He staggered, but stayed upright. Then the reaper took a step back and threw a roundhouse kick that caught Christian in the face. The resulting crack and spurt of blood from his nose made her throat tighten. He dropped, landing with his face in the dirt.

The reaper grabbed Christian's hair and yanked his head off the ground. Licking his lips, the reaper said, "Just a taste now. It will not hurt."

The overly-sweet smell of grapes washed through Brooke's blood like ice water, reminding her of Ryan's death.

Defend.

She couldn't ignore the voice in her head, propelling her to move. She dropped a silent F-bomb, and then shouted, "Leave him alone!"

The reaper let go of Christian and stared at her. The pulse in her neck throbbed. A white-hot dagger of pain shoved through her stomach all the way to her spine. Crying out, she bent over, wrapping her arms around her waist. She wanted to growl, but fear strangled the sound in the back of her throat.

"He is mine," the rogue said.

The rogue's laugh started softly, then built in intensity, the sound clawing its way through her head as he bent toward Christian. She ground her teeth. Rage flamed. Sweat bubbled through her skin. Her fingers ached.

Defend!

She grabbed the back of the reaper's coat and yanked him back. "Get away from him."

The rogue toppled over, and then rolled onto his knees, his teeth bared, his eyes stoned-glassy and burning silver. Christian groaned and rolled to his back.

The rogue shot back to his feet. "He is mine."

She kicked his knee. "I said get away from him, you dick."

His knees buckled, but he caught his balance. Grinning, he said, "I think I like you better. Mmm. Smell so good."

He launched himself at her. Scream sticking in her throat, she raised her hands to block the impact. The reaper crashed into her, and they tumbled in a tangle of arms and legs. The back of her head cracked against the ground with a flare of pain.

He straddled her chest and wrapped his fingers around her throat. "You are going to taste so good, watcher bitch."

He leaned close, his breath like rotten eggs. Brooke rammed her knees into his back. He grunted, but didn't loosen his grip. Gritting her teeth, she fought the spots winking through the darkness. She absorbed the heat flowering from her gut and blossoming into her veins and her burning hands.

She scratched his face, his skin smoldering from her touch. Throwing his head back, he shrieked and tumbled to his side. His eyes flashed hate-filled sparks of silver. Claw marks flamed against his pale cheeks.

Her hands burned red-hot. Without hesitating, she jumped on top of him, seized his face between her palms, and squeezed, digging her fingers into his skin. Heat scalded her, scorched him. Smoke wove between her fingers. Grimacing, she gripped tighter, refusing to let go.

He was going to freaking *die*.

She snarled, "You messed with the wrong watcher bitch, you slanted freak. Keep your hands off Christian." She slammed the rogue's head onto the ground. "Keep your hands off Abby." *Slam.* "Keep your hands off my brother!" *Slam. Slam. Slam.*

The rogue screeched. His face turned crimson, lips peeled back in a rigor-mortis of agony. Her face went cold beneath a layer of sweat. The stench of charred rogue flesh burned the inside of her nose and made her eyes water.

Whimpering now, she ignored the agony and the stench, and kept her hands clasped to his face. A cry wrenched through her.

The rogue disintegrated under her fingers with a long hiss, leaving behind a pile of ash. She flopped onto her back and laid an arm across her eyes, her hands aching. Sweat itched along her scalp. Her body throbbed and trembled; blood thundered in her ears.

At a whispering noise behind her, she wiped her face with her sleeve, pushed damp hair off her forehead, and sat up.

A half-dozen reapers watched her. She forced herself to her feet. Cradling her hands against her stomach, she kept her gaze on the reapers as she moved next to Christian. They rustled closer.

"Back off before I kill you, too."

The reapers scattered, their eyes flashing like shooting stars.

Christian got to his feet and leaned against a tree. Blood seeped from his nose to the corner of his cracked and bleeding lips. A goose egg grew on his cheek under his swelling eye.

"You okay?" she asked.

His eyes opened in a half-lidded gaze. "I'm tired."

He made a half-hearted swipe at the blood spattered on his shirt. He tucked hair behind his ear, his hand trembling like an addict in need of a fix. Groaning, he slid down the tree, leaned his head back, and stretched his legs.

She squatted next to him. "You kind of look like crap."

He opened the eye that functioned and gazed at her for what seemed like an hour. "You saved my life. After what I told you . . . "

"Yup."

"You were like wild fire: beautiful and dangerous and very hot. Just like the first time I saw you." He sighed and closed his eyes.

Her muscles seemed to suddenly lose their strength, and she plopped onto her butt. Despite not trusting him on nine levels, she felt sorry for him. And damn it, her feelings for him hadn't changed.

She said, "I found my power. I guess I should warn you that if you try to kill me, I'll kill you first."

He didn't respond.

"Okay, Reaper Boy. It's time we had a little chat."

Chapter 33

Present Time

Christian's toes hung off the edge of the mountain as he stared over the vacant darkness below. Brooke stood behind him, all that swirling blackness making her leg muscles melt. An owl's call perched on the silence that strung between them.

Pity squeezed her heart at his battered face. She clenched her fists. She didn't want to feel sorry for him. She didn't want to feel anything for him. And yet, the backs of her eyes burned and her throat constricted.

She inspected her hands, where red calluses had formed on her fingertips. "So, what weren't you honest about, other than the curse, poisoned tongue and using me?" As if that wasn't enough.

"I never used you."

"Fine, you just lied to me."

He wiped blood from his mouth with the back of his hand and studied it.

"You said you killed someone after you were cursed. Who was it?"

He faked a smile—a smile that crooked the corners of his mouth while the rest of his face stayed immobile; no lifting cheeks or winking dimples or brightening eyes. "I was arrogant, and stupid. I left Giltine and went to live my human life with my human girlfriend. I hadn't planned on telling her what I was. I never dreamed she'd already discovered truth and would reject me."

"Elizabeth?"

He nodded. "You can't imagine my euphoria of being free. It was everything I'd always wanted, as was Elizabeth. But when I returned to her, she was cold and distant and afraid. Of me. She slammed the door in my face." His fists clenched. "After the shock wore off, I was furious."

Warmth drained from her face. "So you killed her?"

"No!" He swallowed. "Not right then."

"Oh, my God."

He ran a hand through his hair. "It's not what you think. It didn't happen that way."

"But you said another man was condemned for her death."

"I didn't lie about that, but you need to hear the whole story." He waited for her nod before continuing. "Even though she'd rejected me, I couldn't leave her. I didn't eat or sleep. I stayed—watching, waiting."

Her heart rammed against her ribs, but she didn't interrupt. She didn't know what to expect, but there could be no excuse good enough to justify killing a young girl.

His voice was low and soft. "I was there when Renkin came for her. I was there when he admitted to raping her older sister, who'd tried to escape from him by diving into the lake where she drowned. I was there when he ripped Elizabeth's clothes and tried to rape her."

Brooke gasped.

"I was . . . enraged. I had my hands on his throat, and I was pulling his soul with me to the Void, and killing him was the sweetest moment I'd ever experienced. I would have gone through with it if she hadn't brought me back from the brink." He blinked. "He was alive, but permanently damaged. His mind never fully recovered."

"He was the man sentenced for her death?" When he nodded, she asked, "So how did she die, exactly?"

Christian drew a shuddering breath. "She looked at me differently after that. Me, the monster, had saved her from the real monster in her world, the human kind. She realized that, and accepted me for who I was. She loved me."

Ignoring the jealousy pinching her chest, Brooke dug dirt from under her fingernail. "So, what happened?"

"I thought I could just ignore the fact that I could mark people for death. Giltine couldn't force me to do it."

She recalled the words of the curse. Yes, she could see how he would think that.

"I was free. Elizabeth was mine, and we were going to live happily ever after. A fairy tale come true."

His whole body deflated. Her glare melted off her face. When he glanced at her, she looked away and tightened her lips. She wasn't ready forgive him for lying to her, or using her . . . or killing Elizabeth.

"Tell me about her."

Smiling slightly, he gazed over the landscape. "It didn't start off as a fairy tale. Though beautiful, I thought she was spoiled, and I often found myself annoyed with her. But something kept pulling me back to her. It wasn't until she saved my life, of all people, pulling me out of a lake when I was drowning, that I realized she was even more beautiful on the inside. Good and pure, she was everything I wasn't. And despite who I was and what I'd done, she chose to love *me*. My freedom and family had been taken from me, and through Elizabeth I was going to have a fresh start. I'd gone from a life filled with darkness and pain to one of light and hope. She not only saved my life, she saved my soul." His voice broke, and he stopped.

She tugged her ear lobe, listening, watching. Head bowed, he pinched his lips, closing his eyes to shield the glistening wetness.

After a moment he continued. "I was so caught up in what could be, that I didn't take time to consider Giltine's curse. Until I kissed her, I hadn't conceived she'd die from my lips. I thought marking people would be something I *chose* to do, but the choice was never mine to make."

Brooke pushed a rock with her toe. On the one hand, his tragic story made her heart palpitate, splintering the angry shell around it. Glancing at his mouth, she shuddered. Yet his tongue was poisonous, lethal, and she couldn't help but think of a snake in the grass. Holding her breath, Brooke waited for him to finish his story.

"She died in my arms. As I began to realize what I'd done, I became numb, like there was a chunk of ice inside me that gradually melted to send frigid water through my veins." He paused to swallow. "I tried to revive her, tried to find a pulse or hear her heart beat, but there was nothing except the sound of death. I was stupid, a murderer. I was no better than the monster I'd saved her from."

His breath hitched, and he pressed his palms to his eyes. She didn't forgive him—not yet—but her heart broke for him. Standing behind him, she wrapped her arms around his waist, his body shaking against hers.

"William taunted me, blamed me for what had happened. I was crushed, unable to function. Do you know how many times I tried to kill myself? For decades I tried every imaginable way, yet nothing, no one, could end my life. I was immortal, sentenced to face an eternity of guilt for killing my future." Christian sighed and swiped a hand across the back of his neck. "It doesn't matter where I stay; the guilt inside me burns, aches, drives me closer to the edge of insanity.

"I've been haunted by the memory of killing Elizabeth since *1938*. Do you realize how long that is? How year after year after year of losing bits of myself to the darkness, knowing I could never out-live the shame, knowing I could never love again, or kiss again, that I was unworthy of anyone's love. Forever alone. Forever guilty. Disgust with myself turned to anger and, over time, hatred. My heart turned cold, hard, uncaring." His voice softened. "Turning off my feelings was the only way I could live with myself."

Brooke was silent for a long moment. "And me?"

"At first, you were a means to an end. Somewhere along the line, the more I saw and was with you, that changed. You broke every barrier I'd put around my heart. You're the only light in my life of darkness, and I . . . could never hurt you. The best thing for you was for me to walk away and never look back, and I couldn't do that either. I just wanted to kiss you like a normal guy. I'd almost forgotten about the curse."

The flimsy edge of her forgiveness snapped, and she released him. "Almost? And then what? You kiss me, you kill me, and while I'm six feet under doing the horizontal bop with worms, you finally get your happily ever after? That's bullshit."

He faced her. "You're wrong."

"Yeah, right. Which part of that story do I have wrong?"

"Don't you see? There's no happily ever after for me. Once I broke the curse, once I was finally mortal again, the guilt would still follow me for the rest of my life, and if I killed you, the guilt would be double. How could I live with myself?" He gave a bitter laugh. "No, there's only one way I can ever escape my guilt."

"How?"

He gazed over his toe-tips at the dark depths below. "Kill myself. And the only way I could kill myself was to sacrifice you first. You were right about me the first time, Brooke. I'm a worthless dick."

Brooke's mouth sagged. All feeling slipped through her, like a sheet of ice sliding down a warm roof. Christian rubbed his thumbs along his pants' seams so quickly she thought they'd catch fire from the friction. Sucking in her lips, her mind raced, mulling over his painful story. Her heart was split in two, one side longing to forgive him, the other side craving to push him off the cliff for using her.

His head bowed, his shoulders slouched, and he squeezed his eyes closed. "I decided, in the end, that I'd rather live with an eternity of guilt and loneliness, than sacrifice your life for mine."

She clamped her hands together, pushing her thumbs against each other. Forgiving words were on the tip of her tongue, but she couldn't utter them, knowing how close to death he'd brought her.

He tensed, then pivoted and started down the trail. "Forget you ever met me," he called over his shoulder. "And stay away from William. He's dangerous."

Open-mouthed, she watched his retreating back, her heart pumping fists of denial against her ribs. She didn't want him to leave. Not yet.

"Wait!" When Christian paused she asked, "What's his deal anyway?"

"Does it matter?"

"Of course. He's pulled both me and Abby into his world."

Christian turned but didn't move toward her.

"You may be able to walk away from me, but he won't."

"Do you think walking away is easy? I'm trying to protect you from me, the way I couldn't protect Elizabeth." His eyes shone not only with streaks of silver, but with a trace of wetness. His lips were tight, pressed together as if holding back a sob.

Brooke said, "No, I don't think it's easy for you, but do you think leaving me to face William on my own is helping me?"

Christian sighed, studying his boots for a long moment before speaking. "No."

"Then stay. Help me, help Abby."

He took a tentative step toward her before stopping. "When William was enslaved to Giltine, his family rejected him, and he accidentally killed his twin brother—my grandfather. He was in a pretty dark place when I came along, and he thought I could replace Thomas. When I chose to live with Elizabeth instead, he felt betrayed."

"He's hated you for that? That doesn't seem justified."

"I lied and let him believe we could be a family just so he would tell me about the watchers. He begged me not to leave him, and he almost convinced me to not bargain for my freedom, because most never survive. But then I found out he'd been playing me, spying for Giltine so he could get high off unmarked souls."

Hugging herself, Brooke waited for him to continue.

"He's the one who told Elizabeth what I was, and she . . ." Christian stopped to swallow. "Gods how she hated me, telling me she never wanted to see me again. Her rejection after the things I'd done and seen to be with her . . ." He cleared his throat. "It killed me inside. I hated him. I even thought about killing him."

"Why didn't you?"

He shrugged. "What was the point? It wouldn't change things. We're both liars. We're both still secucron. And Elizabeth was still dead."

Brooke had no clue what to say, so she said nothing.

"I couldn't live with an eternity of guilt over killing Elizabeth. Before I got to know you, I thought I could live with a lifetime of guilt over killing you, considering that I wasn't planning on staying alive very long. Besides, I'm already damned. What was one more death on my soul?"

Her mouth clenched, her heart failing for a long moment.

"Until today, I thought bargaining with Giltine was the hardest thing I'd ever done in my life. I thought I was broken beyond repair. I never expected to love you." His voice cracked on the last words.

That pain filled sound crashed down on Brooke. She wasn't supposed to love him either. Yet, she did, and her heart was tearing apart for him. His life sucked, and he was desperate.

Would she have sacrificed someone else to save her brother? Would she have risked all if she could bring him back?

She wanted to say no; but she couldn't say no for *sure*. Shit.

They stared at each other, and then as if by some unseen signal, they were striding toward each other. Arms enveloping her, he hugged her so tightly her feet left the ground.

When her toes touched down again, she snuggled against his chest, breathing in his scent. Yes, everyone deserved a second chance, and she was going to give Christian his.

"I'll find a way to break the curse, okay?"

"Is that a promise?" William asked from behind them.

Pulling apart, they faced him together.

"I guess it is."

"So it worked, he made you fall in love with him." He snorted. "You sap."

"You know what they say, kindness has no enemies."

"Where the hell did you hear that?"

"I read it on a tea bag."

He rolled his eyes. "Your kindness is going to get you killed. If you're expecting a happily ever after, it's never going to happen. You can't *kiss* and make up."

"Why are you here, William?"

"For you."

"What?" she said, stepping back.

Christian squeezed her hand. "Piss off, William."

"Oh, please. I don't want her *that* way." He studied her as she stood silent and unmoving. "You know this thing I have going with Abby?"

"Of course."

A slow smile lifted one side of his mouth. "I promise to stay away from her soul, if you promise me one thing."

Panting, she snapped, "You are such a dick."

"She's not making you any promises," Christian said.

"Mind your own business," William snarled.

She ignored them both. Abby's life could be on the line. "What?"

He pointed to his black eye. "Reapers left me alone as long as I had a watcher hidden away. They eventually caught on that my watcher died, as you can see." He nudged the reaper ashes with his boot. "All you have to do is fry one or two of those bad boys for me so they leave me alone. It's really no big deal, as far as you're concerned."

A deal with William? Not a chance in Hell. "Give me one good reason why I should make any deals with you."

He brushed imaginary dirt from his shirt. "Do you know what happens to a girl who loses part of her soul?"

Thinking of Renkin, her lips tingled as if the blood had been cut off for a long time then suddenly gushed back in. She had a pretty good idea. "Not really."

"She drops into a coma. What's left of her soul is sucked into the Void, where it stays and stays and stays, with reapers taking hits off it here and there. She goes insane, waiting for her body to die. Sometimes it takes a very, very long time; especially for someone as young as Abby."

Brooke's heart pumped blood to her face at such a fast rate she was sure astronauts in space could feel the heat.

"You don't want that for your best friend, do you?" William's tone held a purr.

"I should just fry your ass right now."

"Who's frying ass?" A light bobbed through the pre-dawn light, and Abby reached the Overlook. "Hey guys," she muttered between pants for breath. "This hiking crap sucks. Never again, Billy." She sprawled out on her back. "Shit, my legs hurt."

He grinned at Brooke, then jutted his head toward her friend. "Sure you want to do this now?"

"Maybe I'll just end you now and deal with Abby later."

"I'll have her in the Other World before you can say kiss my ass."

Brooke glanced at Christian. "Is he that fast?"

He nodded, but said, "Don't make any bargains with him."

William's lips tightened. "This has nothing to do with you, you sap."

She searched the trees while searching for an answer. She said to Christian, "I didn't save Ryan, and I can't have the souls of two people on my conscience. You of all people should understand that."

"I do."

Spotting her flashlight on the ground, she scooped it up and twirled it in her fingers. Thoughts fell over each other inside her head, and a theory flickered, briefly, weakly, like a candle in an open window. "It seems like Giltine likes to make bargains."

"Who's Giltine?" Abby mumbled. "God, I'm tired."

"Definitely," William said.

"You want a bodyguard," Brooke said to him, and he nodded. "And you want to break the curse," she said to Christian, who stared at her with no expression. "What does Giltine want?"

"A lover; but no reaper's crazy enough to love that witch," William said.

Abby sat up. "Reaper?"

"A child," Christian said.

Brooke shook her head. "No, what does she want that I can bargain with?"

Silence enveloped them, a silence as dark and heavy as the night. Abby squinted from one of them to the other.

"She wants me; a Nephilim descendant." Brooke lifted her chin.

"No way in *Hell*," Christian blurted.

Abby shot to her feet. "As in angel? What the hell's going on?"

Brooke hesitated, but there was no stopping now. Abby

would either believe her, or run screaming down the mountain. "You know how you're always calling me angelic?"

She nodded.

"Turns out I'm a descendant of one. Surprise!"

"One what?"

"Angel."

"Naphil," William said. "Not angel."

Abby's snort was cut short, as though an arm was putting an invisible chokehold on her neck. "You're joking."

"Not."

One minute stretched into several long moments. Abby peered at her with narrowed eyes, and Brooke forced herself to hold her gaze steady.

Abby seemed to measure her words carefully. "So that savior complex and always telling the truth and always thinking people are nice when they're not and all that glass half full shit . . . that's all for real?"

"Seems so."

"What does that mean?"

"I can, ah, see reapers?" Damn, the words sounded even more insane out loud than they did inside her head.

"You mean reapers, as in hooded guys with a scythe?" Abby made a stabbing motion.

"Yes, but without the scythe."

"You guys are punking me, aren't you? I mean, Brooke's nice and all, but an angel?"

"Technically, she's not an angel," William said.

Abby nodded and winked. "Are there any reapers here now?"

Clearing her throat, Brooke glanced at Christian, and then at William.

"No way!"

"Only half," Christian said. "Our mothers were human."

"Yeah? Prove it."

William closed his eyes. When he opened them, they gleamed silver, cutting through the gloom like beacons.

Abby staggered back. "Well, fu—"

"Anyway," Brooke interrupted. "We need to settle some things."

"Holy shit. You guys settle. I think I need to sit down." When William moved toward her she held up a hand. "Not yet, Billy. I think I need a minute by myself to work on my freak-out plan."

Brooke watched her friend muttering to herself. Abby believed in all sorts of crap. She'd come to terms with reapers and angels in no time. And if she knew her friend, she was going to embrace the knowledge with open arms, a wide grin, and a "Woot! Woot!"

Right now, though, Brooke had to do something about William in order to keep her best friend's soul safe. And she had to fulfill her promise to Christian to break the curse. And she knew just how to do both. "I have a plan."

William snorted. "Can't wait to hear it."

"Christian will take me to Giltine. I can bargain with her and get her to lift his curse. When I come back, I'll be your bodyguard."

"You're not going there, or bargaining," Christian said. "I'm fine."

"Besides, you can't trust him enough to take you there *and* bring you back. Alive."

"Wait just one minute," Abby said. "What do you mean by alive?"

"Ignore him. He's being dramatic," Brooke said. "Then why don't you take me, *Billy*?"

"No," Christian cut in.

William hesitated, and then a smile spread across his face, slowly, like the sun pouring a liquid sunrise on the dawn. "Let's make a deal."

Christian swung her to face him. Brushing her hair from her face, he said, "Don't do this for me."

"It's too late." She pulled away, bracing herself against his pleading eyes before her resolve broke. Speaking to William, she said, "I promise to be your bodyguard if you leave Abby's soul alone."

"My *what*?" Abby squealed.

"He's a reaper, Abby, and you have a soul."

"You wouldn't."

He laughed. "No, I wouldn't, but Brooke thought I would."

She gasped. "You played me?"

William winked at Christian. "Smart girl. I think I like her."

He crossed his arms over his chest. "You're an ass."

"No argument from me." William grinned at Brooke. "We have a deal."

Grabbing her arm, Christian pulled her against his side. "You can't go there."

"Go where?" Abby asked.

"Christian's taking me to the Other World to make a bargain with Giltine to lift his curse."

"Who's Giltine?"

"Goddess of Death. Their boss."

Abby snorted, opened her mouth to say something, and then snorted again.

"You're going to trust this traitor?" William's lips twisted. "He doesn't care about you. He doesn't care about me. He doesn't care about anyone but himself."

"I have it under control."

"All he's ever wanted is to leave the Other World, no matter whom he betrays, no matter whom he lies to, no matter whom he kills." That slow smile worked over his face again, only now it was icy. "Isn't that right, nephew?"

"She already knows about my past."

Brooke cut in. "Giltine will bargain with me."

"If she doesn't? What's Plan B? You think your boy here will just walk away?"

Christian stood immobile, his face as expressionless as a gargoyle, but his eyes flashed slickly silver in the moonlight. "We don't need a Plan B. I'll walk before I let anything happen to her."

"Your Plan B will be to throw her under the bus."

"Shut up."

"I really don't like how all this sounds," Abby said.

Brooke tried to ignore the prickling of sweat on the back of her neck. William didn't know Christian like she did. "It's settled."

"You don't get it. Once he has you down there, he'll turn his back on you, just like he's done to everyone else in his life."

William grabbed Christian's arm, pushed up his sleeve, and thrust his wrist in front of her. A number of deep, red scars glared from Christian's pale skin.

"Including himself," he added.

"Dude, you tried to kill yourself?" Abby asked.

Christian jerked free and rolled down his sleeve. His eyes glowed silver, melting, hot, angry. "Go to Hell, William."

He smirked. "Been there and back. With you. Remember?"

"Oh, my God." Abby took a step back, staring at Christian's face. "Your eyes."

"Reaper, remember?" William leaned close to Brooke's ear, and his warm breath tickled down her spine. "He'll betray you to save himself. It's the only thing he lives for."

Christian hauled him away from her. "Back off. You have no idea what I live for."

"I don't like this," Abby said. "You getting thrown under a bus doesn't sound like a good plan."

"I made a promise." Brooke couldn't hide the tremor in her voice.

"Let me guess. As an angel thingy you can't break a promise."

"Yahtzee."

"Shit."

William said, "No wonder you angels fell from grace. You're a bunch of suckers."

"Wait, wait, wait." Abby held up her hand, her gaze frantic. "Don't do this. These are *reapers*; they kill people."

"I have to. I made a promise."

"Shit." Abby paced, running her hands through her hair.

"Besides, reapers don't kill people," William said. "Well, most of them don't." He tilted his head. "Try not to die, Brooke."

Chapter 34

Present Time

Christian and Brooke stood at the Hang Glider Overlook, a tense silence vibrating between them. Abby and William sat by the trees, their murmured conversation working through the sound of Brooke's pounding heart. Christian was silent and still, his shoulders hunched and stiff. Turning from him, she surveyed the view. The skyline bubbled with dawn's light, and the moonlight began to fade. A few birds warbled sleepily in the trees.

He said, "I jumped from here once."

"You *what?*"

He smiled, but it wasn't enough to get his dimples to react.

"There's no way you could have survived that." She leaned forward to peek over the edge, shuddered, and stepped back.

"I broke every bone in my body. I lost count of the number of souls I had to usher to heal." He took another step in order to peer down.

She studied his scars. "How many times did you actually jump?"

"Just once."

"Are you suicidal now?"

He didn't answer.

Unsure of what to say, she bit her lip and scratched her arm.

"Ready?" he asked.

She nodded, and they knelt in the grass.

Abby squatted beside her. Her eyes were red and her mascara had run. "I don't want you to do this."

The back of Brooke's throat burned. She tightened her lips and squeezed Abby's hand, not trusting herself to speak.

Christian closed his eyes. "Take my hand."

He dropped his chin to his chest, breathing deeply and evenly. The dawn's light highlighted the scars on his face. Brooke's gaze moved to his scarred hands, then lingered on his sleeve, hiding the angry red welts that marked his wrist.

He was a man torn; torn by his past, torn by his present, and torn by his future. Was he torn about not breaking the curse? Would they bargain with Giltine to lift the curse, only to have him commit suicide? Or would he throw her under the bus?

Her bladder threatened to give out, and she pressed her thighs together. No, he loved her. If Giltine refused to bargain, they'd leave. Together. And if she did bargain, they'd have a life. Together.

He inhaled sharply, and her gaze snapped back to his face. His body wavered between shadow and substance, seeming to melt into the night. Releasing Abby, she grabbed his arm.

"No!" Abby's scream sounded far away. "Billy! Do something!"

It went dark; dark and dead and weightless. Brooke's stomach flew up her windpipe and choked her so she couldn't swallow. Her body tingled, as though she was disintegrating, falling to pieces. She tried to hang onto Christian with both hands, but she couldn't feel anything and wasn't sure if they'd broken apart, or if he was even there with her. She couldn't run. She couldn't see, couldn't breathe—couldn't feel anything but emptiness, deep and fathomless and utterly silent. Panic swelled her mind. Unable to scream, she feared she'd be lost in the frigid dark forever.

Her body congealed, suddenly; a painful merging of her cells and molecules. Her muscles and joints cramped with spasms. Brooke landed on her knees. Pain snapped at her kneecaps, and she gasped. Blinking in the blinding light, she uncurled her fingers from Christian's arm and flexed them. There was nothing to break the light; no shadows or fixtures. It wasn't hot or cold, dry or damp.

It was like nothing; not life or death. Just nothingness.

"Where are we?" Her voice was flat, no echo or shade of emotion.

"The tunnel to the Other World," he said. "This is the Void."

"But it's so bright."

"Only to the living."

He stood very still. His eyes had gone slate gray; no blue remained. Tilting his head, he gazed at her.

The panicked intensity of her breathing slowed. White flashed by her, followed by a black streak. She staggered back, then whipped her head to the left, but the streaks had vanished. "What was that?"

"Some souls fly through the tunnel. Their death is instant."

"Crap."

"Those are the lucky ones." He held out his hand. "Take my hand. I'll guide you."

She slipped her hand into his, and let him lead her down the hall. Her eyes widened at the sight of the expansive, black mountain rising high until it disappeared and draped with white and dark figures. Screams echoed, fighting the mad buzzing that deafened her. Her head ached, and the overpowering, sweet smell of grapes made her gag.

Coughing, she asked, "What's up with these reapers?"

"They linger here, taking hits off the souls stuck in the Void. When the lost souls are ready, the reapers cross them over."

Annoyance trickled along her nerve endings. "And your goddess lets them?"

"Technically, they aren't stealing souls, just taking hits from them. The people are still alive. Without watchers to keep them in line, Giltine focuses on the full-out rogues."

Brooke dug her nails into the palm of her free hand. "What happens to someone when a rogue steals his soul?"

"They're lost in the abyss forever."

"Here?"

"No, this is the Void. They're simply gone and they cease to exist; no Void, no crossing over, no light, no sound. There's just nothing. You're aware, but can't feel, can't speak, can't hear. You felt it briefly when we traveled here."

Swallowing, she nodded. She couldn't imagine experiencing that cloying panic for eternity.

"You can't do anything to stop the insanity from rotting what's left of your consciousness. It's a fate you wouldn't wish on your worst enemy."

Brooke tugged her earlobe with trembling fingers. Her soulless brother was drifting forever in that dark hell because of some Other World thug like William. She shivered. And Christian. "So Ryan's suffering?"

"Yes."

She swallowed twice, nodded once, then palmed the wetness from her eyes. "I wish I knew what rogue sentenced him to that hell, because I want to make him pay."

Christian didn't respond. She halted at the base of the black mountain. Narrow trails chiseled in the black surface wound their way to the top.

"Are we climbing that?"

"Yes."

Channeling her new, rogue ass-kicking mentality, she strode forward. When she was finished with Giltine, she'd get out of there and take on the rogues. While Brooke couldn't know which rogue had stolen Ryan's soul, she figured if she killed enough of them, she'd eventually hit Yahtzee. She would avenge her brother's death; she would make every rogue she met pay for condemning Ryan to that fate.

As they climbed the mountain, she tried and failed to ignore the lost souls. They screamed at her. Clutched her jeans and snagged her hair. They pleaded. Tears filled her eyes as she kept her gaze riveted on the worn path.

Her legs and lungs were burning when they reached the top. She stumbled, her weight dragging her forward until Christian steadied her.

"Is that a wall?" she asked between breaths.

"It's the wall to the Other World."

"We're not there yet?"

"This is just the Void. It gets much worse."

She squinted through the gauzy film, trying to make sense of the blurred images. To the right she could see a calming patchwork of green and blue; to the left, nothing but violent slashes of brown and red.

She pointed right. "I take it we're not going there."

He shook his head. Sighing, she took his hand and followed him through the wall. Her gasp froze. Her breath froze. Even the burning in her fingers froze as she checked out the dead landscape, the toiling souls, and the tattered shacks where they were watched by an army of almost-reapers. The combined smell of burned meat, rotten flesh, and sulfur made her stomach churn.

The pulse in her neck throbbed, and her mouth and throat were so dry she thought she was evaporating from the inside out.

Christian yanked the paper out of his pocket and smoothed it with his fingers. "I can't count the times I've tried to destroy these words. I've tried scratching them out, ripping them out, erasing them, burning them, drowning them." Shrugging, he handed it to her.

She brushed her thumb over it. She hadn't noticed before, but the paper was soft and smooth, like thin suede, spotted with bloody fingerprints . . . and her shoe print. "Are these your fingerprints?"

"My father's."

Startled, she was careful not to touch them. "What if Giltine won't bargain?"

He shrugged and focused on something in the distance. Unease slithered around her heart.

"Killed another one, have you? The guilt-ridden martyr just couldn't keep it in his pants."

The corners of his mouth plummeted, and the skin around his eyes contracted. He peered past Brooke and straightened. "Giltine."

Brooke pivoted. Giltine's hair ran wild under her feathered crown. Her eyes were as dark as black holes, set deep into a pale, leathery face. Despite the sultry temperature, an icy wave emanated from her as she scrutinized Brooke. She tightened her thighs, trying to quell the quiver that threatened to loosen her muscles.

The goddess pointed a long finger at her. "You are not dead."

"No." Brooke tried to inject confidence into her voice to disguise the tremor.

Giltine narrowed her eyes.

"I've brought you a Naphil descendant." Christian's voice was just a notch above audible.

"This is a surprise." She took Brooke's chin and turned her head to one side then the other. "Your blood is diluted, but ah, yes, I do believe you are one of my long-lost watchers."

"I'm not a watcher, technically," she whispered.

"You are close enough." Her icy gaze slid down her nose. "The . . . angel . . . has to die, my dear Christian, to break the curse."

"That was our deal," he said in a stale-sounding voice, like bread that had been left out and grown hard around the edges.

"I . . . " Brooke swallowed, her tongue sticking to the roof of her dry mouth. She shot a look at him, but he focused on Giltine and wouldn't return her gaze. "I want to bargain with you."

"Is that so?" Giltine's voice was husky and dark and edging toward dangerous.

"Yes."

"What do you have to offer me?"

"My mad watcher skills."

"If you are not dead, then you already work for me."

Christian said, "But she's *not* a watcher."

Brooke lifted her chin, his moral support lifting her courage. "Yeah, so I don't have to do jack for you."

Giltine's mouth worked as though chewing on words to spit at her feet. "You do not speak to me in that manner. I am Goddess of Death!"

He stepped forward slightly, positioning himself as though trying to block the woman's wrath.

She unstiffened her shoulders enough to shrug. "If I'm dead I'm nothing to you. But if you bargain, I'll work for you."

Giltine's breathing was unbalanced, rasping in short pulls of air as if her lungs had been flattened. "I do not like your insolence. I am in no mood to bargain."

Brooke's heart failed for a second, and her muscles sagged. "Fine, then I'll just leave." Pushing against the wall, her momentum stalled. The gauzy curtain seemed to have solidified. She pressed her hands against it. Solid. She rammed it with her shoulder. Nothing.

"Why can't I get out?"

"You are neither reaper nor secucro nor dead," Giltine said.

Her heart raced. "I'm stuck here until Christian takes me through, is that it?"

She smiled. "Dead or alive."

"Okay, then either bargain with me or kill me." Brooke's

calm voice rang with confidence, belying her trembling body. Giltine loved to bargain; she *would* bargain.

She paced off several steps, and then whipped around. "And what do you want in return?"

Brooke held out the cursed paper. "Lift Christian's curse."

The goddess took the paper without a glance at the words. "No. I will just mark you now and force dear Christian to cross you over."

"You can't do that," he said. "You haven't pulled her name from the Jar of Souls. If you break the rules, Laima might take more than your beauty this time."

She didn't know if he spoke the truth, but judging by Giltine's flaring nostrils and bared teeth, he was right. "Yeah. So let's bargain."

Giltine waved a hand. "I decide who dies, the Jar is merely a game of chance I play to keep things exciting. And you, my dear Brooke, are an insolent child. I do not think I like you."

Christian tensed beside her, his muscles coiling. Tension slid up and down her spine, and Brooke expelled a quiet breath. This wasn't going as planned.

"Reapers have been engaging in a little sport with you, haven't they, my dear Christian?"

"Until Brooke stopped them."

Grabbing Brooke's hands, Giltine traced a fingernail over her fingertips. "Ah. Magnificent."

Brooke yanked free. Even though Giltine hated him enough to curse him, surely she would take the deal; surely she would do anything to have a watcher. "Will you bargain?"

"No. I've given him the gift of death. If he's not reaper enough to mark you, I'll do it myself."

She locked her knees before they buckled. His slate eyes stared at Giltine through his lashes before swiveling to Brooke. His hard gaze froze the breath in her lungs.

"Or, you can just kiss her, my dear Christian. But if *I* mark her, you lose your only chance. Either way, she's going to die."

His gaze drifted to Brooke's mouth, lingered there. As much as she tried to swallow, she couldn't; her muscles had petrified.

Giltine tapped her front teeth with a long, black fingernail, the *tick, tick* counting the endless seconds. "Go on, my dear Christian. One kiss, and you will be free. Is that not what you desire more than anything in your world?"

"I have to kiss him willingly. He can't force me."

"Oh, but you will. Did you not promise him you'd break the curse?"

Oh, shit.

Slowly, slowly, he tilted his head, staring at Brooke with such intensity she couldn't stop the spark of fear that heated her skin. A flash of silver crossed the gray horizon of his eyes. A swallow jerked to a stop in her throat as Giltine's toxic laugh poisoned the air.

Her fingers itched and burned and longed to destroy. Her weapon was locked and loaded. Every molecule screamed inside her to fry him, destroy him, kill him.

He closed his eyes, hiding the sickly silver gleam. "You can't save me."

She studied the dark circles below his lashes, the pale scars that lined his skin, the beautiful, black hair that swept across his brow.

"She'll bargain," she said, and even she could hear the desperation in her voice. "You know I made a promise to you. Bargaining's the only way out for me."

"Oh, did I forget to mention?" Giltine studied her nails. "Earth-bound promises have no relevance in the Other World. As far as I'm concerned, you made no promises to him." She paused and a malevolent smile tugged at her lips. "Or he you."

His face seemed to have been chiseled from granite—unmoving, unblinking, unfeeling. His eyes were ablaze in liquid fire. His gaze froze to Brooke's, and then melted, sliding down to her lips.

A chill raced up the backs of her legs to grip the base of her spine. She'd been so sure Giltine would bargain and now she wouldn't, and she was losing him to the darkness, and she was dead meat, oh crap, why hadn't she listened to William? Her chest tightened so hard it constricted her breathing.

"I'm bored. Maybe I'll just mark you both."

Suddenly, he grabbed Brooke's wrists. With a snap, both her hands were locked behind her. She slammed against his chest. No matter how she twisted her wrists, she was unable to break free.

He freed one hand to grab her hair, forcing her head back. They locked gazes. Brooke's heart thrummed in her chest. The pulse in her throat throbbed.

"I killed Ryan."

Her heart stuttered to a stop.

Christian's eyes gleamed. "I sucked his soul dry and sent him to the abyss. Do you understand me? I killed your pathetic, weak, loser brother."

There was a long moment, bloated with shock, before she slapped his cheek with her free hand. The heat from her hand blistered his skin. With a gasp, he released her. She gripped his head between both hands, smoke bleeding through her fingers.

He didn't fight back. "I'm sorry you couldn't save your brother," he whispered. "I hope you can avenge him some day."

It took her an almost nano-second too late to realize the truth. He'd lied one last time; lied about Ryan just to make her angry, to strike out at him, to kill him. She snatched her hands back.

His eyes teared, wetting the burn marks she'd left on his cheeks. "Brooke, finish it."

She whirled to face Giltine, whose eyebrows were raised and her mouth agape. She gave Brooke the once-over, gaze settling on the tendrils of smoke curling between her fingers.

"I won't kill him for your entertainment."

"You fool."

"And he won't kill me. Are you ready to bargain?"

"No. If he's not reaper enough to take you, I'll do it myself."

"I'll kiss him before you get the chance. We're breaking this curse, and it's your choice whether or not you get anything out of the deal."

"I'd rather rot in the abyss than kiss you," he said.

Brooke flinched, but didn't waver.

"You are an insolent child."

"Brooke, kill me. Please."

Ignoring him, she said to Giltine, "Look, if we bargain, we can all get something we want, including you."

"You presume to know my mind?"

"I know enough."

"I really do not like you."

"You don't have to like me in order to use me. As you can see, I got the juice."

"If I don't wish to bargain?"

Her swallow clicked in her dry throat. "I'll sacrifice myself."

"Gods below," Christian muttered and grabbed her hand. "Don't do this. Not for me. I killed Ryan, remember?"

"Liar." She kept her focus on Giltine.

The goddess spun the ring on her finger. Sighing, her shoulders dropped. "My dear, dear Brooke."

The way she said Brooke's name, low and soft and . . . *motherly*, sucked the breath right out of her. "Do we have a deal?"

Giltine kissed her cheek, then the other. "Welcome to my world, my dear Brooke."

She touched her frost-bitten cheeks, and then shuddered. "Um, the paper?"

"Very well." Sliding the ring off her finger, she held it out. "Take my ring."

"No!" Christian jerked her back a step. "Don't touch it."

One side of Giltine's mouth slid up in a sly smile. "Take it, or there's no deal."

He kicked the dirt, and a cloud of dust poofed. Tension sharpened the angle of his cheekbones and chin. "I swear, if you hurt her, I'll kill you."

"Don't test me, my dear Christian."

The sinking feeling lifted to trap Brooke's heart. Would the ring hurt her? Kill her? It didn't matter. She made the deal, and even if she wanted to run screaming from the Other World, the choice was no longer hers. Pushing her tongue against her teeth, she held out her hand, palm up. Giltine hovered the ring over Brooke's palm then let it drop.

The ring touched her skin indifferently, nothing more than a piece of metal lying in her palm like a dead weight. She hadn't realized she was holding her breath until it gushed out. The tension lines in Christian's face faded as if he'd just gotten a shot of Botox.

She asked, "Now what?"

Giltine blew on the cursed paper before handing it to her. "Slide it through the ring."

She did as she was told. The paper burst into flames, and ashes scattered to the ground like gray snow. "That's it? The curse is lifted?"

Giltine raised an "as if" eyebrow and held out her hand. "My ring, please."

She handed it over, and Giltine slipped the ring on her finger.

"Is this a trick?" Christian's eyes narrowed at Giltine, dropped to the ring, then back to her face.

She held out her hand. "Take my hand."

He rubbed his thumbs along his pant seams, staring at the ring, his Adam's apple jiggling in his throat when he swallowed. He touched her hand with the tip of his finger, jerked back, and then very slowly held it.

His eyes widened. "Gods below. It's true."

She released him then turned.

"Wait."

Giltine halted, and after a second that stretched like a year, turned to face Brooke with raised eyebrows. "You are beginning to test my patience, my dear Brooke."

"I want to know what happened to my brother."

Giltine spun the ring on her finger, interrogating her with her gaze. "And who is your brother?"

"Ryan Pettigrew."

"Ryan Pettigrew was not marked by me. And what happened to dear Ryan?"

"A year and a half ago, he got sick with a high fever, and a rogue came into his room and . . ." She cleared her throat to keep it from cracking. Christian slipped his hand into hers, and she continued, "Ryan's dead, and I want to know if he's . . . gone."

"You saw this?"

She nodded.

"What of the rogue?"

"He vanished. There was smoke, and this sizzling noise, and there's a burn mark on the rug."

"Your brother was a watcher, it would seem."

"Oh."

Giltine held out her hand and admired her ring. "Even dying, Ryan's watcher power was strong. Even in death, he destroyed the rogue." She dropped her arm to her side.

"But you didn't mark him?"

"Occasionally watchers lose the battle against rogues, especially if their defenses are down, though if Ryan killed the rogue, the rogue surely didn't succeed in taking his soul. The ordeal must have been a lethal blow to Ryan's weakened body. I assume his soul was intact and that he passed Laima's judgment. Your brother has never set foot in my world."

Brooke's trembling channeled from her hand into Christian's. He gave it a squeeze.

"Very well then." Giltine turned and strode away, then stopped and studied her. "I'll be watching you."

"I'll be watching you too."

Giltine popped a delicate snort, and then, without another word melted into the desert's shimmering heat waves. Christian's breath gushed out of him. His flat gray eyes looked vacant without their blue shards.

"You tried playing me one last time, didn't you?"

His smile was lopsided. "Busted."

"So, I guess that's it. You're free from that damn curse."

Sighing, he leaned his forehead against hers. "I can never, ever thank you enough."

She didn't have time to ponder his freedom, or his gratitude. Nausea gripped her stomach in a blistering fist, and her head ached with fevered intensity.

She wiped sweat from her forehead with the back of her hand. "I am so done with this place. Let's make like birds and get the flock out of here."

Chapter 35

Present Time

The ground pressed its cool lips against the back of Brooke's neck. Birds warbled, encouraging her to open her eyes. Nausea threatened to hijack the contents of her stomach. Groaning, she struggled to sit up, and then held her head between her hands.

"Brooke?"

She blinked to bring Christian's face into focus. Her mouth was parched, her lips cracked. She caught the flash of sun breaking over the hills, and mental knives stabbed her skull. "My head hurts. And I think I might puke, so keep your distance."

"You're dehydrated."

She pressed her fingertips into her temples. "Well, that got tense down there."

When he didn't answer, she snapped her gaze to his face. He stared over the horizon, hands shoved in his pockets, shoulders slumped. A breeze swept a lock of hair over his eyes.

"Wait one damn minute. You're not planning on killing yourself, are you, Reaper Boy? Not after everything we just went through."

"Why the hell were you going to sacrifice yourself for me, Watcher Girl? Are you insane?"

She crawled to her knees, and when her head stopped spinning, hauled herself to her feet. She swayed a moment, dizziness pulsing through her head. "I wasn't the last time I checked. Besides, you were going to sacrifice yourself for me. Or have you forgotten?"

She ventured close enough to take his hand.

He bowed his head and squeezed her fingers. "I never thought this day would come. I thought after breaking the curse, I'd be able to free myself from guilt."

"What happened to Elizabeth was an accident. You can't blame yourself. At least you know she crossed over."

He wouldn't look at her. "But what about the souls I condemned to the abyss? How do I redeem myself for what I've done?"

"I don't know, but we'll think of something. I'm not letting you leave me."

He ran his thumb over her knuckles, perusing her with truth-finder intensity. "You mean that?"

"Yes, and you know I can't lie."

"I expect you have a couple of lie-loopholes up your sleeve." The tension in his eyes, face, and shoulders broke with a long sigh. He closed his eyes. "I don't want to leave you. Ever."

"Better not, because I'd really hate to have to kick your ass."

One of those sexy half-smiles flicked in her direction, making her heart jump. "Hmm, that sounds like it could be fun."

Giving a shaky laugh, she ran her free hand through her hair, but didn't get far before her fingers hit a knot of tangles. "God, what's up with my hair?"

"You've never looked more beautiful, actually."

She snorted and ducked her chin.

"You're blushing."

"You can't know that. It's not light enough."

"Oh, I can feel it."

A shudder rippled through her body. She pressed her knees together.

He stepped closer to the edge, pointing down and to the right. "See that horse stable? That used to be a dairy farm."

"Okay, I think that's close enough, Reaper Boy." She dragged him back. "You're mortal now, so back off before you kill yourself."

"Would that bother you?"

"Well, duh."

He winked. "You feel up to hiking back down?"

"Let's do it."

She drew a ragged breath, and let the tension slide from her neck and down her spine. She became hyper-aware of the trembling in her limbs as she walked alongside him. When she stumbled, he linked his fingers through hers. A cascade of bird calls chased them down the mountain.

Sunlight broke through the trees when they hit the road, sparkling against her car. His motorbike was parked near the dense woods, its blackness sucked in by the shadows. Abby slept behind the wheel of her car, William pacing in front of it.

When he saw them, he leaned against the hood and crossed his arms over his chest. "You're still alive, so I'm guessing my nephew didn't sell you out."

"Careful, William. It almost sounds like you care."

"I don't care about *you.* I care about my bodyguard. You're no good to me dead."

Sweat played along her hairline. Groaning, she sagged, laying her head on the roof of her car. "You're frigging impossible, you know that?"

Christian sighed. Loudly.

"Hey, just protecting my dick reputation." William reached through the open window, then tossed her a bottle of water.

She caught it. "This doesn't seem like something a dick would do."

"Drink your water and shut up."

After she downed the entire bottle, she gasped for breath. "Thanks. I feel better."

He shrugged.

Christian said to him, "I'm sorry I wouldn't listen to you about Giltine. You were right, I was wrong."

"You've always been a sap."

"Can you forgive me?"

"No."

"William!" she said.

"Hey, you can't just erase the past."

"No, but you have plenty of time to write the future."

He looked at her as if she'd just shot milk out of her nose. "What Hallmark card did you steal that lame line from?"

She one-shoulder shrugged. "Just saying."

"I don't know whether to like you or hate you." His tone held just enough bite to tell Brooke he wasn't totally kidding.

"Wouldn't it feel better to get your issues with each other out in the open?"

"No, it would not feel better. You two saps belong with each other." William waved his hand. "Anyway, what happened with Giltine?"

"She agreed to my bargain, and Christian's free from his curse." She ignored another eye roll from William. "And you have your bodyguard."

"Good. I'll let you know when I need you. Probably sooner rather than later, so stick around."

"Wait." She tossed the empty bottle inside her car. "I think we might have a conflict of interest here."

"What?"

She leaned toward him, sniffed, and wrinkled her nose. "Don't piss on my leg and tell me it's raining."

"Oh. That. You're going to overlook that, right?"

"No."

"Fabulous. What else do you want from me?"

"If I hear you sent one more soul to the abyss, you're on my hit list. You got that?"

He tightened his lips. "You're changing the deal."

"Overlooking your rogue life was never part of the deal. I'm just setting down the rules."

His cheek muscles rippled, but he said, "Fine."

"Smart boy. I think I like you."

One corner of her lips lifted at William who looked like he'd just sucked worms through a straw.

"I'm getting out while the getting's good." He rested his hand on Abby's shoulder. "I'll be in touch."

"What do you think you're doing?"

"Leaving."

"Not with her."

"Chill. I'm just going to hang with her, not suck her soul."

The fire in her gut snapped awake. "You're changing the deal."

"The deal was to lay off her soul, not to lay off her." He smiled. "I'm just setting some rules."

She ground her teeth, annoyed at him for turning her own words against her. Her fingers itched and burned and yearned to grab his neck.

"I don't think I'm willing to take the chance you won't slip up."

His eyes brightened with silver streaks, and he licked his lips.

"Stop reacting to me!"

A flush rolled up his face. "What do you expect, genius? You're about to detonate like Mt. Etna, and you expect me not to fucking notice?"

She watched the sick gleam in his eyes. "Jesus."

"Brooke," Christian said, and the word sounded strangled, as though an invisible arm had a chokehold on his throat. "You need to calm down."

She ran her tongue along her teeth before taking a deep breath, then another, then another. Her hands were burning, flaming crimson.

"What's going on?" Abby's voice was thick with sleep. Panting, she met her friend's blinking gaze.

"Oh, my God. Stilts! You're on fire! And your eyes are freaking glowing, like an atom bomb just exploded inside your head. Someone get a bucket of water, stat!"

The car door opened, then shuffling footsteps. Brooke heard the movement through a fog.

"Just give her a minute," William said. "She'll be fine."

"And Billy, your eyes . . . they're glowing, too."

"No reaping," Brooke murmured.

"Just give me a minute and I'll be fine," he said.

She stuffed her hands in her armpits and concentrated on dousing the angry flames inside her. She pictured glacier-riddled lakes, waterfalls, dripping icicles. Squatting by her car, she closed her eyes and pressed her forehead into her knees.

Finally, her ragged breathing smoothed out. The mental glaciers melted, dripping cool water through her veins, extinguishing the fire.

"Better?" Christian asked.

"Much." She stood, leaning heavily against her car.

"Are you dangerous?" Abby asked William. Her voice was a cross between hopeful and fearful.

Brooke sighed. Some things never changed.

"Sometimes. Does that scare you?"

Abby dropped her chin and looked up at him through her lashes. "It's kind of a turn-on."

Brooke rolled her eyes. "I think I've seen enough."

He held out his hand to Abby. "Come on, doll, let's find somewhere more private."

Brooke made a T with her hands. "Hold on. What are you planning on doing?"

"Sorry, I don't kiss and tell."

"Don't mess with me, William."

"I *like* her. She doesn't act like a nun with too much starch in her wimple, like some people I know."

"Wait a sec," Abby said. "I thought you were only supposed to stop the reapers who steal souls. What's your problem with Billy?"

"Your boyfriend has a bit of a past."

"You are so *bad*." Then she smiled.

He chuckled. Brooke twisted her lips. On the flip side, Abby would probably be in love with someone totally different by next week, anyway.

Brooke pointed at William. "If you so much as sniff her soul, you and I have a problem. You feeling me?"

"Okay, okay. Let's go, doll."

"Oh, Billy wouldn't hurt a fly. Later, Stilts. Call me, but not before the crack of noon. I'm beat."

She glared at the car as Abby backed over the curb and onto the road.

"I'll be watching you, William," Brooke called.

He twittered his fingers out the passenger window.

"This is so not cool."

Christian said, "I don't think you can stop him from seeing her."

"I can do whatever I want."

"You have a deal with him. You can't break it."

"What am I supposed to do? I don't trust him."

He shrugged. "Just watch him."

Sighing, she stretched. "What a freaking long night."

"Yes." After a moment he said, "Can either of your parents see reapers?"

"Not that I know of. My dad sensed something off about you, but they were pretty freaked out when I mentioned reapers once." She studied her fingernails . . . where had all that dirt come from? "How come they can't when I can?"

"It must be a recessive gene."

"After centuries, one surviving watcher could have hundreds of descendants."

"True."

"There could be more out there."

"True."

"So, I guess you don't need me anymore."

One side of his mouth curled, and a dimple winked. He stroked her jaw with his knuckles. "So very not true."

Shivering, she traced a finger along his skin, just under his swollen eye. The blood had dried and cracked. "You look terrible."

"If I usher souls, Giltine's poison will speed my healing."

"You can still do that, even though you're free from her?"

"Even though I'm mortal, and I'm free from having to usher souls, it doesn't change who I am. I'm still part securcro. I used to loathe that life, despised my addiction to Giltine's poison, but now I know crossing souls over isn't a bad thing. I shouldn't be ashamed of who I am. A lesson I learned from an old friend."

"Who?"

"His name's Forrest. You'll meet him some day."

"Maybe that's your answer."

"What was the question?"

"How you were going to find absolution." She picked up his hand and studied his scarred fingers. "Killing yourself was never the answer. Helping people, helping souls, is."

He hesitated. "That wouldn't bother you?"

"No. We could be a team. I fry those rat-bastard rogues, and you usher those lost souls. We could be, like, comic book heroes."

He smirked. "Would you wear a Wonder Woman costume?"

Laughing, she slapped his arm. "Nice try, but no."

After a moment, he nodded. "Maybe you're right."

"I know I'm right. It's who we are, and well, complaining about it is about as useful as boobs on a bull, right?"

He gave a lazy twist to his lips. "Yes, ma'am."

"Do you feel different?"

He cupped the side of her face and stroked her cheek

with his thumb. Her lips parted. "I feel free," he murmured against her neck.

She trembled.

"Maybe we should make a test run," he whispered. "Make sure the curse is lifted."

She licked her lips, glanced sideways, and then laughed, a little too loud. "Um, you mean kiss?"

His gaze swept down to her mouth, then slid back to her eyes. Her face muscles tightened under his fingertips. Her thigh, pressed against his, clenched.

He dropped his hand to his side and stepped back. His words sounded distorted, squeezing through his stiff lips. "Are you afraid of me?"

Her cheek missed his fingers, though she couldn't deny the sudden clamminess between hers. She wanted to kiss him—she'd be totally slanted if she didn't—but what if they kissed and she died?

"I'm not afraid of *you*."

"You don't think the curse is lifted."

The hurt in his voice was like a lethal blow to her heart. "What if it isn't?"

He stuffed his hands into his pockets and stared at his feet. "Do you think Giltine lied?"

"No." She drew the word out in two syllables. "But she has a way of twisting words, doesn't she?"

"Not this time. She didn't say anything, only destroyed the paper."

Her heart throbbed, *kiss him, kiss him*. He tilted his head and studied her with a slight curl to his lips. She shifted from one foot to the other.

"So how many watchers do you think are out there?" Her voice trembled and a liquid smile softened his face. "There are a lot of rogues, and, um . . ." He played with a strand of her hair. "Um . . . maybe I could use some . . ." His fingertips grazed her skin below the ear. "Help."

"Can I kiss you now?"

Without answering, she grabbed his hips and pulled him against her. The hardness of his thighs pressed against hers made her breath slam back in her throat. Her insides unwound, slowly, like a snake gliding around a tree.

"Well?" he murmured.

His lips touched the pulse in her neck. Heat slithered through her body. He chuckled right before his tongue grazed her ear.

She tilted her head back, letting warm breath slide along her jaw.

"You'll have plenty of time to take on rogues." His low voice melted her from the inside. "Tomorrow."

"What rogues?"

His smile was all kinds of pleased. Even his dimples look pleased, winking at her. He trembled against her. Not trembling like an addict desperate for a fix, but trembling like a guy trying very hard not to lose control.

His gaze coasted to her mouth, lingered there for a moment before meeting her eyes again. "Should I stop?"

Her heart made like a woodpecker on steroids. "Hell no."

"Good."

So he kissed her.

His tongue ran along her lips until they parted, and then slipped inside. She moaned in the back of her throat. Cupping her face, he deepened the kiss.

Brooke's lips melted with his. Her fingers tightened in his hair. He took his time, exploring her mouth, and she savored the feel of his tongue against hers.

He stopped the kiss. "Heart still beating?"

He had to be able to hear her heart, which slammed against her ribs. "Yeah, but maybe we should try again, just to make sure."

His mouth hovered over hers, his breath mingled with

her breath, and when he spoke, his lips brushed her lips. "If you insist."

He kissed her again, a warm, deliciously slow kiss that sank heat to her toes.

Brooke's pocket buzzed, snapping her out of the hazy kiss-fog. She fumbled for her phone and checked the message. "Great, Mom's kind of pissed. I have to go."

"Okay." He licked her ear.

"I think you need to, ah, let go of me."

"Fine."

His lips brushed against hers, once, twice, and then held still as his tongue grazed the outside of her mouth. She was still sighing when he pushed away, opened her car door, and waved her in.

She slid behind the wheel. He shut the door, and she rolled down the window.

"See you later?" he asked, forearms leaning on the door.

"You bet."

He inhaled deeply then stepped away from the car.

"Hey, Reaper Boy."

"What?"

"No goodbye kiss?"

There was something so . . . *boss* about the way his lips curled, kind of slow, and sweet, like syrup sliding like a seductive tongue over a stack of pancakes. For one painful moment, she forgot how to breathe.

"I thought you'd never ask, Watcher Girl."

He kissed her, making her feel so alive.

Lightning Source UK Ltd.
Milton Keynes UK
UKHW012309301218
334781UK00009B/402/P

9 781682 917893